A Cooper School Novel

Life

Breaking In

A Cooper School Novel

—— Jan Levine Thal ——

> *I meant to write about death, only life came breaking in as usual*
>
> ~ Virginia Woolf

Ordering Information:

Special discounts available for **book clubs, corporations, associations,** and others.
For details, contact the publisher at director@vanvelzerpress.com.

The characters and events in this book are fictitious. Any similarity to real persons, living or dead, is coincidental and not intended by the author.

Paperback ISBN: 978-1-954253-38-4
Hardback ISBN: 978-1-954253-39-1
eBook ISBN: 978-1-954253-40-7
Audio ISBN: 978-1-954253-41-4

Library of Congress Control Number Available from Publisher

Printed in the United States of America
FSC-certified paper when possible

Van Velzer Press
3792 W. Creek Road
Brandon, Vermont 05733
(802) 247-6797
VanVelzerPress.com

This book is dedicated to Holly Yasui, a writer, activist, and dear friend who Covid stole from us.

Her family's experience with the U.S. internment of Japanese citizens made her a fighter against all bigotry.

I try to live up to her example.

Train Line

Cooper
School
Flambert
Lake Ontario
Poughkeepsie
New York City

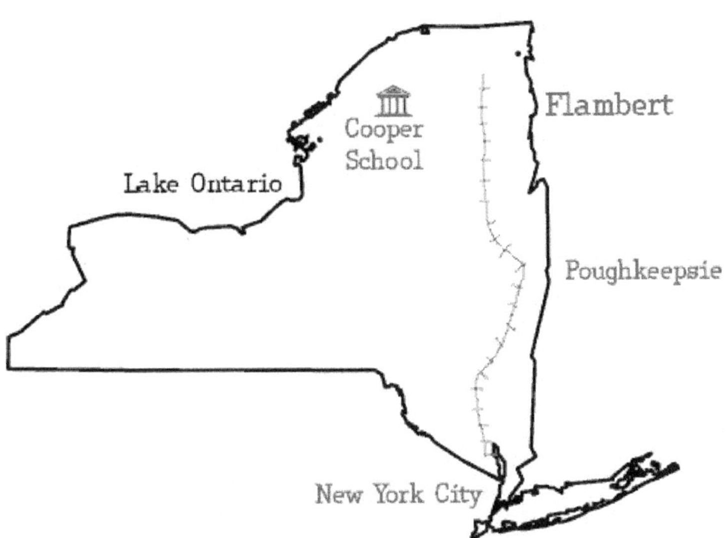

CHAPTER 1

The killer wanted to add a verbal flourish but knew better. Teenagers' texts were generally awash with poor grammar and willful misspellings. For anyone reading this one, suicide would be the inevitable conclusion.

YR falt!!! U no who UR

Stella lay flat on her back on her pathetic single bed, the particle board at its head hand-decorated with glued and scratched images from a video game the killer surmised she'd chosen for its name, Stela, so like her own. Her open brown eyes stared straight up in a sightless void. Earlier, as she breathed her last terrified gasp, their live version gazed on the killer's Hazmat suit.

The killer screwed the top onto a partially full bottle of faux-fancy iced tea on Stella's bedside table; its added cocktail of a lethal toxin and the paralytic had stopped her from fighting back. As that bottle went into the killer's tote for later disposal, a new tea bottle emerged from it, identical except without the paralytic. The killer allowed one self-indulgent chortle, relishing the inevitable public outcry to come as word of Stella's death would soon spread from a distraught parent to the community. The pay was, as always, generous, but beside the point.

Some artists work for the love of it. Such a pity so few would ever know just how brilliantly Stella had been executed.

* * *

For Callie, the day's end was always bittersweet. Her energy was finally allowed to flag. She could literally and figuratively kick off her shoes and let down her heavy brown hair. Her students were off to their next projects: homework — *yeah, right* — or confiding in friends, or playing sports or music or rehearsing theater or consuming snacks. Whatever it was, students were on their own until they joined faculty house parents for dinner.

Callie missed the young women already. She missed their synapses firing as they eagerly dissected the literature she taught, she missed their arguments with one another. She even missed the prickly ones who professed boredom with fiction. *I'll get you, my pretties. If Jane Eyre doesn't suit you, wait for Octavia Butler.*

Cooper School was a boarding school founded over a century ago for "talented young ladies of limited means." Callie was determined to make it worth their while. Thanks to careful financial management, Cooper had huge resources and the latest technology. Staff was well paid and had many benefits. Though the girls paid no tuition, they gave up time with their families to live in these north woods, hours by train from New York City.

The students may have been mainly Irish and Italian immigrants at the beginning, but today they were every race and ethnicity, speaking a fistful of native languages. Cooper School admitted no boys and no rich people, which some found irritating, mainly rich people and parents of boys. The girls were expected to work hard, behave well, and give back to the community. Most were exemplary. Thus, their huge acceptance rate into the Ivies with full ride scholarships.

Right now, though, Callie's mission was in abeyance. Right now, she wanted fresh air and a challenge for cramped limbs. The warm September days were still long and a run along a wooded path called to her. She had time before dinner at her boyfriend's.

New England fall, universally acknowledged to have the best foliage in the galaxy, was in full riot gear. Reds and oranges blared at Callie through the window, overhead and underfoot, mocking her sedentary indoorness.

Just then, Hazel charged into Callie's classroom, her fair complexion flushed, grey curls flecked with paint and tangled in post-class disarray, talking before she entered. "We got trouble. Right here in River City." Hazel was a colleague, a dear friend, and the source of endless random quotations.

Callie found Hazel's blithe reference to the musical *The Music Man* oddly reassuring. *Can't be that bad.* "What do you mean?"

"Turn on your phone."

Callie saw an urgent text from Coop. "Emergency. My place."

The two women hurried across campus, dotted with classrooms and housing, stately old trees, and fallow gardens. The air was warm, a few maples still green without a hint of the gold and orange others were showing off like fancy frocks. As the warm afternoon air warred with the oncoming crisp scents of fall, Callie was grateful to be in shirtsleeves for a few more weeks. Unannounced, a shiver overtook her.

At a trot, the teachers speculated about the emergency, secretly hoping it reflected badly on people they didn't like. Callie grew up with few resources and a healthy distrust of people who had too many and didn't appreciate them. Recently, her own fortunes reversed. Since she'd become wealthy beyond imagining, she'd made a vow to spend this fortune wisely. But creating good works turned out to be harder than it looked.

"All I want," she'd told Hazel back when the troubles began, "is to buy the land next door to the school and develop a women's center. They act like I'm trying to kill off their first-born males. With all their piousness, you'd think they'd know women were the saviors, not the killers." *Even Moses didn't save himself; the midwives launched him into the bulrushes and the pharaoh's daughter fished him out.*

Callie had no living relatives and had long ago gratefully embraced the warm welcome from Hazel and her family. The older woman was Callie's source for school history and for gossip about the nearby town of Flambert. Between them, they jokingly used the French pronunciation of the town's name, though the official pronunciation was English "with a hard hurt—minus the H—— at the end," as Hazel would say. Perhaps most endearingly, Hazel had cheered on Callie's unlikely romance with their boss, Harold "Coop" Cooper.

At the end of their dash across campus, Hazel and Callie simultaneously noticed Craig's car parked outside the converted mansion the Coopers called home.

"The school's lawyer is here." Hazel loved referring to her husband by his accomplishments. She'd married him only a handful of years earlier and was still rather smitten.

"I hope he just came for dinner and not some legal emergency." Callie jiggled crossed fingers at Hazel as the two women entered the century-old building.

Designed for the splendor required by the school's founder and first principal in the early days of women's suffrage, the mansion's once-elegant ground floor now housed a dining room and study areas for the students assigned to this house. Only the top two floors were the Cooper family residence, chock full of antiques and memorabilia collected by the generations of Coopers who had run the school since Gwendolyn Cooper founded it in the early 20th century.

Waving to students and faculty in the common area, the two women tore up the stairs, bursting into a tense conversation between Coop and Craig. Raised voices were punctuated with the clanking of Coop cooking at the kitchen end of the great room. Neither Callie nor Hazel interrupted, waiting to unpack the gist of the argument.

Coop spoke with a deliberateness that Callie knew meant he was either furious or frightened. "We need a better public presence."

Callie moved to Coop's side and because they were not alone and she needed to be busy, she began constructing a salad. Coop kissed her perfunctorily but unlike his normal practice, didn't stop her preparations to issue strict instructions. Normal seemed off the table at the moment. She could count on one hand the number of times she'd heard Coop argue with Craig, who was not only the school's lawyer but a close friend.

Callie and Hazel exchanged worried glances as Hazel placed a hand on Craig's arm. Craig focused on Coop. "It's important to release our statement immediately. We can update the website tomorrow when we know more."

Coop shook his head. "She deserves better."

Hazel clapped her hands for attention—a technique that worked wonders in her art classes. "What. Happened?"

Coop stirred furiously. Craig told Hazel and Callie to sit. Perhaps because Craig rarely gave direct orders, both complied.

"A Cooper girl killed herself."

Callie felt her limbs weaken. "Who? How?" Both men answered simultaneously, arguing with one another in the process, so sorting out facts from their commentary took a little doing.

Callie mentally braided the frayed threads into a coherent story. A sophomore named Stella Kelly had swallowed a lethal dose of something a few hours earlier. The teenager was still warm when her mother found her. Mrs. Kelly gave her daughter CPR while waiting for police and emergency medical personnel, who arrived in short order with equipment and meds. Despite everyone's best efforts, the girl couldn't be revived.

So much for The Music Man.

In the small town of Flambert, the news had spread quickly. Hazel's daughter, Alexis, who worked with the police, called her stepfather. Craig called Coop as he was already speeding toward the school. Now Craig, a portly African

American man in his 50s, raised his hands for attention. Callie remembered seeing him use this gesture with great power in a courtroom.

"As you all know, Cooper School's relationship with the town is fragile. We need to express sympathy without allowing the town even the slightest excuse to blame the school. Our statement does that." Craig passed his tablet to Hazel and Callie, displaying the school's brief statement of regret and condolence. "I'm sorry this had to go online before you could speak directly with the students."

"Does Dr. Chen know?" Hazel referred to Chen Hu-Wei, the school's vice principal and physician.

"Yes. The medical examiner called him to Flambert to consult on the autopsy."

Callie wondered how the police chief would handle this. She felt he was neither experienced enough nor discerning enough to be competent. "Could the death be accidental?"

"Doubtful." Craig squeezed his wife's hand. "Did you know Stella?"

Hazel suppressed a sob. "Yes, I worked with her individually. She had a real talent." Hazel looked to Callie. "You?"

Callie considered Stella's photo on the school website. "No. She must be—have been—in one of the underclass English courses." Coop was teaching those this year while Callie developed her plans for the women's center.

Coop pressed his lips together. "Yes. She was from Flambert. She left a message yesterday that she wasn't feeling well and was going to her mother's place in town for a couple days. If she'd asked permission, I'd have said no." As the school's principal, Coop generally insisted that all students stay on campus when school was in session, even the few townies.

Without touching him, Callie could feel his grief. She sought his eyes. "I'm so sorry. But you couldn't have known."

Coop shook his head, unwilling to accept any absolution. He beckoned everyone to the table.

"Who's downstairs with the girls?" Ever-practical, Hazel

poured water and worried.

Coop named a couple of teachers who were the house parents for the student cabins associated with this house. "We called an assembly for tonight after dinner." His phone rang and he left the room as they began to pass the food.

Nobody ate much or said much. Setting aside a plate for Coop, Callie shoveled leftovers into containers and filled the dishwasher. Craig and Hazel left for the assembly.

Coop returned from the long call looking grim. "Dr. Chen says they're waiting for a tox screen, but they're fairly certain the poison was self-administered."

"Did she leave a suicide note?" Callie knew that notes weren't common but hoped Stella had left an explanation.

He waved off the plate she'd made for him. "The police say her friends received a text blaming some bullies." He took in a sharp breath. "I need to call Mrs. Kelly. Go ahead to the assembly. I'll be there shortly."

Once outside, Callie was swept into a sea of girls, teachers, and staff, some weeping openly, some pale with fear, all headed toward the gym, the only Cooper School building large enough for a school-wide assembly. Unready to talk about Stella, Callie put on her stone face, crafted from teen years in juvie. No one approached her.

The gym was rife with the odor of ancient sweat from generations of athletic shoes and chlorine wafting from the basement pool. Outdoor light filtered through undusted windows, streaking the air and floor with melancholy.

Craig took his place at the temporary front of the assembly, under a basketball hoop. The Flambert police chief stood next to him. Callie flashed back to the chief's controversial appointment by his brother, the mayor. *Would it be too catty to teach the students about nepotism?* She liked and respected the previous chief, who had believed Callie's insights that led to convicting a rapist. The new guy wouldn't give her the time of day, no doubt because she and the mayor didn't see eye to eye about the women's center. Callie wondered if he had enough experience to deal with a student suicide without missteps and gaffes.

Callie joined a group from her advanced English composition class in the bleachers, observing Hazel and other teachers likewise seated among their students, a tacit acknowledgment that they would need adult support. Alexis stood against the wall, one arm slung over the shoulder of her girlfriend, Shauni Rodriguez, the school's soccer coach. Shauni's green eyes were puffy from crying and her mahogany skin had an ashen hue. Callie remembered from the school website that Stella had been a soccer player and made a mental note to check in with Shauni later.

When Coop entered the gym, the hubbub quieted to whispers and sobs. At 6 foot 4, with the muscled frame of a lifelong athlete, and slightly overgrown silver-streaked black hair, he was an imposing figure. Generally, the students adored him, though one once asked when he would turn back into Bruce Banner.

Callie chortled when she heard about it, simultaneously making a mental note to teach students about how to construct metaphors based on truth. Coop was not an angry man and certainly had not transformed from a small scientist. He did have an engineering degree, though, among his other PhDs. *Happier times will come when all I have to consider is teaching techniques.*

"I'm sorry to share the news that a Cooper student died earlier today. Evidence suggests that Stella Kelly took her own life."

Callie admired that Coop systematically made eye contact with as many girls as he could, as if to say he was not afraid of their grief. "These next few weeks will be hard, especially for Stella's friends. So please share whatever you're experiencing with teachers, advisers, and coaches."

Heads swiveled as students assessed possible mentors. The senior next to Callie sniffled quietly. Callie squeezed her hand. Another student leaned into her from the other side. *Good thing I brought a box of tissues.*

Coop's forty-something face creased with kindness. "You

may have received a text from Stella pointing a finger at bullies. Please share them with a teacher if you have received one." He looked around again. "I doubt I have to remind you that school policy prohibits cell phones use during classroom hours. However, for now we aren't penalizing anyone for breaking those rules. We want to support you through this with whatever you need. And please, if you know anything about the bullying, speak up. Now or privately."

Next, the police chief spoke. *A tale told by an idiot, full of sound and fury signifying nothing.* Nobody remembered what he said when asked later.

As girls whispered to one another, Callie's fists balled. Her first instinct was always to fight, not flee. *Bullies beware.*

Coop raised a hand for silence. "As you all know too well, I can be blunt." An acknowledging titter ran around the room. "But this has to be said. At some schools, one suicide inspires another and another. Don't let that happen here. In more than a century since the Cooper School began, we've had only two suicides. The other was decades ago. You don't have to suffer alone. If you're afraid of someone, or know someone is being bullied, we'll protect you. If you notice that someone else is having trouble, let us know." Coop paused, as if waiting for his words to sink in. "Questions?"

Hands rose from girls anguished that someone who was right there breathing this morning was permanently scratched off. Coop and Craig patiently listened to each student. Craig fielded questions about legal issues. When Coop finally called for the last question, a senior named Harriet raised her hand. "Yes?"

Harriet stood. "Stella was murdered."

CHAPTER 2

Murder? What? Now that the specter presented itself like Hamlet's ghost, nobody could ignore it, least of all Coop and Callie. Their morning coffee conversation was consumed by it.

"Are we cursed? Do we bring murder to us?" Callie knew she was being melodramatic but each of them had a murder in their past—her mother, his wife; each killed by a psychopath hiding in plain sight.

"Honey, you know I'm not superstitious. We're facing this because we deal with infinitely more people each year than the average couple. This situation, well, public opinion could really hurt us. Let's reserve judgment until we talk with Harriet." Coop offered her a perfect omelet, complete with garnish and a side of fruit.

"Coop, what did the police chief say about Harriet's claim?"

"He's not inclined to share his opinions with me."

Callie sighed. "I liked the old chief."

Coop nodded. "That was a great retirement party."

"I remember. He invited us to visit him in Florida." For a moment she wished they could go there right now. Leave this mess for someone else to handle.

"I try to stay out of local politics for obvious reasons, but it's pretty well known I'm not a fan of the new guy." Coop took a breath and shifted his tone. "If you're going to the meeting, you have to leave now." He kissed her and handed over the materials she needed.

On Callie's drive to Flambert, she tried to squelch a desire to turn around, return to the school, and join Coop's discussion with Harriet. But there was another pressing task that only she could do, as scary as it felt. She had to defend the women's center to the Flambert town council or lose the land she wanted. Callie wished she could forget the teen experiences that whined through her veins like a siren whenever she felt threatened. They made her feisty and sometimes rude. *Right now, ladylike would be good.*

Council President Anjali Verma was the obvious lady at the Flambert Council table. Well-spoken, reasonable, even thoughtful. Civilized. Yet Callie heard threats under the honey. Callie visualized pummeling the president until she cried. Lady-like be damned.

There is no salvation for us but to adopt Civilization and lift ourselves down to its level. Thank you, Mark Twain. Callie's focus see-sawed from the meeting to the fate of Stella Kelly. Under-the-table texts with Coop revealed his discussion with Harriet was unproductive. The student had no idea why she thought Stella's death was a homicide but insinuated that Stella had enemies. Callie wanted to cry or scream or shake Harriet until she said something useful. *Completely inappropriate.* Callie was abruptly brought back to the council meeting when her attorney's elbow grazed hers, a signal to pay attention.

Lawrence White's piles of fancy degrees and slew of experience meant he had an enviable vocabulary when he was, say, arguing in front of the U.S. Supreme Court; here he spoke in plain English. "I believe the council has violated its own ordinances." He rose respectfully, buttoning his jacket as he continued to lay out their missteps, though he must be going quietly mad. He no doubt knew it was useless to explain basic legal concepts to people who had no interest in following the law if it didn't suit them and would cite anything from a cookbook to a religious tract to "prove" their assertions.

Who here knew Stella? Why aren't you as upset as I am?

Anjali tapped her gavel, but it couldn't be heard amid the grumbling from council members and townsfolk.

Anjali's henchman and husband slapped the long wooden table, a louder call to attention. "Yer sayin' we're anti-female." He was apparently offended by the word "women," which nobody had said in at least ten minutes. A ruddy man in polyester, he owned a string of gas stations across New York state, which evidently qualified him to be mayor. His bullying of business and personal associates alike was constant fodder for the local grapevine. Yet, he'd served the town for years, and his cronies were half of the eleven council members in this tiny room in the center of this gossipy upstate town.

Instead of jumping over the table and tearing out someone's throat, Callie s turned to Lawrence.

He addressed Mr. Polyester. "I beg your pardon?" Lawrence never begged anything from anyone and was surely fed up with the willful misunderstandings and misdirection of the proceedings. His polished, well-informed parries to Anjali and cohorts would be a joy if they convinced the council—as they rightfully should—not to sandbag Callie's dream of a women's center.

Callie allowed herself a moment of daydreaming. In that scenario, Stella was alive and well and creating mind-blowing art in the women's center studios.

Anjali tapped her gavel again, this time more effectively. She spoke to Lawrence, as if Callie were invisible. "What my esteemed colleague means is that we don't oppose a women's center *per se*. We'll sell this land to the project that best serves the town." The words *esteemed colleague* caused snickers around the table. "Your client's architectural plans are inadequate, and you have no environmental impact statement."

A woman in a faded sweater raised her hand.

"The chair recognizes Council Member Dorothy Kelly."

Callie also recognized Stella's mother. She'd spoken to Mrs. Kelly briefly in the few minutes before the meeting, acknowledging her grief and reiterating Coop's offers of support. The women's center, if it ever came into being, would provide free grief counseling among its many services. Typical of Anjali, she hadn't yet said a single word of comfort to Mrs. Kelly.

Dorothy apparently came to the meeting so soon after Stella's death for one reason—to oppose Anjali. She glanced around at the big guns with the courage that won her election after election. "I support the women's center. I'm a single parent and I'm not the only one around here. Most of us gotta work full time to pay the bills. The council cut the after-school program at the public school, which is not a safe situation for our kids. The center's gonna have a free one. Let's give them a chance to fix their proposal."

Anjali surveyed the group and seemingly determined she'd be outvoted and possibly shouted down if she told Dorothy no. Instead, she directed a disapproving stare directly at Lawrence. "Attorney White, you haven't cleared the land use with the Mohawks and—"

Lawrence, one of only two African American attorneys in Flambert, bristled when anyone waved the flag of minority rights in a way he thought was unseemly. "The town purchased the land a century ago. The tribal elders have never laid claim to…" Lawrence rattled on about land purchase and use history that affected this particular parcel. Callie once again lost focus. Though Lawrence was technically correct, Callie disagreed. Several members of the Mohawk nation were at the back of the room speaking quietly with one another.

She scribbled a note to Lawrence. **Must meet with Mohawk elders.** Lawrence nodded almost imperceptibly while finishing his point.

Anjali dismissed him with a wave. "We have two offers. The women's center and … another. We'll consider both applications at next month's meeting. Ms. Franklin, you have until a week before that meeting to submit an updated proposal."

Lawrence continued standing as if to stake out territory Anjali was trying to wrest from him. "We have one other request."

Anjali displayed the regal bearing of a Brahmin, though her family had no money. As if grieved to be forced by the public setting to maintain a semblance of democratic procedures, her voice oozed impatience. "Yes?"

Lawrence could out-regal the best of them, however. "We request that the council issue a public statement of condolence to the family and friends of Stella Kelly."

Even though the statement had been Callie's idea, tears sprang to her eyes as she heard the words aloud. She saw Dorothy Kelly cover her face with a hand.

A wave of further annoyance crossed Anjali's face but she knew she had been bested in the game of "I care the most about this town." After a quick unanimous vote, she directed the council secretary to create such a statement and banged her gavel for adjournment.

Callie blinked in the fall light as she stepped onto the stone steps outside, remembering her first time in this building that housed the council, as well as Flambert's only courtroom, police station, and jail. It was the same day she admitted to herself that she was in love with Coop, and the same day police arrested him on trumped up charges. Despite threats of prison, he'd greeted almost everyone warmly, from the arresting officers to the judge.

But not the council president.

Coop and Anjali had clashed from high school forward. These days they maintained a thin veneer of cordiality. When Callie asked Coop to come today, he'd said it would be like bringing a snake to a mouse festival. Callie giggled at the image, attracting a withering stare from Anjali as she passed by. *She can't read my mind, but she knows she's the punch line.*

Mrs. Kelly was last to leave the building but seemed gratified that Callie was still on the steps. "Hello, Ms. Franklin."

"Callie, please." Callie grasped the woman's offered hand in both of hers. "How're you doing? Is there anything I can do?"

"Thank you so much for asking for a public statement. May I meet with you and Principal Cooper when I come to collect Stella's belongings?" Mrs. Kelly's usual vigor was muted, and deep circles sagged under her eyes.

"Of course." Callie fished out a business card and scribbled her cell number on the back. "Let me know when you're coming." Callie generally kept a distance from all but her closest friends, but now she impulsively held out her arms to Dorothy. Surprised but grateful, the grieving mother accepted the embrace. Callie wished Anjali had stayed to see what she should have done as a leader of this little village, or simply as a human being.

* * *

Sitting at Coop's kitchen table days later, Callie ripped open Anjali's one-page letter, reading with growing disgust. Discarding the paper, she slapped the table. "This isn't an official communication. It's an ugly joke." She wanted to throw the council president and her mayor husband and his police chief brother into a ravine. *Upstate New York has lots of them.*

Coop looked up from his laptop. "Must be the ski resort." He gestured toward a glossy flier ready for the recycling bin.

"They won't approve a women's center because they want a ski resort?" Callie crumpled and balled the offending letter and then the flier, pitching them against the wall. "Why don't they put some effort into addressing teen suicide instead of ruining my life?"

Her dream center sprang to her mind like disconnected bars of a forgotten song. It would be a complex of eco-friendly buildings, bustling with myriad services and classes amid the lush mountains and clear streams. Callie saw outdoor walks and trails, classrooms, a theater, a pool, music practice rooms. Soundproofed studios for meditation or counseling. Stella could have been referred there when the first suicidal thought emerged. Incongruously, Callie's long-dead mother joined the vision—not as she'd last seen her, a naked crumpled emaciated body covered with blood, but sitting gracefully in a shaft of sunlight, oblivious of her movie star beauty, laughing with her sister, Callie's beloved aunt Sophie.

"What can I do?" Callie touched the dove necklace she always wore, a gift from Sophie, asking for heavenly help if such a thing existed.

Coop grinned. "That question is a tad open ended, but if you want suggestions——" He raised an eyebrow, angling his head toward the bedroom.

"Oh, shut up." Callie rewarded him with a lingering kiss, but before their lust could permanently derail their day, she slid away and distracted herself by gathering hiking gear. "What's the deal with Anjali? Didn't she learn anything from going to Cooper?"

"She was an A student. Attended Vassar where she also did well. Could have gone anywhere with that degree. But she came back and settled here." As the school's principal and owner, he took pride in each girl's accomplishments. "Probably because she married the mayor."

"Doesn't that worry you? About her mental health? He's so ethically bankrupt."

Coop reached for his phone. "No accounting for who people love."

Callie groaned. "Who are you calling? 1-800 Save Me from Stupidity?"

"Dorothy Kelly." After a brief conversation, he said a thank you then hung up. Rescuing the letter, he smoothed it out. "Paper trail."

Callie was ready to burn the thing. *And my bridges with it.* "I made an offer way over the asking price. Isn't the town broke? Why are they turning down cash?"

"Dorothy bought you some time. She's grieving the loss of her only daughter and she fought for you. You owe it to her to get better plans."

She sighed. "I know you're right. I just feel so unanchored."

"They gave you a few weeks." He scanned the letter for other details. "Dorothy says right now the council is evenly split." He slid the letter into a file folder, labeling it in his neat hand. "We also talked a little about Stella."

"And?"

He painted the sad picture. Stella was found in her only party dress, accessorized with her favorite jewelry. She'd applied fresh makeup to her freckled Irish face, only to leave the world distorted by the ravages of the poison. She looked as if she'd been stood up for a date, though her text was about bullies, not a broken heart. Both Dorothy and the police were perplexed. Callie wished she could ask the police for details but knew they had no reason to share with her.

Coop changed the subject. "Did Lawrence go over the town regulations with you?"

"Yes, but my memory of them is jumbled."

"The letter suggests you need to adhere more closely to them." He pushed a folder of Flambert city policies toward her. *Damn this man is always prepared.*

"And once I dot all those ts, they'll go after me some other way, right?" Callie gathered her thick brown hair into a ponytail, jerking so hard the band broke. She growled and stomped around, looking for one of the half dozen hair elastics she tended to leave around Coop's apartment. With his usual uncanny ability to read her, he opened a kitchen drawer and handed one over. Not for the first time, Callie missed Coop's daughter, Nora. The two women had a common trait: orderliness was not their forte.

Coop arranged his work into methodical piles, a skill he had yet to teach his daughter or his sweetheart.

Tidiness ... Something about Stella's death is too tidy.

Returning her thoughts to the center, Callie thought about advice from her attorney, who had almost as many accolades from top-notch institutions as smarty-pants Coop. "I knew the center plan was a little rushed, kind of half-baked, but the council isn't famous for paying attention to details—or its own regulations. Until the meeting, I thought it would be a simple transaction. Flambert needs to sell the land, I made a strong cash offer. Everybody should be happy."

Coop shrugged as if to say she had plenty to learn about being rich. "Dorothy says the ski resort matched your offer. Now you'll need to wow the council."

Callie tried to find it soothing to slather on sunscreen. "But Anjali recommended the architect I used. Doesn't hiring local—"

"Make you a local? Maybe it just makes you a dupe. Time to find another architect." Coop snapped his fingers. "What about that lady—"

Callie interrupted automatically. "Woman."

He rolled his eyes. "—woman. College friend. The, um, architect?"

"Right. Phoebe. Yes. Wow." Callie threw herself into Coop's arms, kissing him. "Really great idea." She emailed Phoebe that second. "She won't read this till she gets home from work. Let's go."

Within minutes they crossed the well-groomed campus grounds. Another half hour and they were well up the mountain locals called Lovers Peak. Birds and insects offered rhythmic accompaniment to their adventure, and small animals rustled nearby. Callie inhaled the moist honeysuckle fragrance, trying to shut out the world at the bottom of the mountain. From time to time, they talked of Stella. From time to time, they touched on what the center could provide for the whole region. Mostly they were each lost in their own thoughts. Neither the woods, nor vigorous climbing, nor Coop's company soothed Callie.

* * *

Phoebe called after dinner. "What's the big SOS?"

"A student committed suicide and I don't feel I can give enough attention to the students or the school because of the stupid Flambert City Council." Callie briefly described the current dilemma. "The council is pushing me to rush new plans or lose the opportunity with the center on this perfectly located piece of land and all I can think about is Stella."

Phoebe sighed. "I get it, Callie. You always had a soft heart under that tough exterior. I'm really sorry about your student. The only thing I can—*maybe*—help with is the center. Tell me more about it."

Callie described the complex she wanted. "And performance spaces and a gym and a warm water pool and a hockey rink, a soccer field and.."

Phoebe guffawed. "You and what hedge fund? You're always broke, and I thought your boyfriend owned a school, not a Fortune 500."

"I inherited money not too long ago. Plenty. Long story for another time. Right now, you have to help me defeat the Evil Empire." She described the dreaded ski resort.

"What's the big hurry? Other land will open up." Phoebe sighed. "In case you haven't heard, we're in a recession. You can probably get a good deal right in the same area, maybe even a better spot."

"This land borders the Cooper School land. And it's free and clear of all claims, including the historic Native American treaty claims."

"It sounds a little . . ."

Impossible? Unrealistic? Childish? Stupid? Shut up, Callie. "A little . . .?"

"Complicated."

"As you know, some bad stuff happened here." Callie shook away the memories, more than two years past but still too recent. "The center is a step toward healing."

Phoebe interrupted, "Yeah, yeah, I get it. The center's your Genovia. Castles. Julie Andrews. Okay, let's say I bite. Where do I come in? And is Chris Pine involved? Because I could use a date with a movie star—"

Callie inhaled courage. "Help me rework the plans to fit city regs."

Phoebe sighed again. "Honey, I'm a junior associate. You need an expert on public-use complexes, someone with a lot of time. I design parking garages and work a sixty-something-hour week just to keep my job."

Callie's age-old fear of abandonment caused her pulse to quicken. "Don't say no. Please don't. You're my last hope, Obi Wan K' Phoebe."

Phoebe giggled. "Whoa, the Callie who never showed her hand is sure gone. Hello Ms. Drama Queen. For heaven's sakes, Callie, every community needs a place like that. Build it somewhere else."

"No, no. It has to be here. This is where it all happened. Where Miriam died."

"Miriam?"

"We're naming the center after her." Callie punched several pen holes into the glossy ski resort flyer.

Coop looked up from his book with a clear reprimand. "Callie."

Callie's voice crept louder, feeling at odds with Phoebe and Coop. "Both of you?"

"Both of who?" Phoebe sounded irked.

"Whom. Don't you mean whom?"

"Oh. My. God. Call me back when you come to your senses." Phoebe disconnected.

Coop didn't move. "I don't appreciate you using Miriam as a bargaining chip."

"Phoebe doesn't know who Miriam is." Callie hardly did. She'd seen photos and videos of Coop's late wife and heard sweet family stories from Nora but getting murdered had a way of erasing all but the highlights.

Coop slapped his book shut. "That's not the point and you know it. What's going on? You practically bit her head off. Over grammar. She's your good friend and you need her."

"She can't help. Nobody can. I'm going home."

Callie slammed the door of Coop's apartment, running down the stairs, past a scattering of students, and through the outside door. Headed to her own cabin, she half wanted Coop to follow.

As she stormed up the path, the sheer energy of walking shook loose a couple of truths: She wasn't mad at Coop -- he was right to call her out. And she wasn't mad at Phoebe-- she was right, too. *I'm mad because I have to ask for help and I hate that. So instead, I act like a spoiled brat and everybody knows it. If this is what being rich makes me do, maybe I should just put all the money on a barge out to sea.*

Her pace slowed as she came to a familiar bend in the road. Here a madman shot at her. She shivered despite the warm summer night. After a moment, Callie slowly dragged herself onward to her cabin. She went to bed fuming at herself and hoping for forgiveness.

Nightmares invaded her sleep. Stella. Anjali. The police chief. She woke exhausted and on edge. Callie waited until the sun rose. A reasonable hour. She called Dr. Chen. He, evidence suggested, had a different definition of reasonable because he let the call go to voicemail. Her message asked whether it was possible that Stella was murdered. Then she drifted back to sleep.

An hour later, Callie woke with a rueful checklist in her head.

One. *Call Coop and apologize.*

His response: "I know, sweetheart. I love you." He always knew, and he always loved her.

"Can you cover my classes today?"

He laughed. "Cheeky to ask for a favor so soon." He let her wait a moment. "Sure."

Two. *Take the train to NYC.*

Easily done. A few hours later she was under the constellations at Grand Central, wishing she believed in astrology—or any predictive magic.

Three. *Go see Phoebe.*

Hailing a cab, she searched her memory for literary apologies. She was a literature teacher, for heaven sakes. Surely one would come to mind. Back in college, Callie and Phoebe frequently repeated a William Carols Williams poem they called **Sorry, Not Sorry** though his title was **This is Just to Say.**

I have eaten
the plums
that were in
the icebox

and which
you were probably
saving
for breakfast

Forgive me
they were delicious
so sweet
and so cold

I don't think "sorry, not sorry" is the message I want today.

CHAPTER 3

Callie straightened her spine to her full five seven as she approached the building that housed the architectural firm where Phoebe worked. It was designed to impress, yet all Callie felt was a bit intimidated. A first-floor guard. A lobby full of busy professionals on their way to wherever busy professionals go in *The* City. A glassed-in elevator with a view of the busy streets, ever more coldly imperial as it rose. Callie wanted to hug the Chrysler tower just for appearing in her line of sight, an elegant Art-Deco antidote to the glass and steel straight lines nearby.

On the top floor beyond the elevator, gray tinted glass doors slid apart revealing a sleek modern desk. A redheaded young man at a computer sneered behind a brass nameplate reading **Elton**. His sculpted face and toned physique suggested a model instead of a receptionist. *In New York, everyone has an agenda.*

Elton's half-response to her query reminded Callie of the years when her rough edges routinely elicited disdain from gatekeepers. Maybe she could never truly hide her past. But today, in her own estimation, she looked pretty good. Expensive outfit. Good haircut. Evidently, this guy didn't buy the disguise. *Disguise. Did Stella have a killer and was he or she a wolf in sheep's . . .*

While she was still considering appropriate parries to the redhead, he snapped a finger and pointed at some expensive-looking chairs. "Have a seat." He made no move to help, despite a headset that suggested he could call Phoebe without significant effort.

A plump woman burst through an office door, carrying rolls of blueprints. "Elton, why did none of my clients receive … Callie Franklin! You're here."

"Phoebe." Callie leapt to embrace her friend. "Please forgive me."

"Don't be silly, you were—are?—upset." Phoebe surveyed Callie's coiffure, wardrobe, manicure. "Wow, you weren't kidding. A teacher's salary couldn't buy that look."

"You look great, too." Callie remembered fashion magazines appearing among her classmate's study materials with greater frequency than, say, notes. "Did you design that?"

Phoebe shrugged at her own outfit. "No time to sew these days. It's *prêt-à-porter*. Off the rack. Still fabulous."

The redhead snickered, apparently unconcerned that they knew he was eavesdropping.

Phoebe turned toward him long enough to deliver a withering glance, then aimed her joviality at Callie. "The road to *haute couture* is paved with starving artists. Bizarrely, I like to eat and pay rent. So much for becoming a designer like Maisie Wilen." Pushing wild curls off her face, Phoebe thumped heavily marked blueprints on the receptionist's desk, issuing terse instructions. When Mr. Smirky finally appeared compliant, she returned to Callie. "Sorry, hon. I'm swamped."

"Let me take you to lunch."

A bevy of suits, apparently more senior than Phoebe, appeared from side offices and beckoned her toward a conference room.

Nodding at Callie, she lowered her voice to almost a whisper. "Deli on the corner at one; preorder for me so I can inhale it."

She disappeared into her meeting.

Callie texted Nora who worked in an art gallery in Chelsea.

In midtown for a few hours. You free?

Nora responded immediately.
Gallery packed today. Next time.

They'd been close when Nora was still at Cooper School. After two years of art school, Coop's daughter was currently on a gap year to work among the up-and-coming of the art world. Now twenty-one, Nora seemed determined to keep her father and Callie at arm's length. Disappointed, Callie wandered Manhattan, peering at jewelry she could finally afford but would never buy. She strolled past Central Park's carousel full of laughing children, settling with the *New York Times* on a bench outside the deli to wait for lunch. Too antsy to read, she called Coop. "Hey."

"Did she say yes?"

She sighed. "I'm fine. How are you?"

"Callie, I love and adore you—I'll prove it when you get back. In detail."

"I'll hold you to that." She could almost feel his touch. "Should I worry about Nora? She's too busy to meet me."

"I worry about her all the time. It doesn't help."

Callie sighed again. "Have you heard from Dorothy?"

"Yes." Coop hesitated. "She heard about Harriet's claim and is really upset."

"I'm sure. Maybe she knows whether to take Harriet seriously. I left a voicemail for Dr. Chen, but—"

His tone changed, sliding down to register something Callie couldn't quite identify. "Dr. Chen says there's something we need to know about Stella's death. He wants to explain in person. We'll see him tomorrow."

Now for the question she waited to ask. "Have you forgiven me?"

"For running away whenever things get tense?"

"I wasn't .... well, okay. Yeah." She hated how well he

knew her. *And love it.*

"And there's something else…" It wasn't like him to stop mid-sentence.

"Tell me."

"Not on the phone."

Gotta get home.

At that moment, Phoebe arrived. A few minutes of perfect kosher pickles and pastrami over the din in the delicatessen pushed the two women back to the outdoor bench.

With a dramatic flourish, Phoebe poked Callie. "You always told me it was all good back there in Pennsylvania."

"I lied." Callie fingered her dove necklace. "You were at Columbia grad school, I was a teacher's college dropout…"

"For good reason, Florence Nightingale. You were on full-time bedside duty for your Aunt Sophie." Phoebe looked away. "Sucks that she died so young."

"Sucks." Callie flashed on the three of them sitting in Sophie's kitchen before her aunt fell ill; they were murdering Ella Fitzgerald songs. "Thanks for the flowers."

Phoebe shook her head. "If I'd known your situation, I'da sent something more useful."

Callie raised a shoulder. "I liked the flowers. Even though I was laid off from data entry and had no idea how I was gonna pay the bills."

"You did good. Great teaching job. Guy of your dreams. And an inheritance you failed to mention before." Phoebe smirked.

"I hated Coop when I first met him." Callie showed Phoebe a photo on her phone. "Now I'm over the moon."

Deliberately issuing tasteless gurgles and grunts, Phoebe asserted judgment. "Hot."

"Hands off." Callie narrowed her eyes.

Phoebe knocked her cardboard cup against Callie's. "All yours, honey. Besides, he owes you.."

"How do you figure?"

"You caught his wife's murderer."

"Oh, that." Callie faked eye-fluttering modesty. "And

don't forget, I helped put a rapist behind bars. It was nothing. Nothing at all."

Phoebe's voice sharpened. "I know you. You're already trying to figure out what happened to Stella. Be careful, Callie."

Callie looked down. "Why would that senior say she was murdered?"

"How would I know?"

Callie changed gears. "I wish Aunt Sophie, or my mother, had lived to see me succeed. This women's center is partly for them."

"Blah blah. Save it for the press release." Phoebe appraised Callie. "You'll be the hottest nonprofit executive director on the east coast. You still have the best hair ever and apparently work out like a marine. What happened to your scars?"

Callie self-consciously flipped her hair off her shoulder, ignoring the reference to her youthful brawls. "Hot? I'm thirty-three. In your world, isn't that elderly?"

"Seriously, hon, I'd give my Prada sandals to work on your center." Phoebe methodically dismantled her cup. "But even if you can pay me—"

"I can."

"I can't afford to give up my secure job for a short-term project." Phoebe picked at the edges of her cup. Suddenly, she raised her index finger and drew a dramatic circle in the air.

Callie's spirits dared to lift a smidge, recognizing the gesture. "Aha. You have a brilliant idea."

"It's a long shot. But a partner at my firm, Jillian Wilson, is the best public-spaces architect in New York." Phoebe smiled. "She's into eco stuff, so she'll hate the ski resort."

Callie allowed herself Emily Dickinson's "thing with feathers." *Hope.* "Why a long shot?"

Phoebe tossed her newly re-designed empty cup toward a trash barrel and missed. "Jillian's a really big deal and always has a whole boatload of projects. Her walls and shelves are covered with awards."

"Too busy, then?"

"Or too something. She might refuse to work with you for

no good reason—because she hates your shoes, or all women's centers, or upstate, or that it's Tuesday."

Callie nodded. "Got the picture. And?"

"Lots of ands. For one, that bony little creep Elton is her nephew. Everyone at the firm despises him. We're all insane worker bees while he spends all day Googling expensive gizmos. He's constantly taking off on ski or hiking or hunting vacations, depending on the season. The last person who complained about him got booted, so nobody says anything. Jillian believes he can do no wrong. He works on all her projects even though he's basically useless. That means you'd be stuck with him if she—" Phoebe stuffed the fallen cardboard cup into the trash can and clicked her phone. "What the hell." She nodded at her friend. "Elton, put me through to Jillian."

On the walk back, Callie tried not to let her excitement rise just because Jillian agreed to see her immediately. It still was not a sure thing. Upper east siders tend to disdain a tough kid with a record, however well-disguised.

Elton showed Callie into Jillian's office, following an elaborate stretch no doubt intended to convey bored indifference at not being included.

The woman behind the giant antique inlaid desk appeared to be in her sixties, queen sized and well-dressed, gray hair styled to show off designer silver earrings. She wasted no time on small talk. "Tell me about your center."

Cascades of talk and a dozen sketches later, Callie shook Jillian's hand. "I have to ask—"

Jillian, as always, interrupted. "Why I'm doing this?"

"Yeah."

"I'm a feminist. I believe in making things better for all women. Unlike you young people, I'm not into being as ruthless as men."

"Um—" Callie decided against correcting Jillian's misrepresentation of several entire generations.

"My father designed a school modeled on Cooper. I've always wanted an excuse to get up there and poke around."

"I see."

"You probably don't." Jillian turned to her computer. Beyond her, the twentieth-floor window revealed the lights of the city blinking into the night.

The summary dismissal couldn't diffuse Callie's elation. Jillian had rendered Callie's half-baked vision into real drawings on real paper in just hours. Callie danced along the hallways, carefully slowing to a professional pace when she passed Elton's desk. She needn't have bothered. Focused on what appeared to be a website about ski equipment, he never looked up as she walked by.

Once outside, she called Phoebe's cell. Even though Phoebe was in her office, they'd agreed that it was best for Callie not to appear too friendly in front of Phoebe's colleagues, all of whom seemed to be working late and any of whom could undermine Callie's relationship with Jillian if they thought she was too connected with an underling. Even Phoebe's office phone was off limits.

Tucking her own cell between ear and shoulder, Callie sat on a bench and changed to comfortable shoes. "I owe you big time. Jillian is something."

"Don't you love her suit? Tadashi Shoji." Phoebe could correctly identify any designer couture from a hundred feet. She lowered her voice, apparently unwilling to have nearby colleagues hear her query. "What did she say?"

"She'll do it. She'll even come up to the council meeting and explain the environmental advantages of the center. Is that normal?" Callie stuffed her heels into her backpack.

Still speaking softly into her cell, Phoebe snickered. "Normal? Nothing about her is normal. And she's changeable. Don't be surprised if she sends a minion at the last minute. Fingers crossed it isn't Elton."

"Brought to you by the letter E."

"What? Never mind. Where's Flambert?"

"A few hours on Metro North. Faster if you drive—the train hits every milk town in the entire state." Callie owned a hybrid car but preferred the train. She secretly loved the stop-start rhythm moving her from life to life, plus it gave her time to read.

Phoebe harrumphed. "Then, you're stuck with Elton. Sorry."

"Why?"

"I doubt Jillian's set foot on public transportation in the twenty-first century. Elton's her driver and personal assistant. At least he's familiar with the area. He vacations in upstate New York. He brags about it to anyone who will listen."

Callie heard an office phone through the cell.

Phoebe sighed. "Just a sec."

Callie could hear only the cadence of Phoebe's voice, no actual words. The sounds rose and accelerated, then became quiet and terse, then ended abruptly. When Phoebe came back, her voice sounded unsteady. Uncharacteristically, Phoebe exhaled an audible sob. "Can't talk here."

"What's wrong?" Callie wasn't sure what she could do but owed her friend at least a sympathetic ear. "Isn't the workday over? Come out with me until my train leaves."

"I have hours more but..." Phoebe sounded too teary to say no. "Wait for me across the street."

Callie checked the time and called Coop. "The good news is that Jillian's a genius who may well save the center. The bad news is that I probably won't make the next train."

"New boyfriend?"

She snorted. "Yes. We're taking a room at the Plaza for an hour."

He offered an exaggerated snore. "You know the Plaza isn't a hotel anymore and never rented by the hour, right?"

"Anything rents for an hour if you pay enough."

"So sad you've succumbed to the arrogance of the *nouveau riche*."

"You suck at jealousy." Callie tsked elaborately. "Phoebe wants to talk. Something's wrong—and this time it's not because of me. Don't know how long it will take."

"Least you can do." They both said 'love you' and disconnected simultaneously.

Callie watched for her friend amid the surge of

professionals hurrying home. Phoebe appeared, steering Callie into a nearby diner. "Let's go here. The food is awful, so it won't be crowded."

Settling into a cracked vinyl booth, Callie ordered coffee, regretting it as soon as she caught its scent. "What's the big mystery?"

"I'm done being the other woman. Done."

Callie allowed herself one selfish moment of wishing she hadn't asked. "Other woman?"

"A partner at the firm…" Phoebe trailed off.

"Married?"

"Very." Her cell dinged and she texted a few words. "Jerk."

"Do you love him?"

"Callie, you're so great. Most of my friends launch right into lecturing." Phoebe's tale unfolded in fits and starts. A dapper older man with zillion-dollar taste and glib half-truths. Long work hours. Midnight dinners. Office couches that progressed to hotels to weekend getaways. "Maybe I love him—but I thought I loved the others, too."

Callie's phone alarm sounded that it was time to leave. "Others?"

"I'm a serial home wrecker."

"Oh, Phoebe. Jump off that merry-go-round." Regretting her judgmental tone, Callie reached for her friend's hand. "How can I help?"

"Get me out of the city."

Callie gathered her things and hugged her friend. "I'll ask Jillian to put you on her team. If she agrees, you can stay with me—maybe you can help figure out what happened to Stella."

"So now I'm Watson? Robin?" Phoebe patted the tears sliding from her eyes to keep from smearing her mascara. "Beats moping around my shoebox Brooklyn apartment watching reality TV. Or worse—rom-coms."

"Heaven forbid."

"And we know how well that romance blueprint works out for me." Phoebe waited while Callie's Uber arrived. "I'll call you tomorrow. If I last that long."

"Now who's the drama queen?"

CHAPTER 4

Aboard the train chugging northward toward home and midnight, Callie was plagued by a repeating loop of anxieties. Stella's death. Phoebe's predicament. Nora's distance. Over-commitment. Hope against hope for the women's center.

Coop's words, *not on the phone,* returned and returned. Was someone else dead? Was Cooper School in trouble?

Minds are tricky, though. Words from Charles Schultz, the Peanuts guy, popped into her head: *Don't worry about the world coming to an end today. It's already tomorrow in Australia.* She peered around to see whether anyone wondered why she was giggling uncontrollably alone in a train car. Fortunately, almost nobody sat nearby and those few seemed uninterested in any life but their own.

She distracted herself by scribbling To Do lists, tackling the New York Times crossword, and half-reading a well-reviewed novel that she abandoned at page 75.

One million uncomfortable musings later, the train arrived at the Flambert depot. Callie phoned Coop. "Need anything from town?"

"Do me a favor and pick up some papers at Craig's office." Coop sounded tired and remote.

"At this hour?"

"Meadow's waiting for you."

"On my way." Callie considered the advantages of having a

secretary, or better, a personal assistant, who would work until all hours doing her bidding.

Could I stand to hire someone who'd know my deepest secrets? Who did Stella trust?

Callie parked in front of the mostly dark law offices. A modest sign read: **Landers & White, Attorneys at Law.** Inside, the firm's modesty disappeared. The reception wall showed off awards and commendations as well as tastefully framed photos of both partners posing with politicians and international celebrities. Callie wondered if the display impressed or intimidated their detractors. Surely their supporters valued the lawyers for more than a four-second encounter with the Pope.

A young receptionist in jeans greeted Callie. "Oh yeah. Papers for Coop. It'll take me a minute."

Haven't you been waiting for me for hours?

Meadow didn't seem in any hurry. "Hey that's super sad about that girl who died."

"Yeah, it's hit us all pretty hard. Did you know her?"

Meadow shrugged. "To say hi."

Callie pushed back her hair, grabbing that moment to find a neutral subject. "Applying for college soon?"

The young woman flipped back black braids with pink tips. "Saving up. Right now, I'm learning Kanien'keha."

"Sorry?"

"The Mohawk language. I'm gonna major in Native American art history."

"Sounds good." Callie rubbed her eyes, more tired from the rollercoaster day than from the late hour. "As long as I have a few minutes, is Lawrence still here?" She hoped the words *few minutes* would light a fire under the young woman.

Meadow nodded. "Oh yeah. He works all the time." She buzzed the intercom.

Lawrence White appeared in moments. He greeted Callie with a smile, ushering her into a well-appointed office. "Do you want anything? A coffee for your drive to Cooper School? Whiskey because it's too late for caffeine?"

Callie didn't sit. "Another time. I didn't mean to bother

you right now. But I'm dying to know what you think." She'd texted him the news.

"Jillian Wilson. I'm a huge fan. I have a book of her green buildings somewhere here." He searched through a shelf of oversized volumes, handing Callie a hefty tome. "Having her on board is a big leg up. I'll re-initiate the permit applications for the women's center tomorrow."

"Don't work too late. You need your beauty sleep." He was, as an objective fact, handsome. But he seemed oblivious to it. Teasing him was very satisfying.

Back in the lobby, architecture book in hand, Callie noticed a new photo. "Is that Craig with Barak Obama?"

Meadow turned off the office computer and reached for her backpack bedecked with buttons and badges promoting Native causes. "Yeah, a month or so ago Craig got some big prize and so did Obama." The framed award was above the photo. "Old smart black guys or something." Meadow offered an untidy pile of files. "Here's the stuff Coop wanted."

Callie accepted the files and dialed as she walked out. "Hazel, your husband hung out with Obama?"

Hazel's voice was groggy. "What time is it?"

"Oh sorry, did I wake you up?" Callie squinted at the phone screen to see the time.

Hazel cleared her throat. "It's only eleven. Probably shouldn't be in bed."

"Many apologies. I'll call tomorrow."

"Where are you right now?"

"Leaving Craig's office."

Hazel sounded a tiny bit more alert. "I can get up. Come over. I'll make you a late-night snack. And I can remind you I *did* tell you about that award."

Callie was at her car door. "You know I love your cooking almost as much as your chiding. Gimme a rain check. Coop didn't sound quite himself and I should get home."

"We'll do dinner when you've got time."

Callie grinned, making a mental note to bring wine. Fine wine. Something else she needed to learn about as a proper rich person. *Do rich people know stuff, or do they just know the guy who knows? Do I know a guy? Should I hire a real detective for Stella?*

The half-hour drive from Flambert to Cooper School was alive with the rustle of trees and the aroma of the final hurrah of wild berries. *Someone should pick those.* Soon this stretch of road would house either an exemplary women's center or a crowded and disruptive ski resort. Wrinkling her nose at skunk odor, she closed her windows and drove on, turning at a wide drive under the lighted sign reading **The Cooper School.**

Inside Gwendolyn Cooper's former mansion, Callie passed the empty first-floor common room, mostly unlit save some safety lamps. Lights out for students was an hour ago and the faculty had retired as well. As Callie reached Coop's second floor apartment, the door flew open and Coop pulled her close. Melting into his embrace, she wallowed in a newfound sense of belonging, especially now that among Coop's extensive collection of books and antiques and mementos, some family photos included her.

Decades ago, someone knocked down the walls dividing up the early 20th century manor, ridding it of small useless rooms, creating open spaces on each floor. Downstairs they formed student dining and study areas. Here in the living quarters, the kitchen, living room, and library joined as one large and inviting environment, with many large windows. A master bedroom and bathroom completed the floor, while the attic above remained Nora's bedroom and studio.

Coop held Callie a moment longer than usual. Without speaking, they ambled together to the couch by the fireplace. On the coffee table, a pair of snifters and a bottle of brandy sat next to an elaborate dessert.

"I've been gone maybe a dozen hours." Callie tried to read him, but he was more skilled than she at hiding feelings—and she was a Gold Star expert. "What's wrong? What couldn't you tell me on the phone?"

Coop poured amber liquid into the snifters. He hesitated so she knew it was bad news. "Dr. Chen says there's no way Stella could have acquired the poison that killed her. It's used to kill persistent vermin in industrial sites. It's very tightly regulated."

Callie silently set her glass on the table as waves of fear shook her. "Suicide is bad enough. But murder? Who would murder Stella?" *And how did Harriet know?*

Coop's piercing black eyes found hers. "I wish we knew. Hu-wei says the Flambert police lab couldn't identify the particular toxin but figured it didn't matter since they thought she died by her own hand. He convinced them not to write it off as rat poison but instead to send it to the national lab at Bethesda. I'm glad he's there, though he'll be largely MIA from here while the case is ongoing."

Before Coop hired him, Dr. Chen retired from teaching at a medical school and had a national reputation among forensic scientists. The local lab frequently consulted him on forensic matters but usually they needed only an hour or two of his time. His original plan had been to briefly consult on Stella's case but as he realized how inexperienced the local scientists were, he felt he had no choice but to stay in the lab full time until the case was solved.

Callie grasped for another scenario. "Maybe it was a prank gone wrong? Or a terrible accident? Kids trying to get high on substances they didn't know would be fatal if ingested." *Any explanation besides murder.*

Coop rubbed tired eyes. "There were no fingerprints. No out-of-place DNA evidence. No sign of a killer except a rare poison."

If Callie had been asked how she felt right then, she wouldn't have known how to answer. The deep sadness about Stella's death and the gut-twisting anxiety about the future of the school were now accompanied by a fiery anger directed at the psychopath who killed a precious student.

Callie let some of the pieces fall into place before she spoke. She realized that she, like the town, had been wondering where the school went wrong. "If the murderer got hold of Stella's phone, the text is fake and the bullies are fictional, right?"

"That's another thing we need to find out." He sighed wearily.

"Another thing?"

Coop seemed uncharacteristically defeated, leaning back for a moment with closed eyes. He reached for her as he spoke. "The coroner's report will be out later this week and confirm that it wasn't suicide, but for now, the town believes Stella was being bullied at Cooper School. Maybe that's why the killer did it."

Callie was skeptical but kept her voice as neutral as possible. "Who would want to undermine the school?'

Coop could always read her, despite her best efforts. He raised an eyebrow as if to say, *You doubt me?* He looked down at her, literally and figuratively. "Lots of candidates in Flambert, the town has a love-hate relationship with this school."

Callie longed for the Coop who was always positive and practical. *This Eeyore "we're screwed" guy needs to go away.* She tried an argument she didn't completely believe. "More people love us than hate us."

He scowled and gulped the brandy too enthusiastically. "Only a few townies go to Cooper, but enough alums are around to dispel stupid myths. And everyone knows we contribute to the town in many ways. Sadly, the mayor and police chief are not so positively inclined; they tend to repeat every negative rumor that ever circulated about the school and their constituents do the same."

Callie longed to point out that he was lecturing her like a newbie but decided the better part of valor was playing along as the apprentice. Perhaps he needed to narrate the whole story— to help him think. "That's why the girls are required to do community service."

"Not why, exactly. We believe in service for the students' benefit. Service certainly does keep the community familiar with our students and vice-versa." He nodded ruefully. "We've never faced torches and pitchforks, but opposition for sure. Some is anti-intellectual, some is racist since our students are a robust mix of cultures and ethnicities, some is griping over our many acres of tax-free land because of our non-profit status. Unfortunately, we have just enough enemies that there could be a psycho among them."

He reached to refill his glass and Callie stopped him. "I think we need to be sober for this."

He clenched his jaw instead of snapping at her, silently breathing for a long pause. Then nodded. "Yeah." He set his snifter on the table next to the untouched dessert.

"Maybe the murderer…" Callie paused to take in the word murderer. "Maybe the murderer isn't a psycho. Maybe they coldly and calculatedly picked Stella because she was low-hanging fruit. For some agenda that isn't about Stella herself."

He offered a grim frown. "She was so vulnerable. It's so easy to lure a young woman off campus if she needs…" he hesitated. "I don't know what."

"What does Dr. Chen think?"

"He's a scientist. He'll only conclude what the evidence tells him. Nothing about the evidence suggests a motive yet."

Callie felt as lost as he did. "What's our next step?" She meant the murder inquiry.

He had something else on his mind. "Dr. Chen may be working with the investigation for the rest of the semester. I need someone to fill in as Vice Principal, someone who can take on his tasks, like talking to students in a crisis." He paused, waiting for her response.

Callie tensed as his meaning dawned on her. "You'd like me to step in."

If she said no, it would be World War III. If she said yes, how could she teach, develop the women's center planning and construction *and* be an administrator simultaneously? *What if I wreck everything? Coop seems depressed, I'm worried about everything and can't focus.* Shelley's poem galloped through her brain, offering little comfort:

'My name is Ozymandius, King of Kings,
Look on my works, ye Mighty, and despair!'
Nothing beside remains. Round the decay
Of that colossal wreck, boundless and bare
The lone and level sands stretch far away.

Will the center become my Ozymandius?

Coop murmured as he kissed her forehead. "Callie. Don't be a drama queen."

Damn, this man can read me.

Coop rose from the couch and loomed above a volcano oozing molten chocolate that rose from a bed of crumbles on a fragile crystal platter. Like a master chef, he dished the dessert onto caramel strings. A giant—literally and figuratively—he could intimidate almost anyone but nowadays usually chose finesse instead. Not tonight. "At this late date, you're the only one I can ask. Everyone else who's qualified is unavailable."

"So am I." Callie could count on one hand the times she'd wept before she met him. With him she felt it was safe to be honest. Unaccountably that meant tears of all sorts. He was used to drying her eyes. She cradled her head in her arms and dissolved into weeping.

He didn't move to comfort her. "The center isn't even approved yet. And might not be. Even if it is, you won't break ground for at least a month, then you will have a few months of down time during the winter. Dr. Chen might be back by then."

That seemed overly optimistic. "I can't just get out a shovel and dig a foundation. Planning. It takes a form of planning I need to learn. I can't run a major real estate development and simultaneously take on a new job. I don't even know exactly what Dr. Chen does. Two steep learning curves at once. No, Coop, I can't." The bitten-back tears were getting in the way.

"Callie, the school needs you. Stella's murder is going to throw a lot of things into disarray." Coop wasn't exactly mad, just forceful. But mad could be close behind.

I hated the murderer before but now I really hate … God, how can I be so selfish? Callie couldn't yet know what her timeline would be if the council approved the center, but she was sure Anjali would make the deadlines almost impossible to meet. That meant building through winter, in good weather and bad. Around here, snow fell in feet, not inches. Every vehicle and every pair of boots was a testament to protection against abusive cold over fashion. Callie pictured herself as The Little Match Girl, holding a tiny candle and expiring outside while Anjali and her cohorts—

Coop barreled on. "I'm not saying burn your blueprints and give up. I'm just asking for help." Coop stirred a salted caramel sauce that didn't need stirring, apparently counting to ten or to three hundred million.

Callie pressed her lips together, swallowing a sharp retort. Had monomania undermined her priorities? She'd snapped at Phoebe and forgotten that Craig and Hazel had met the Obamas. *Get a grip, Callie.* She pushed dessert around on her plate. "What about the math teacher who coaches drama? He could delay his classes—"

"Stagecraft training in Austria. On leave for fall semester."

She ticked off other faculty members in her head.

He ticked them off out loud, rapidly naming every staff member who was the least bit qualified. Besides Callie. "You filled in for Nora as office manager all summer. You know enough about the school to cover for Dr. Chen."

Her phone rang. *Please be a national emergency or a Martian invasion.*

He growled at the instrument. "Don't answer."

Martians, I'm telling you.

Phoebe's name appeared on the caller ID. Callie showed it to Coop and answered. Phoebe delivered rapid-fire paragraphs. "Jillian agreed to include me. I'm coming up with her. She says I'm staying to oversee the project." Phoebe continued, heaping details upon details until Callie was lost. But one thing was certain. Phoebe was the solution. Callie hung up and faced Coop, taciturn yet magnificent in his unspoken fury. "Phoebe's coming. She'll co-manage the center so I can work here and there at the same time. My schedule's going to be a major war zone." Callie speared a strawberry as if to demonstrate combat skills. "But…"

Coop exhaled audibly. "You'll do it?"

"Either because I'm crazy or because I love you." Now she could relish the brandy.

"I think your mental health is intact."

She reached across the table for his hand. "My boyfriend might suffer."

"Forget it. I'll find someone else." He half-smiled.

She jabbed him with a finger. "Don't budget a salary. You can't afford me."

He kissed her. "And such a short time ago you were grateful to be teaching for peanuts."

"That reminds me. You need a substitute English teacher while I'm getting the center established. Maybe as long as a school year."

"On it." Now he grinned with his entire face, reminding her they were on the same side.

Suddenly they were both ravenous. Tension eased, they gobbled the dessert and exchanged the details of their days. She reminded him he'd promised to show her a good time. He pulled her to the bedroom, leaving lights blazing and dishes unwashed. He peeled away her professional garb. She tugged at his t-shirt as he stepped out of his jeans. The rest of their clothing fell, followed by kissing, excellent kissing, deep kissing, and…

* * *

Unease woke Callie a few hours later. Coop snored softly at her side, his arm flung across her protectively or perhaps possessively. Straining to listen, she wondered what she sensed. She heard only crickets and frogs repeating their endless autumn song through a screened window. *Crickets die in the fall. Is that what I'm hearing? Death?*

Then it came. A soft knocking. Drawing on a robe, she tiptoed to the apartment door. *What if it's Stella's killer?* Another knock. "Yes?"

"I lost my key."

Callie unlocked the door. Coop's daughter fell into her arms.

"I'm in trouble." Nora buried her head on Callie's shoulder.

CHAPTER 5

Nora made a move to shush Callie before Callie was able to summon Coop. "No. You first." The young woman soundlessly closed the door to her father's bedroom and flung herself into a chair by the fireplace, now cold and ash-free in the warm fall weather.

"What kind of trouble?" Callie waited, silently asking for help from Aunt Sophie. *Please not drugs. Or cancer.*

"Tea. Make tea like you used to."

Callie hoped that delaying tactics meant Nora was exaggerating. "You're awfully bossy for someone who scared me half to death." She turned on a burner under the water kettle.

"I'm in love." The young woman, short and sturdy with wild multi-colored hair, delivered this news like a death sentence.

Or pregnant. "Are you pregnant?'

"What? No!"

Callie bit her inner lip to keep from laughing in relief. "Oh."

"Oh?" Nora lolled in the chair.

Callie pulled out the tea that Nora liked best. "I was worried you were on the lam from the law or had the nuclear codes. You know, Trouble."

"To quote the kid in *Love Actually*, what's worse than the total agony of being in love?"

The two of them had watched the movie together more than once. Its dialogue had become their private language. Callie snorted. "I'm Liam Neeson in this scenario?"

"No. I love you more than Liam. Think of *Nell*. Yuck." Nora made a vomit gesture. "Hey, I'm super sorry about the Cooper girl who killed herself." Nora shrugged with a very small nod. "Don't think I ever met her."

"Dr. Chen thinks she was murdered."

Nora sat up straight. "Holy shit. This school just can't stay out of the crapper, can it? Did it happen on school grounds?"

Callie caught Nora up on facts and rumors ending with a question. "Do you know Stella's friend, Harriet?"

"Not really. She's on the soccer team, right? Ask Shauni."

Callie considered for a moment. Callie and Coop frequently socialized with Shauni and Alexis. "Surely Shauni would have shared whatever she knew by now."

"Yeah, but maybe she knows something she doesn't know." Nora wagged her finger. "Don't you read detective fiction?"

"Back to you. Boy or girl?" Callie silently reveled in the young woman's willingness to share confidences after so many months of distancing.

"Boy or girl what?"

"Your sweetheart. I don't like to assume."

Nora smirked. "And yet you thought I might be pregnant."

"Answer the question."

"Arthur."

"Arthur?'

Nora sighed her *you-never-remember-anything* sigh. "The owner of my gallery."

"Where you intern?"

Nora corrected Callie's lingo. "Where I'm a gallery rat."

Callie didn't roll her eyes, which she felt showed great restraint. "Loving him is trouble because?"

"He loves his wife."

Callie groaned. "Something in the Manhattan water?"

"What?

"My friend Phoebe. She's coming here as part of the architectural team partly to get away from her married man."

"And she's okay with you telling me?" Nora seemed a tiny bit thrilled that an adult's story was akin to hers.

"She'll probably tell you herself about a minute after you meet her. Oh, and she's coming with a seriously terrible but hot guy, Elton. Don't fall for him, too."

Nora poured boiling water over tea leaves in a cute silver dipping ball. "Have a little faith, Callie. I didn't just 'fall for' Arthur. He took over my world, invaded my every thought. It's killing me. I want to get over him. I doubt I could even look at another man." She almost wailed but squelched it into a whisper. "How do I stop thinking about him?"

"No idea. I've only been in love once, and I never stop thinking about him, even when he pisses me off." Callie pulled the robe closer.

Nora slopped hot water over the edge of the mugs she carried. "Ouch. Trouble in paradise?"

"Your dad and I had a stupid argument. It's settled but my stomach isn't."

Nora passed a cup of tea to Callie. "I love the way you and Coop fight. You can be mean, but you don't give up on each other."

Callie caught sight of herself in a mirror, her appearance unconsidered in the fighting and eating and sex. She finger-combed her thick dark hair, a futile gesture. "Your dad is … Don't tell him, but I suspect I'd forgive him anything."

"Imagine being Coop's daughter and then trying to date. Most guys my age bore me. Nobody's that smart. Or as strong as Samson and has all their hair."

Callie acknowledged that Coop was a wonder. "How old is Arthur?"

Nora furrowed her brow as if calculating. "Same as you and Dad."

"I'm nearly 34. Your Dad is 43. Pick a number, any number."

"Not the point. Arthur's the first guy I've met who could

even come close to measuring up. He smells good and dresses like a dream and he's totally hot. He knows everything about art, *everything*. I could listen to him forever. All the top artists come by the gallery." Nora shook her head, perhaps at her own folly. "Course, his wife's like a supermodel."

Callie knew she couldn't find a winning argument but had to try. "Honey, the feelings are intense now but ... When I was your age—"

"Seriously?" Nora chortled.

"What?"

Nora stifled outright laughter. "*When I was your age? Seriously?*"

"I guess you're not all that broken hearted." Callie raised an eyebrow.

"You're wrong. I'm devastated but what can I do? I was ready to write it off as just a crush. Then he kissed me."

Inadvertently Callie remembered a song by the Crystals her aunt used to sing. She half- expected Nora to continue with *I felt so happy I almost cried.* Instead, Callie frowned. "That doesn't sound good."

"It isn't, of course. Of course. But it was sooooo fantastic and romantic and perfect. We were alone in the gallery and talking about art and stuff. Next thing I know we're making out on the bench in front of the Cindy Sherman. That's why I came home. I gotta focus on something else." Nora's bleary eyes suggested her entire ability to focus was ebbing. She stood up. "Going to bed. I took a few days off from work to get over this, so don't wake me at your usual ridiculous hour." Hugging Callie, she clumped up to her third-floor bedroom.

"Sure. A few days to get over heartbreak. Easy peasy." *Why did Stella leave "for a few days?" Maybe Nora's behavior holds the key.*

The least meaningful crush could derail the most practical young person. Against her better judgment, Callie let Coop sleep. When his alarm sounded at six am, she already had his cup of coffee in her hand. "Coop, don't freak out."

His sleepy morning voice held a groan. "Love conversations that begin 'Coop don't freak out.'"

Callie summarized Nora's story. He was a good listener and didn't interrupt through all her stop and starts and retelling. "I'm glad she came home."

* * *

Both Coop and Callie left for work while Nora slept. Callie headed for the gym in search of Shauni Rodriguez, a former student who was now the physical education teacher and soccer coach. Callie tried to convince herself she was visiting the coach as a condolence call for losing a student. But admitted that she had a few questions. As it turned out, so did Shauni.

Shauni grew up in New Jersey and was direct as always. "Did Stella kill herself? She didn't seem the type."

"You knew her?" Callie was surprised.

"Not really. She sometimes walked Harriet to practice, and a couple times talked with me about trying out for the team next year." Shauni was sorting equipment and continued working as they talked. Partly, Callie suspected, to cover her emotions.

"What about Harriet? Why would she say Stella was murdered?"

Shauni shrugged. "Beats me. She's always thirsty for the spotlight. Maybe she really thinks Stella wouldn't kill herself. Maybe she just wants to feel like she's helping. I dunno. But if she knew anything, y'know, real, she'da told you by now."

Callie broached her second subject. "Nora came home."

"She texted me on her way last night. Me and Alexis are getting together with her later. Those two can talk about everything they learned in kindergarten or whatever."

"I won't ask you to break any confidences, but—"

Shauni offered a wry smile. "We won't let anything bad happen to her." She fidgeted with a pen on her desk. "Favor?"

"What do you need?"

"Like you know, I'm commuting from Flambert every day. It's a major hassle. Dr. Chen said he'd assign me on-campus housing. Could you?"

"I'll see what I can do." Callie hugged Shauni and departed.

She called Coop as she left the gym. "Why doesn't Shauni have staff housing?"

"The only available cabin was a crime scene and then had to be renovated." His rapid-fire fact-dump suggested that she should have known that.

* * *

As the days wore on, Callie felt at the mercy of other people's eccentricities, with little down time except her routine forays to the gym or runs in the woods. Calls to the police and to Dr. Chen gave her little additional information about Stella, information she longed for.

Nora took a formal leave from the New York gallery and temporarily resumed her position as office manager. Wonderful for the school, less so for Callie and Coop, who were always getting SOS texts. Nora decided to quit her internship permanently, minutes later declaring she would return to Chelsea and tough it out. Then flip flop again. Often Callie took time she couldn't spare to hike with Nora, soothing a million fears and misgivings. More than once Coop held his daughter while she cried. Shauni and Alexis helped as they could, but heartbreak is hard to cure.

Nora was not Callie's only time suck. Dr. Chen's administrative records were meticulous, but he was a man in his 70s and some of his notes puzzled Callie, causing her to call him at the lab far too frequently. She always tried to sneak in a question about Stella's death and he always parried that he wouldn't comment on an ongoing investigation, even to her. The lab personnel, wisely, designated him as the chief investigator on Stella's case, which made him even more close-mouthed about sharing information.

Then there were students. Callie squeezed her teaching

duties into each day, grateful to have the previous year's lesson plans to fall back on. Teaching office hours were too short and she felt … inadequate. Daily she harangued Coop about finding a replacement, even though she knew he was doing what he could.

* * *

The council meeting loomed. Phoebe messaged plans and revisions from her desk in New York, each with a subject line more urgent than the last, each time accompanied by a complaint that correspondence was Elton's job, but he'd never do it. Despite several abrupt video conferences with Jillian and endless budget discussions with the contractor, Callie felt hopped up all the time—and not in a good way. Through it all, Coop did and said all the right things to both Callie and Nora, but Callie felt him retreating into the remoteness he displayed when they first met.

Hazel was Callie's rock. Before meeting Hazel, Callie had been close to only three people—her mother and her aunt, who were both gone, and Phoebe, who'd moved to New York after college while Callie foundered in Pennsylvania and then moved to Cooper School. It was an embarrassment of riches that both Phoebe and Hazel would be nearby as soon as Phoebe moved to Flambert. *If only I had time to enjoy them.*

Escaping to Hazel's classroom, Callie moped. "How did my life devolve into over-commitment and general irritation?"

"Idyllic doesn't last forever, does it?" Hazel looked over Callie's notes for end of semester grading, provided in her role as substitute Vice Principal. "I hate to tell you, but you've mixed up my classes. Underclass students can't enroll in advanced art."

"I suck at this job." Callie sat on a classroom chair and fake-pouted. "I'm a complete failure." Two years earlier, Callie had taken a mid-year position as the English Lit teacher, replacing Coop's beloved late wife, and everyone's absolutely favorite teacher. Enter Callie, who had not quite finished her teaching degree, had taught very little, and was distracted by strong feelings for Coop it took her awhile to admit. She feared she'd fail the students who, like her, came from no money and had obstacles by the ton. Now she had to step up to different responsibilities and once again face her own inexperience.

Hazel waved off Callie's fussing as she continued perusing the list. "Wait, wait, the student is—was—Stella. Her file has a note; Dr. Chen gave her special permission. She was extremely talented. So, you were right." She pointed to a sophisticated sketch on the bulletin board. "That's hers."

"I keep wondering why her. Why would anyone want to hurt Stella?" Callie examined Stella's work, hoping for a clue.

Hazel brought her back to a laser focus. "Stella had very few friends. Artsy and a townie—perfect target for bullies. No idea how she and Harriet became friends."

"Do you think they were lovers?" Callie looked for Harriet's work on Hazel's wall.

"No, I'm fairly certain they both preferred male partners." Hazel pointed to an unskillful portrait signed by Harriet. "I think that was meant to be Stella. Unfortunately, their friendship didn't give Harriet any talent."

Callie sat on a chair by Hazel's desk. "Tell me about Stella."

"Like many young artists, she hadn't quite found her way. She had a lot of talent and probably would have grown into her vision eventually." Hazel trailed off.

Callie tapped the desk, newly energized. "It had to be a boy."

"Sorry?"

"Stella left a message for Coop saying she felt unwell and was going home. Coop would have sent her to Dr. Chen's clinic instead, as school protocol dictates. Students don't have access to cars and the taxi company has no record of her ordering a ride. She might not have been suspicious if somebody sweet-talked her into going with them, maybe into having sex in her bed while her mother was at work—"

Hazel always flinched at teenage sex, though her own daughter met Shauni at age 18, and Hazel loved them both dearly. "Maybe Harriet knows something about the boy?"

Callie nodded. "That could be why she's being so cagey." She texted Coop and Craig, explaining this new theory.

Hazel's eyes misted over. "Dorothy didn't even know Stella was home until she found the body."

"You've seen Dorothy? How's she doing?"

"Not great. I've been by her place a couple times. She's taking Stella's death really hard. At first, she blamed herself for not knowing what would drive Stella to suicide. Some days she insists Stella would never kill herself and if she did, would never have sent that text. When the news came out that Stella was murdered, it was like she started mourning all over again." Hazel's focus went fuzzy. Taking a deep breath, she went on. "Luckily, her voters really love her. They've filled her place with flowers and her refrigerator with casseroles."

"We sent flowers. When my aunt died, my friend Phoebe sent flowers and it was more comforting than I expected. I hope Dorothy felt the same." Callie hugged Hazel and put on her jacket. "See you soon."

A few minutes later Callie entered the admin building. Surprised to find Nora absent from her desk, she moved to Coop's office door and raised her hand to knock—a courtesy they always extended one another when working. Hearing raised voices, she hesitated.

"Dad, don't get all bent out of shape."

Callie knocked.

"Not now." Coop's terse response to her knock sounded exasperated.

Callie opened the door anyway. "What's going on?"

Coop shot a thunderous glance her way, which softened when he saw who it was. "Callie, come in and close the door. I thought you were someone else."

"And yet I thought you'd recognize my little tapping." No one laughed.

Nora sprawled on the couch, choking through tears. "He's

mad at me, not you."

Callie summoned her classroom voice. "Somebody explain."

"Nora hasn't told us the whole story." Coop waved what appeared to be a letter from Planned Parenthood.

Nora wailed, stomping in a circle. "You had no right to open my mail. And I'm not pregnant."

Again, he roared. "But you could be. That's why you were tested."

Nora pouted. "I took three home tests before that. They were all negative, too."

"Thorough. That's good." Callie sat abruptly. "Wait. You had sex with your boss? What happened?"

Nora collapsed into major weeping. "Big mistake. Big. I know it. But we only did it once."

Coop stood. He gripped the edge of his imposing desk, as if steadying himself.

"It was my first time. My only time." Nora sat up. "Not counting the rape."

Callie spoke too loudly. "Rape isn't sex." *For the hundredth time or the thousandth.* Nora's attacker had been a trusted teacher. As if that was not traumatizing enough, he turned out to be a serial rapist who partnered with another criminal responsible for Nora's mother's death. Although the events occurred before Callie arrived at the school, she could see the details as if she had witnessed them.

Nora howled, "I'm a total loser. A double loser. I had two penises in me and they're both creeps."

Coop's voice shook. "You did consent this time, right?"

Nora wailed as if histrionics explained everything. "I'm in love with him."

"And his wife?" Callie heard the echo of her conversation with Phoebe.

"She's nice. And gorgeous. But she's wrong for him. He

loves me."

When will women stop being clichés?

The office phone rang. As the person nearest, Callie answered. "Harold Cooper's office."

"Arthur Bement here. I'm looking for Nora Cooper."

∞

CHAPTER 6

Coldly Callie said, "One moment, please." She pushed Hold and spat a curt word at Nora. "Arthur."

Coop reached for the phone, but Nora beat him to it. "Dad, don't make this worse." He hovered, but she twisted away from him and spoke into the phone, "Hello, Mr. Bement. I can't speak with you right now. I'll text you later."

Noticing the "Dad" from the girl who usually called her father "Coop," Callie willed him to do the right thing. Probably not because she willed it, he waited for Nora to hang up and pulled his daughter close. Nora went stiff, the way toddlers do when a loving parent tries to calm them down. But a few seconds later she relented and relaxed into her father's embrace.

Callie felt fury rising. "If he's calling you here after you quit, he's a sexual harasser. We could threaten a lawsuit." *I should ask Lawrence whether that's really true.*

"No," Nora squealed as if physically injured. "Arthur didn't do anything wrong. If I wanted to hurt him, I'd call his wife."

"Having sex with your employee is—"

Nora interrupted. "Get off the soapbox. You two had sex when Coop was your boss."

Coop and Callie exchanged glances, sheepishly admitting Nora was right.

Before either could speak, Callie's cell sounded. Phoebe's voice vibrated through the phone with the chugging of a train.

"My train arrives in about an hour. By the way, be grateful the weasel isn't with me."

Callie took Nora's hand. "We need to talk about this more but right now I have to pick up my friend at the station. Can we table it without you feeling dismissed?"

Nora squeezed Callie's fingers. "You're so funny. I know you'd never dismiss me. I'm ready to stop talkin' about this. Okay, Dad?

Coop, like Callie, heard the "Dad," and took it as intended, an acknowledgement of how close they were despite their fights. "For now." He turned to Callie. "What brought you here?"

As she stood to leave, Callie reviewed the checklist in her head. "What do I need to do for Dorothy?"

"Pack up all of Stella's things, including whatever her teachers have in their classrooms." Coop had prepared a list of Stella's classes, which he handed over.

Nora blinked as if realizing the world had troubles that were not hers. "I'll help."

Callie smiled. "Great. Can you get started while I collect Phoebe from the train and get her settled?"

Both Coopers nodded, an identical physical gesture that always amused Callie.

"Later." Nora took the list from Callie and departed.

At the door, Callie stopped short. "Coop, Phoebe will stay in my cabin while she's here, okay?" Expecting a distracted approval, she was perplexed at his frown.

"Fine. She's your guest for now but ... she's not here on school business and you're only acting VP. If the center's approved, we'll need the cabin for the substitute English teacher."

Callie waited until she was out of his earshot to let loose a loud animalistic growl.

She met Phoebe's train with coffee and takeout. They ate while they crammed Phoebe's pile of belongings into the car like a jigsaw puzzle. As they drove through Flambert on their way to the school, Phoebe identified architectural styles. "This town is so adorable."

"Wait til you see my cabin. All oak floors and mountain views. My first real home."

"What about Sophie's place?" Phoebe sipped carefully to avoid slopping coffee as Callie negotiated the country road.

"I was little when Mom and I lived with Sophie after my dad died. Of course I'm grateful to her for being my north star." Callie's finger grazed the dove necklace. "But I only have a sketchy memory of it."

Phoebe nodded as she recalled details. "Oh, right. That was before your mother married Blake."

"And I did live in that one-room hellhole in Troysville before I moved here but I wouldn't call that home."

Phoebe laughed. "My place in Brooklyn could be described the same way."

Callie swerved to miss a pothole. "Whichever project gets the contract, I expect Flambert will have to fix this road. Maybe you should re-think New York."

"New York City is the center of the universe. And has better roads than this." Phoebe clutched the hand grip. "I'm glad Blake was long gone when I met you."

Callie pictured Blake's cold, mausoleum-like house, tastefully decorated with expensive furniture and nothing for a child. "A new daddy who lived in a palace sounded like a fairytale too good to be true. It was."

Callie confided in Phoebe long ago over late-night dorm popcorn that her stepfather murdered her mother when Callie was eleven and her own attempt to intervene by shooting him landed her in detention. "When I got out, I stayed with Sophie but we both knew it was temporary until I finished school. Then, well, you know. She got sick and died."

"Yeah." Phoebe fell silent for a while. "You have your own cabin, but don't you mostly stay with Coop?"

"Mostly. I need to escape coupledom from time to time." *Or when I'm having a meltdown.*

"Copy that." Phoebe raised her thumb.

Callie paused before she delivered the news. "Coop is

kicking us out."

"What? You like this guy, right?"

Callie nodded. "Love him. But if I start working fulltime on the center—"

"**When,** not if—"

"Crap. He's probably right. The cabin's not really mine." Callie hated that Coop's ethical compass was routinely more reliable than her own. "I guess I could build my own place."

Phoebe patted Callie's arm. "Now you're speaking my language. I can design you a home on the center grounds. Or in town. Or somewhere else. How 'bout a cabana in the Caribbean? I'm a novice at big projects but single-family homes are my jam. Want a swimming pool? How about a personal movie theater?"

"Let's rent an apartment in town for the winter. That'll give us time to plan."

"You're the weirdest rich person I ever met."

"Who you callin' weird, weirdo?"

The 'conversation' continued in much the same vein, punctuated with explosive bouts of laughter until Callie pulled next to the cabin. Phoebe surveyed Callie's spacious one-story house nestled among fir trees, complete with wrap-around porch.

"You call this a cabin?"

"See what I mean?"

Inside, Callie fired up the wood stove. Though the autumn day was still warm, she anticipated a chill as the sun went on its merry way. She brewed tea while Phoebe explored the house, yelling one delighted exclamation after another. "Wow, purple and gold tiles in the bathroom? Could be really cheesy but this is classy. Way cool." Her footsteps sounded as she moved on. "This spare room is dreamy."

"My friend Hazel Landers, the art teacher, lived here before she got married. She gets the credit for the elegant touches." Callie interrupted Phoebe's tour and convinced her to rehearse their presentation for the next day.

"Who's on the council? Do I need to kiss ass or be

professional? Flirty or businesswoman of the year?" Phoebe opened her laptop. "I can show them the blueprints, but a lot of clients don't want technical stuff, just pretty pictures of the final product. Details or big picture?"

"Coop knows better than I do. He'll brief you on personalities over breakfast. Here's the basics." Callie opened her own laptop and brought up the council site. "Eleven members. Six are local business owners, the other five are a hodgepodge. One is Mrs. Kelly, the mother of that Cooper girl who got murdered. The council president is married to the mayor. And they're relatives of the incompetent police chief. Does that help?"

Phoebe rolled her eyes. "Stupidity and corruption. I can work with that."

They tried a couple of different overviews of the presentation, picking and choosing among Phoebe's many slides. Yawning as they finished, they said goodnight.

Before Callie let her weariness win, her mind drifted to Stella. *The police are useless. I need to make a murder action plan.*

By mid-morning the next day, the two women and Lawrence were enduring the boring opening remarks of the Flambert council meeting. Callie pinched the inside of her hand to keep from fidgeting. *Roll call, for heaven's sakes. Can't they tell they're all there?*

The ski resort's lawyers and architects looked appropriately quasi-rich and quasi-athletic. Invited to speak first, they presented a circus of graphs and charts about their so-called green land use and the incoming money avalanche that would bolster the town of Flambert and the surrounding county. As nearly as Callie could tell, their 'facts' were either madly speculative or completely false about everything from the number of jobs it would create to the environmental impact.

Under the guise of note taking, Callie texted Phoebe and Lawrence rude observations about the saucer-eyed council members who seemed ready to strap on their Nordics. She fought a rising defensiveness. At her side, Phoebe assiduously messaged Jillian, seeking rebuttal ammunition.

Predictably, the council needed a break after the dog-and-pony show and called a lunch recess. Phoebe went outside to call her boss.

Coop arrived bearing sandwiches for Callie's team. Callie watched Coop work the room, shaking hands with council members—trading stories as if he were Switzerland-neutral. Envious of his apparent comfort in the role of favorite son, she also felt a certain pride knowing he was parachuting behind enemy lines with her best interest hidden in his imaginary flak jacket.

Lawrence spoke to Callie quietly. "Phoebe sent me the presentation. It's good but I don't know whether this council will understand how good it is. You need something flashy, like the ski resort presentation."

Enhanced whispering arose among the opposition. The cause of the disturbance was Jillian's arrival, Elton in tow. The world-famous architect overtook the room like a blizzard, greeting the ski resort's row of legal suits with a storm of waves and air smooches as if to imply *Why are we important New Yorkers in this godforsaken place?* She shrugged out of a floor-length white duster: "fabulously expensive silk weave" according to Phoebe. Directing Elton toward the council secretary, Jillian murmured to Lawrence, "You needed a bigger gun. Me."

Lawrence smiled in gratitude, star struck.

As Elton transcended his usual lethargy to arrange figures and illustrations on easels and to set up a huge screen, Callie looked around for Coop, hoping he'd appreciate that this time *she* had the connections.

As if he read her mind, Coop was at Callie's side, offering a hand to Jillian with a deference just short of kissing her manicured fingertips or one of her huge rings.

"Harold Cooper, how the hell are you?" Jillian whispered something in French that Callie could have sworn was, "We'll always have Paris."

He laughed heartily as he casually touched Callie's shoulder. "I knew Jillian a lifetime ago from Quaker school. She moonlighted as a French teacher during her early days as an architect. *Bonjour, Madame Gordon.*"

Madame? Callie struggled to hide her shock that Jillian had another last name. Not only had she allowed a man into her life, but she'd married him and taken his name? Phoebe looked completely stunned. Her text was a series of emojis, some of them rather rude.

"Is Professor Gordon well?" Coop ushered the women toward their seats as the council began reassembling.

"Oh yes, he's still teaching film at NYU. Neither of us can bring ourselves to retire. The descendants are all out of college but——" Jillian squinted her eyes at Anjali as the council president banged her gavel for order.

The next hour made the ski resort's presentation look tawdry and amateur. Using the fanciest of advanced computer technology, Jillian projected the Miriam Cooper Women's Center images Phoebe and Callie had selected on her huge screen. She manipulated the visuals, dismantling them like a dollhouse, uncovering everything from ductwork to roof shingles. Slyly, she undermined the ski resort's claims, first with her environmental impact report and later with offhand remarks about protecting the woodlands through classes and workshops on forestry and nature conservancy that Callie hadn't previously considered.

Sure, why not? I need a few more tasks.

Evidently reeling from information overload, the council adjourned, promising to make a decision in a few days.

Callie called Hazel and asked if she had room for Jillian and entourage for dinner.

"Of course, dear. I invited Lawrence and Meadow, too. Are we celebrating?" Background noise suggested that Craig was helping in the kitchen, not entirely to her satisfaction. "Use the other cutting board. Dicing means little cubes." At Callie's laugh, Hazel returned to the phone. "Can't talk right now. Just come."

Nora went on foot to "get some exercise," which Callie surmised meant "get some privacy" on her phone while she talked to someone Callie hoped was not Arthur. A sullen Elton drove Phoebe and Jillian, leaving Callie to ride with Coop. She blabbed on about the meeting, detail by detail. He responded in monosyllables, politely not pointing out that he'd been there. She shook her head. "Damn. I used to be better at this."

"At what?" He pulled up behind Jillian's town car at Craig's.

"Suppressing stuff. Not downloading every detail of the day."

Unbuckling first his seatbelt then hers, he wordlessly drew her into a kiss that made her wish they were going straight home. Breathing hard, her mind grasped for something, anything, to ground her. "Hey, what was that Paris stuff between you and Jillian?"

His brow furrowed, as he tried to make sense of her question, then smoothed in sudden recognition. "*Casablanca*."

"The city in North Africa?"

"Anti-fascist movie. 1940s. Humphrey Bogart and——"

"Ingrid Bergman. Yeah. I've seen it."

Coop seemed uncharacteristically nostalgic. "Jillian's husband showed it to our French class. Can't remember why."

"And?"

"I was floored by the film. When I raised my hand to express whatever teenage critique I was ready to expound upon, she insisted that I speak in my very rudimentary French. God knows what I said. Whatever it was, she ridiculed me on many subsequent occasions. 'We'll always have Paris' is from the film. It's their code. Rick and Ilsa." He took her hand. "Do we have a code?"

"We'll always have that embarrassing first interview?"

"Hey, I hired you anyway, didn't I?" He looked away, a little too casually. "Madame Gordon was my first schoolboy crush. I was sixteen. She was—I dunno—twice that?"

"I'm not jealous." Callie squeezed his hand.

"Should I love that or worry?"

Callie rolled her eyes. "You're an idiot."

At that moment, Craig opened the front door to the house, calling to the two in the car. "Trouble in paradise?"

"Why does everyone keep saying that?" Callie got out of the car and marched into the house.

Coop followed. "*Trouble in Paradise.* Another great movie—"

Callie patted him indulgently. "Fascinating. Let's join the others."

Hazel's food was ambrosial as always and the wine plentiful. Surprisingly, Jillian was the hit of the party. Despite her upper class *bona fides,* she regaled the group with tales of irrational New York bureaucracy and muddy construction sites. Elton, slappably snotty most of the time, seemed fascinated with Meadow and the entire Mohawk nation. Meadow, in turn, seemed taken with his ski-instructor good looks.

Callie's inner warning lights flashed like a strobe; something was wrong, there just weren't enough clues yet to pinpoint it.

As the party broke up in the wee hours, Jillian brought the jollity to an abrupt halt. One foot raised to get into her car, she announced confidence that the center would win the contract and they had no time to waste. "Phoebe, you'll need an administrative assistant."

Buoyed by the wine and Jillian's confidence, Callie interrupted, despite many warnings never to do so. "A recent Cooper graduate might—"

Jillian could interrupt anyone she pleased. "I'm sending Elton back up here."

Elton and Phoebe glowered at one another through their nodding smiles.

Jillian, blithely unaware, tossed her final grenade. "Phoebe, I'm sure you can rent a place before Elton arrives that has office space and living quarters for each of you."

Sure, add those to the budget. Why not?

Goodnights were exchanged by all as Elton pulled the car out of a snowy parking space and pointed it toward New York City.

In self-conscious imitation of Coop, Callie spent the following morning mumbling random soothing words while Phoebe fumed in rapid-fire New-York-ese interspersed with strings of unladylike cursing. "He'll spy on everything I do and make my life miserable. Is Jillian testing me? Where can I buy untraceable poisons? Fuck. I really mean it. Fuckety fuck fuck fuck."

Untraceable. "We should research that. For real." Callie explained that her current temp position in Dr. Chen's job was because he was busy trying to identify what had killed Stella. "I think the investigation could use all the help it can get."

"Callie, the last time you had that attitude, somebody nearly killed you."

"I'm smarter now."

Phoebe looked doubtful. "Let's find a place to live before we get ourselves arrested for interfering with an ongoing investigation."

Tromping up and down many flights of stairs, they inspected every rental in Flambert—a village with little more than a downtown but too many recession-induced failed businesses—finally deciding on a three-story former dress shop with ample commercial space and apartments on each of two upper floors.

Phoebe gave Jillian a video tour. "Pre-war. Pseudo Italianate ... Maybe fifteen hundred square feet per floor." Eventually, Phoebe slammed her notebook against her thigh in frustration, indicating the call had ended. "Small. She says maybe the spaces are too small for six months. Compared with Manhattan, where a 400-square-foot efficiency goes for a zillion? Where the hell does Elton live? The governor's mansion?"

"She said no?"

Phoebe shook her head from side to side, over-acting out No. "It was one of her nos that mean yes. She says it can work if you pay for a few upgrades."

"I guess if you're important enough, no can mean whatever you want it to." Callie ran a finger along the smooth oak of the built-in cabinets. "It's pretty clean. Elton will have a classy two-bedroom place to himself. You'll be living better— even with me as your roommate—than your place in Brooklyn.

Phoebe drew herself up to a full five foot four. "Hey, don't knock Brooklyn. I still go to the Mermaid Parade every year."

"The mermaid what?"

Phoebe gave Callie the *ha I know more than you do* look. "The biggest art parade in the country. Only handmade floats and costumes allowed. You know I'm a designer at heart, right?"

"Sure." Callie considered the glass built-in cabinets, the high ceilings, and the graceful bay windows fronting the street on all three floors. "After Aunt Sophie died, I moved into that efficiency of linoleum and tar paper. This looks good to me."

"Those were the days. Between us we could afford one sandwich." Phoebe snorted. "Jillian wants a bunch of updates to this place. She even said she'll pay for them—and her penny-pinching is legendary. Guess you don't get rich any other way. Unless you're you." Phoebe grinned. "Apparently her precious nephew must have only the most expensive frou-frous of the 21st century."

Phoebe separated the keys to the top floor, handing one to Callie. "Ha. We get the top floor, the penthouse so to speak. Elton gets the sandwich floor. The old shop will be our office."

With Elton's arrival imminent, Phoebe negotiated a lease while Callie arranged for furnishings and improvements. Even with Flambert's limited resources, Callie was impressed by how quickly a corporate credit card could deliver. Eight hours later, as Elton parked his Tesla, the HVAC and Wi-Fi were operational, the cleaning crew was packing up, and several fancy-stuff rental companies had nearly finished furnishing the office.

Callie's mind kept wandering to the murder. *Who enticed Stella away from the safety of school grounds? Wait. I have an untapped resource...*

CHAPTER 7

Alexis was a tech expert any police department would pay handsomely to keep. Flambert lucked into her services only because she hadn't yet left home for one of the elite institutes that wanted her. She and Shauni were saving to attend college together somewhere in a year or two. Callie was accustomed to asking Shauni about her work at Cooper School but Callie rarely asked Alexis about police business. Today was an exception.

As she headed out, Callie encountered Elton observing the array of non-designer goods in the office. Elton's sculpted face contorted with fake pain. "I've been banished to Siberia. Ersatz Siberia, not even the real thing. This town doesn't even serve a decent latte."

Callie gently pointed out that Jillian purchased a pricey espresso maker for him and another for the office. He sneered and looked over the rims of thousand-dollar glasses. "Don't underestimate me, Ms. Franklin."

Callie extricated herself from the promise of further unpleasantness and jogged the few blocks to downtown Flambert. The police station, the court, the jail, the city council and other offices made up a sprawling patchwork of wings and walls constructed over several decades and appointed in old-fashioned wood and plaster. Alexis's work area, by contrast, was a riot of high-tech gear and monitors full of moving numbers and images beaming blue light.

Alexis shouted a welcome. "Callie! What brings you here?" She hit several buttons to silence the buzzing and beeping on her screens.

Callie surveyed the office to make sure no junior techies lurked nearby at various computers and was satisfied they were alone. "I have a huge favor to ask."

"I know nothing about that horrible ski resort."

Callie shook her head. "Stella Kelly."

"Ongoing investigation. No information."

Callie pressed forward. "Just one question."

"Ongoing —"

"Was Stella seen around town with anybody?"

"I can't give you any information." She shifted from emotionless to friendly as she changed the subject with a barely perceptible wink. "Hey, I heard the Main Street Bar & Grill is tasty." A local pub full of dark wood and dark corners.

Callie bookmarked the address into her phone. "Know anybody who works there?"

"Maybe ask for," Alexis paused for a moment as she looked something up on her computer, tilting her screen away from Callie, "Daryl." She stood. "I love talking about food but we both have to earn our keep, right?" Alexis's plausible deniability hung in the air as Callie departed.

At school, Callie stopped several girls she thought might have known Stella and asked about a possible sweetheart. Generally, everyone seemed certain that Stella had no one.

Except Harriet.

The young woman looked worried. "Ms. Franklin, do you think her lover killed her?"

"Did she have a lover?"

"I'm not sure. Just lately she said she had a secret. I thought it might be sex, but she didn't tell me." Harriet said goodbye and ran to class.

At dusk, as Callie mounted the steps to Coop's apartment, she reflected on Harriet equating love and sex. *At her age I only knew about sex. Not love. And Stella?*

She wanted to mull over Harriet's words with Coop, but

his kiss felt perfunctory. The slightest rejection evoked her years of mind-numbing data entry, alone, undervalued, and underpaid. *I can be nobody anywhere.*

Coop's usual knack for following her unspoken thoughts didn't fail. "Guess we're both distracted at the moment. I need a do over." He kissed her again, this time telegraphing every moment they'd ever shared without clothing. "You first."

Callie hesitated. For most of her life, keeping secrets was a survival skill—from her criminal stepfather, the kids in juvie, whomever. When Aunt Sophie died, Callie lost her last truth guardian and barricaded herself against heartbreak with high walls of distrust and low thresholds for meaningless lovers. That all changed when she met Coop, a man she now loved ferociously. And here he was, asking her to be open and honest. *How can I refuse?* "Let's get bar food for dinner."

To her surprise, he agreed. He grabbed the keys and they headed out the door. En route to Flambert, she explained why this particular bar.

His dark eyes were shaded. "I don't suppose I can convince you to leave the investigation to the authorities?"

"I won't get in their way. I just want to do a little poking around."

He rubbed the crease between his eyes as if staving off a headache. "Be careful not to poke a bear or a bomb."

"Promise."

Main Street Bar & Grill was a surprise. She expected a seedy place of shadows, complete with an imaginary Stephen King at a booth in the darkest corner, writing award-winning horror novels he barely remembered through an alcoholic haze. Instead, it was a busy place with trendy pop music, pool tables, and a dance floor full of young people.

A hostess approached them, menus in hand. "We're really busy tonight but I can seat you at the bar if you'd like."

Callie squeezed Coop's hand to keep him from objecting. "Yes, please." She smiled at the harried young woman. "Is Daryl working tonight?" The hostess pointed to a bartender covered with piercings and tattoos.

As they mounted their barstools, Callie signaled to him.

"What can I get you?" He wiped the bar in front of them, setting their flatware and napkins on the half-dry surface.

Callie showed him a photo of Stella. "What do you know about her?"

Daryl grimaced. "Reporter or police?"

"We teach at Cooper School. She was our student, our friend."

Daryl looked from one to the other. "I told the cops I remember her because her fake ID was too fake. Then her boyfriend gave her his drink right in front of me, so I threw them out."

"What was he like?"

Daryl poured water for them. "Skinny white kid. Older than her by maybe ten years? Athletic. No scars or ink. No beard or stache."

"Hair? Straight or curly?"

"Dunno. Wore a Yankees beanie."

Callie took notes. "Did they come here a lot?"

"Never saw her before but I know his face. No name. Look, you two gotta order. I have other customers."

The meal was forgettable, but Callie left the bar satisfied. "I'm going to ask Dorothy about Stella's boyfriend."

Coop steered his truck toward her new apartment to check it out for the very first time. "If she's like me, she knows nothing about her daughter's private life."

She heard the hurt behind the words. "What's wrong?"

"Nora texted Bement. It wasn't the kiss-off I was hoping for."

"You read Nora's texts? Ever heard of the First Amendment?" Callie sat back.

Coop peered out the window like a guilty schoolboy. "Couldn't help it. Her phone buzzed. She was in the bathroom."

"Couldn't help it?" Callie scowled. "Did you tell her?"

"Oh, yes. You missed quite a battle."

Unsure about how to respond, Callie let her focus roam.

"What'd she do?"

His neutral response belied his worry. "Train to the city."

She had a new thought. "Have you ever read my texts?"

"Callie, I've never read anyone's before today. I barely read my own."

"Tell her you're sorry." Callie dialed Nora, but the call went to voicemail.

"I've left six messages."

Callie wasn't sure how to be loyal to both of them. "What did you say?"

"Have a little faith, Callie." He pulled up in front of her building.

"Nora said the same thing and…" Callie took a beat. "What was in her text?"

His jaw clenched. "I see. It's not okay for me to read it, but okay for me to share it?"

Callie huffed. "It upset you. I want to know why."

He rarely yelled but the raised voice was implied by the intense words. "The guy's a snake oil salesman and Nora can't see it."

"She's in love." Callie rubbed sleepy eyes.

Coop's quiet voice snapped. "That's your idea of love? Blind and mindless, tricks and lies?"

Let me de-escalate. "Coop, can you remember being in love at twenty?"

"I was in love with the right woman. By the time I graduated from high school, I was committed to Miriam."

"Yeah, and when she broke it off, you romanced every supermodel in New York. You were extravagant and cruel—" Callie's words were his own, his earliest personal revelations to her. Was it a betrayal to repeat them, even to him?

"Why do you think I'm worried?"

Callie sputtered. "Oh, sorry. I don't mean I apologize. I don't. But I'm sorry that—"

"That my chickens have come home to roost? That I have to pay over and over for indiscretions I committed two decades ago?" His dark eyes blazed. "Maybe it's justice."

"Justice? Coop, really? Self-pity?" Callie shook her head. "This is about Nora, not you. And if I'm right, it could give hints about Stella's behavior."

"I can't talk about this right now." His phone rang. A phone always rang in the middle of things. "Yes?"

Callie watched his face change from a petulant teen pretending to be an adult to the real thing. "She's here. I'm putting you on speaker." He pressed the button.

The phone voice was clear despite iffy rural phone service. "Alexis here."

Callie was immediately apprehensive. Any calls this late usually meant something bad. "Is Hazel okay?"

Alexis's voice shook. "It's Dr. Chen. Someone broke into the lab, knocked him out." She'd grown up in Flambert where physical violence was typically a bar fight or a guy abusing his wife. Never a stranger attacking a scientist.

"Is he—" Callie couldn't continue.

"The night cleaning crew found him. Saved his life. He's in the hospital."

Coop's free hand joined Callie's. "Serious or not?"

Alexis raised her voice to be heard over hospital noises. "We won't know for a while."

"Why would anyone attack Dr. Chen?"

Alexis sounded tired. "It must have something to do with Stella."

Coop stiffened. "Why do you say that?'

"The attacker stole all his research. The samples, the notebooks, everything from the Stella Kelly case."

Callie and Coop spoke almost simultaneously. "On our way."

Coop drove. Callie fretted. When her phone rang, she failed to check the ID, confident it was about Dr. Chen. Bad plan.

Jillian assumed Callie recognized her voice. "I've spoken with Anjali Verma. She'll fax you the contract tonight. Now hire a construction company."

Despite the hour, Callie knew better than to protest. "I'll

get right on it. What else needs done?" The call would end when they got to the hospital, even if Jillian was mid-sentence.

"Elton sent me your notes. That girl Meadow says the third company on your list, McComber & Sons, is Mohawk. I like minority contractors. I'd prefer to hire women but can't find a big enough female-headed company anywhere near you…"

Jillian wasn't a collaborator. She issued decrees. Apparently, Callie was only expected to write checks. *Fine. Where's the pen?*

With a hint of slur, Jillian spoke as if accusing. "Do you know about the election?"

"Excuse me?" *Bite your tongue hard, Callie—the taste of blood might help.*

"Anjali says the local spring elections could completely change the votes on the council—and we know how easy it is to buy elections these days. Flambert will upgrade the road from the town. If the new council leans to the ski resort, those bastards could rescind our contract on any technicality and claim they have to give it to the resort because they already paid for the road. We gotta get the center done fast and right."

"Of course." Callie was only half listening.

Jillian apparently sensed this distraction. "I don't think you understand how urgent this is." Jillian was barking and audibly imbibing something Callie suspected wasn't water. "The business owners on the council hate educational nonprofits. Cooper School sits on a large tract of tax-free land. The center will be another one."

Despite her desire to hang up, Callie was hooked. "They're against education?"

"They're against private schools they think are snotty and elite."

"Our girls are from poor backgrounds and the teachers are hardly rich. And we accept a few townies every semester."

"They're also suspicious of poor people. A lot of your students are nonwhite and foreign, which those yahoos find scary. They think the center will preach gay marriage and fluoride in the water."

Callie hadn't followed politics since volunteering in the Pennsylvania peace center her Aunt Sophie founded.

Jillian apparently assumed these pronouncements were common knowledge. "And now that girl gets herself killed." Which was apparently the fault of the school, or Callie, or general incompetence. Jillian rambled on, lacing facts with extravagant opinions.

Callie shifted the phone to the other ear, assenting periodically until Jillian stopped short, evidently expecting Callie to say something. "Sorry?"

"They're gunning for us." Maybe Jillian was inebriated. Or paranoid. One thing was certain: she wasn't necessarily wrong.

After what felt like fifty thousand iterations of Jillian commanding Callie to complete a slew of tasks "first thing tomorrow," the call ended.

Callie texted Jillian's demands to Phoebe and Lawrence, punching each letter, finally sitting back as Coop's vehicle barreled toward the hospital. Stars, the moon, fireflies, the warmth of day still clinging to the air, rustling leaves that would fall too soon. She took them in to cherish later when things were set to rights. In the past, she was impervious to the natural world and all her emotions generally boiled down to anger. Only recently had she allowed herself to feel anything else. Worry over Stella and Dr. Chen with frustration about Jillian's demands twisted through her. She needed action to bring her back to reality. "What do you know about the McComber construction company?"

Coop tuned into her need for facts instead of emotion. "Good company. One of the sisters went to Cooper."

Callie was puzzled. "Aren't they rich? How'd she qualify?"

"They started out as Mom-and-Pop carpenters. She graduated in—"

Callie sidestepped the detour to yet another Cooper girl's success story. "Jillian's worried about the spring elections. Tell me about them."

Coop's face creased with every one of the ten years he'd

lived longer than Callie. He shrugged.

"Please, Coop. We can't help Dr. Chen until we get there."

His eyes flickered in the dark, gathering light from the moon, perhaps. "If the mayor's friends get voted in, they'll find a way to halt construction and get you out. Less likely if it's already finished, to no chance if it is in operation."

Callie tried not to whine. "But we have a contract."

"Small town councils have an ugly way of upending their own decisions. They frequently weasel out of legal obligations."

"Jillian said something about the Mohawk Nation?"

He nodded. "The Mohawks have a long-standing suit claiming treaty rights to specific acreage in upstate New York. Cooper School isn't part of it. Gwendolyn—"

"Gwendolyn? Oh, right, your great-great-great-whatever grandmother." As the hospital came in view, her focus shifted back to Dr. Chen.

"—signed a land deal in the early twentieth century, which gave the school undisputed control of our land and the Mohawks fishing rights on Cooper waters." He steered into the parking lot.

"And the center land?"

"Legally, no land anywhere near here is disputed, but some people might use the suit as a reason to screw with the facts and question the history of areas that aren't included right now." He opened the door and they hurried into the emergency room.

Does it ever end?

* * *

The doctor treating Dr. Chen was—*what else*—a Cooper grad. A willowy Ethiopian who settled in the freezing north for heaven knows what reason, her dark, serious eyes looked at them askance. Coop had some difficulty convincing her that he and Callie needed to visit Dr. Chen even though it was approaching midnight and they were not relatives. She finally agreed to give them a few minutes.

Callie usually considered Dr. Chen eternally vital. Despite his years, he was an avid sportsman, energetic, and always responsive to the needs of students and faculty. Tonight, though, he looked old and frail for the first time. The stark white bandages on his head contributed to a deathly pallor. He was awake, clearly in pain, yet greeted them with his usual grace.

"I'm going to be fine." He smiled wanly. "I'm more concerned about losing the samples than the blood from my head."

Coop was a little too jaunty. "You're a survivor. We need you to get well and back to the school. Your replacement is—" Coop wrinkled his face and pinched his nose, jerking his head toward Callie.

"Hey!" Callie fake pouted.

Dr. Chen smiled again, indicating that he got the joke but didn't have the energy to produce a laugh.

Coop offered to call Dr. Chen's family in Shanghai. "My Mandarin is rusty, but I can at least reassure them."

Callie squeezed Coop's hand. "Mandarin? You keep surprising me."

Dr. Chen nodded with appreciation. "I'll give you the password for…" he trailed off and closed his eyes, drifting into slumber. His doctor shooed them out of the room. She assured them a nurse would call if anything changed.

In the waiting room of this small but well-respected regional hospital, they found the police detective in charge of Dr. Chen's assault, George Belanger. Callie assumed he'd tell them nothing about an ongoing case and they'd have to trick him into giving up even a sliver of a clue. The ruddy young man, however, was eager to share his analysis. *I'm so naïve. This is Flambert, and this is Coop who knows everyone.*

Detective Belanger's story had too many details and not enough of a coherent narrative, but Callie surmised that Dr.

Chen had been working late in the coroner's lab, finalizing his report on the poison that killed Stella. The lab door was unlocked, but as the detective pointed out, most people in rural upstate areas left their doors unlocked. The wounds on the doctor's head suggested that he turned, possibly after hearing someone enter, and was hit on the head, rendering him unconscious and with no memory of the attack. His research, notations and samples in the nearby refrigerator were all neatly labeled so the attacker could easily identify the lot and whisk it all away.

The detective directed most of his story to Coop, whether because of a gender bias or because Coop was familiar and Callie was a stranger. But his eyes fastened on Callie when he delivered his final thoughts. "Anyone who tries to figure out who killed Stella is in danger."

The details of the attack would be common knowledge throughout Flambert and the Cooper School before lunch the next day. Suspicions would arise among anyone whose husband had gone out unexpectedly or whose sister couldn't be remembered at the bar she usually frequented. One of them probably did it. *Why would the murderer take this chance?*

Detective Belanger handed Coop a business card. "Feel free to call me."

Callie wasn't sure what would prompt either her or Coop to call the man but was glad to have a police contact who wasn't the chief.

Coop and Callie agreed that the school needed an assembly after breakfast. Callie texted an alert to the entire school population, set to wake them at cock's crow. Then she texted Phoebe, explaining that she'd be late getting in and apologizing for not pulling her weight. She hoped her final **I'm so Elton** would make Phoebe laugh.

* * *

When Callie and Coop returned to visit Dr. Chen the next day, he seemed much better and insisted he could go back to the lab. "I need to get to work on the samples right away."

Before they could object, his doctor spoke. "The samples are all gone. The notes are all gone. You talked with the detective last night."

"Oh. You told me that earlier, didn't you?" He leaned back on the pillow, deflated.

She nodded kindly. "This amnesia is probably temporary. You may never get back the memories of the time right around the attack, but you'll eventually remember everything else. That is typical of a head injury."

Following the doctor's lead, Callie tried to be upbeat in asking whether he needed anything from his cabin.

"Please don't trouble yourself. They're taking good care of me here." He, too, tried to be positive, but was not an experienced liar like Callie. His face was sagging, his spirits were down.

"Last night you mentioned giving us a password." Callie wondered if it was for school-related data.

He stared at her as if he didn't quite comprehend the words. "No, I can't think of anything like that. Perhaps I'll remember later..."

Coop assured him that there was nothing to worry about and that he was staying in daily contact with Dr. Chen's family in China.

The doctor led them to a conference room. "I have permission from Dr. Chen and his family to fill you in on his situation."

Under the table, Coop took Callie's hand. He knew, as he always did, that when she was uneasy, she said little and revealed less. He nodded to the doctor. "Go on."

"Dr. Chen's injuries are serious. He remembered more last night than he does today. Even a younger man would probably have headaches and a Swiss-cheese memory for some time to come. Given Dr. Chen's age, we don't know what to expect. With injuries of this sort, the patient may experience additional issues—physical unsteadiness, even mental disorientation. We're sending him to a rehab facility. Unfortunately, the closest one with the right services is in Albany."

On the long ride to the school, the cold truth hit both of them. Coop spoke first. "Did it sound like the doctor was saying she didn't think he'd recover enough to get back to work?"

"I was trying to ignore that." Callie swallowed hard. "I can't imagine the school without Dr. Chen."

Coop spoke carefully. "Then we need to hire an English teacher for your job, so you can take on his duties indefinitely. Callie, I'm sad to say, the replacement for your teaching job could be permanent."

Permanent. Callie knew he was right, but she felt as if he'd punched her in the stomach. "Why not a new vice principal instead? Then Phoebe could have her place to herself, and I could keep my cabin and the new person could get Dr. Chen's and—"

"Let's give Hu-Wei a chance to recover and come back."

"You're right, of course. That's the ethical thing to do. I hate it when you're right and I'm wrong." She pretended to pound her fists together like a fighter.

He smirked. "I know."

"You also know how much I love teaching."

Coop pulled over to the side of the country road, still a few miles from the school. "I do know, Callie. It's why I hired you and why your students love you. I hate losing you as a teacher, too."

She took his hand, hoping the simple gesture would help her cause. "Maybe in a year Dr. Chen will be back, then I'll hire a manager for the women's center so I can get back to the classroom."

He gazed at her with familiar affection. "And maybe the planets are made of chocolate cake."

"What?"

"I'm not saying it's not true, I'm saying there's no proof."

He chuckled at his own silly joke.

"Coop, seriously, could you hire a temp for me instead of a permanent replacement?" *Who am I if I'm not a teacher?*

He guided the vehicle back onto the road. "Okay. I'll think about it."

CHAPTER 8

Moving out of her Cooper cabin the next day triggered more grief than Callie expected. Coop offered to help but she was afraid if he saw how sad she was, he'd feel responsible. She'd prepared materials for her first teaching job at this table, encountered an intrepid raccoon by this kitchen island. Here she kissed Coop. Here she left him when she shouldn't have. She didn't possess much, even now, and the few pieces of her life that were her own fit a little too neatly into a series of plastic tubs.

She accepted help from Phoebe and Hazel, both surprisingly quiet as she went through unspoken goodbyes. *I will miss that tree. And that one. And that one.* As she left the cabin, now as devoid of personal belongings as when she'd first arrived, she marked the many changes since her first day there. For one, she'd learned to dress for the upstate New York winters. She smiled, remembering the inappropriate boots she brought with her, thinking they made her seem sophisticated. As she embraced her 33rd year, she felt pride at how well she had adapted to this life. Despite injuries on her first attempt, Callie was now a skier. She'd become comfortable as a teacher, wrapping her arms around the wonders of English literature. She had good friends. She and Coop were, well, an item that everyone knew about and approved. An inheritance came out of the blue and lifted her out of poverty forever. *How much of this will still be mine in the next chapter of my life?*

Once the last room was swept and her tubs were arranged neatly into the vehicles, it was almost as if she'd never set foot in this magical place under the trees. She sighed. Hazel sighed.

Phoebe looked from one to the other. "Are you two okay?"

"I already hate the new English teacher, whoever she or he may be." Hazel was a loyalist.

Phoebe hooked them both with a conspiratorial declaration. "Tonight. Adult beverages."

Callie and Phoebe lugged the tubs up two flights into the Flambert apartment they now shared, upstairs from Elton so they could only hope to annoy him with their footsteps. As they passed the office, Elton looked up from his laptop briefly, but didn't offer to help.

"Now I see the distinct advantages of an elevator building." Phoebe flung herself onto their sofa, sucking air. "We're not ever allowed to move again."

After unpacking most of her things, Callie once more texted Nora and once more got no response. *How can I ever be a parent? I'd be a nervous wreck.*

Hours later they convened at a small Flambert tavern called the Pine Tree. Callie chose it because it had no pool tables and no dance floor. As bars went, it was quiet and serene.

Hazel offered a toast. "To Dr. Chen's recovery."

Callie spoke quietly, almost to herself, "And to finding out who killed Stella."

Hazel shook a finger at Callie. "You mean to the police finding out who killed Stella."

Callie flushed but said nothing.

Phoebe, apparently determined to change the mood, clinked her glass against Callie's. "To Elton, without whom our lives would be so much easier."

Hazel drummed in an exaggerated gesture. "Girls' night out means never having to mention Elton."

Phoebe ignored that. "Aside from the whining about how provincial everything is, he's seriously incompetent. If he'd been hired to undermine the center, he couldn't be more effective than he is now. Thank heavens for the cloud. At least we have backup for everything he loses or destroys."

Callie considered for a moment. "Does everyone back up everything to the cloud these days?"

Phoebe nodded. "I don't know about everyone but it's standard business practice."

"And does the cloud use a password?"

Phoebe raised an eyebrow. "For heaven sakes, Callie. Haven't you been on the internet in the past hundred years?"

Callie laughed as the gears in her head turned.

Phoebe wasn't a mind reader and on her second drink wasn't catching the hints. "I've been trying to trick Elton into asking for a transfer back to Manhattan, but, sadly, he wants to stay."

Hazel sipped a tiny glass of liqueur, which she said reminded her of her days at Bryn Mawr several decades earlier. "He hates it here. Whatever for?"

"He's dating Meadow."

Callie's head contracted with pain. Meadow had been a Cooper student and seemed well-suited for the law office. Didn't that mean she was too smart to fall for Elton? "What could that girl be thinking?" She asked the bartender for ice water and Hazel for a painkiller.

"I'm not sure thinking is the main activity." Phoebe guffawed, a bit more salacious due to the beer. "Despite Elton's complaining, he seems more at home here than I expected. He says he used to come up to this area to ski every year. I'm surprised one of you hasn't seen him hanging around Craig and Lawrence's office. He's practically stalking Meadow." Phoebe looked around the bar, sparsely populated on a Tuesday night, as if Elton might be anywhere. "And she's over at our office," Phoebe crooked her fingers for air quotes. "*Delivering* papers from Lawrence all the time."

Hazel searched her bag for Advil. "Does Jillian know?"

Phoebe shrugged. "She's thrilled. Puts Meadow on a pedestal and always totally misses Elton's shortcomings. No accounting for taste. Or kids. Speaking of which, heard from Nora?"

Callie stuck out her lower lip like a toddler. "She asked me to give her some room…" Explaining hurt too much.

Phoebe used her swizzle stick to pick through the mixed nuts, searching for cashews. "But?"

"Maybe I'm hypersensitive." Callie held out her palm for Hazel's pills.

Phoebe coughed on a nut. "Yeah. Everyone knows *that's* your problem."

"Cynic." Callie washed down the pills.

Hazel patted Callie's hand. "What's wrong?"

"I don't know. The first text wasn't right. It was cutesy shorthand, but it wasn't Nora's cutesy shorthand. And now she won't answer at all."

Hazel's brow furrowed along well-earned age lines. "Is Arthur dictating to her?"

"Or commandeering her phone?" Phoebe set her beer down.

"What if new language choices are just her way of being frosty? No question she's mad at Coop." Callie turned to Hazel. "You had a teenage daughter. How do you tell a cry for help from a shut-the-hell-up?"

"As Tom Stoppard said, 'It's a mystery.' Before she came out to me at fifteen, Alexis was curt and rude for almost six months. You can imagine how relieved I was that she was struggling to reveal her sexuality and not, say, a drug habit." Hazel studied her empty glass for a minute as if contemplating a second drink. "But it took you to get her to tell me she'd been raped." Sniffing back tears, she pulled a lavender hanky from her bag.

Callie's turn for hand-patting. "She was trying to protect you from a maniac." Her mind insisted on taking her to the very places she was avoiding. "What if Stella's guy's a maniac? My mother married one. They're not as uncommon as one might hope. What if Arthur is one?" How far they were from Arthur's gallery packed with cutting-edge work by promising New York artists. Here, the air smelled of beer and popcorn and the wall adornments were photos of local teams and a scattering of yellowed calendar photos of scantily clad women.

Phoebe made patterns on the table, overlapping the wet rings of her glass. "The art world is gossipy, and everyone talks about Arthur Bement's gallery. Back when I was working for a designer, I heard lots of rumors about him seducing his gallery staff, but none that he's violent. Besides, what are the chances Nora would get two in one lifetime?"

"Maybe Nora has a warped view of how to choose men." Callie's memory strayed for a split second to the inappropriate young guy she'd bedded when she and Coop were apart. "What if Stella did, too? Every teenager isn't smart enough to choose someone like Shauni."

Hazel agreed. "I'm a lucky mom."

A noisy group of women entered the bar, whooping and backslapping. Wearing bowling shirts bedecked with matching logos, the new group settled at a large table. One bellowed to the bartender, "Coupla pitchers for the winners." Others shouted food orders.

"There goes our quiet night." Callie eyed the group and noticed a familiar face. "Mrs. Kelly's over there. Shall we say hello?"

Hazel hopped off her stool without waiting for consensus. "By all means. I took her a casserole a few days ago and she was still pretty low. Glad to see she's starting back to regular activities."

As they approached, Dorothy beckoned. The team shared knowledge via a lighting-fast game of telephone around the table: "That's Hazel, she's in my book club." Or "She's Alexis' mom" or "That's Coop's girlfriend" or "The big girl with the wild hair is from New York."

Soon they were all chatting amiably. After covering the game, the weather, and food, the three women moved to leave. Callie was surprised that Dorothy joined their migration out the door.

As they ambled into the parking lot, still chatting about

nothing, Dorothy smiled at Phoebe. "Do you mind if I speak with Callie and Hazel about school business?"

Phoebe returned Dorothy's smile. "I'll walk home. I need the exercise." She turned her attention to Callie. "Are you sober enough to drive?"

"Not even buzzed anymore. Can't speak for Hazel, though. Luckily, I'm her driver."

Dorothy led Callie and Hazel across the lot, away from the bar noises. She spoke quickly. "I was going to call each of you, so I'm glad to find you together. If Stella was murdered and Dr. Chen attacked, are the other girls at the school safe? Am I safe?"

Callie kept up the appearance of calm concern that belied a deeper panic. *Oh hell, I was just wondering about this myself.*

"Have you talked to the police?" Hazel pushed gray curls off her face, a gesture Callie recognized as meaning they would be businesslike, drink or no drink.

"The chief says there's nothing they can do if I don't get an outright threat." Dorothy raised her hands in frustration. "The old chief woulda done something."

Callie felt a hint of winter in the air, matching her gut feeling. "Do you feel unsafe?"

Dorothy leaned against a car. "I dunno. I already get tons of hate calls cause I voted for the center instead of the ski place."

"Thank you for that." Callie guiltily counted her blessings that she wasn't an elected official.

"That's awful." Hazel glanced at Callie. "Are the calls anonymous?"

Dorothy nodded. "Some are. Some aren't. Some act like I should know who they are. Like, I'm pretty sure the mayor has called more than once. And it's not just calls. I get tweets and email and so on. The worst is when they say things like, I hope you go like your kid."

"Oy vey." Hazel's words, a Yiddish expression she used often, meant she was shocked but didn't know what to say.

Callie's stomach turned but she focused on needing to help. "I met a detective at the hospital where they're treating

Dr. Chen. Do you know George Belanger?"

"Yeah. I know all the cops. Belanger's one of the investigators on Stella's … murder." Dorothy stumbled over the word. "I didn't even know Stella was being bullied until I read that note." Dorothy looked down at her worn athletic shoes. "If she even wrote it. And now I'm getting the same treatment."

Hazel touched Dorothy's arm reassuringly.

Dorothy began to shake almost imperceptibly. "I was real proud that she got into Cooper. It's so hard for townies to get in. But maybe somebody thought she didn't deserve—"

Hazel shook her head. "It's hard for anyone to get in. We turn away five qualified girls for every one we accept. And many more unqualified ones. Stella was hard-working and talented. She belonged at Cooper."

Callie peered through the dark at Dorothy's dimly lit face. "Why did you say, 'If she even wrote it?'"

"It didn't sound like her. She was so proud of her good grammar, always correcting my mistakes." Dorothy looked defeated. "Would her last words be so—?" She paused. "I don't have evidence. Just a gut feeling."

Callie plunged on. "A bartender at Main Street Bar & Grill said she met her boyfriend there. More than once. Did you meet him?"

Dorothy tensed. "The first I heard of a boyfriend was from the police. I always wondered if she was gay because the only person she ever really talked about was Harriet. Oh yeah, Harriet calls me from time to time."

Hazel recoiled. "Threatening you?"

Dorothy raised a hand for no. "She keeps saying she wants to tell me something. In person. I guess I've been avoiding it because I didn't want to hear about her affair with Stella."

"You wouldn't approve?" Callie was surprised.

"Oh, I'm not against the gays. It'd hurt my heart if Stella was in love and didn't tell me. Now I wonder whether Harriet knew the guy. I'll text her right now." Dorothy immediately started typing.

Hazel sighed. "Nowadays I know so much about Alexis and Shauni—more than I want to sometimes—but a few years ago, I was like you. Wanting to know and not wanting to know at the same time. Callie's like that, too."

Callie crossed her arms. "No, I'm strictly monomaniacal."

Dorothy tilted her head questioningly.

"I only want to know. I think both Nora and I would be better off if she'd talk to me. And her dad."

CHAPTER 9

A terse phone call from Coop roused Callie at some pre-sun hour. "Harriet is missing." Callie was not yet used to waking in the Flambert apartment and had a moment of disorientation, then mumbled at him to tell her what was going on. "The students who share her cabin reported her gone when they got up a few minutes ago. Her phone and ID are still in the cabin." Coop's voice wove fear and anger into a discordant growl. "The police are on their way. The whole school is up and looking for her."

Callie assured him she'd be there as fast as she could throw on clothing and tell Phoebe. She planned to inform Elton as a courtesy, but his car was already gone. Probably to the gym as usual. Or, with any luck, he'd gone off on one of his several-day holidays as he tended to do every couple weeks.

When Callie arrived at Cooper School, evidence of a massive search effort was everywhere. Groups had fanned out across the grounds. Some were going door-to-door throughout the campus in hopes that Harriet had fallen asleep in a classroom or in the wrong cabin. Others walked forward in long lines, arm length apart, moving into the woods calling Harriet's name. Callie found Coop and the police chief going over the searchers' reports laid out on a folding table, fighting to keep the papers down in the morning breeze.

Suppressing a desire to cry pitifully and demand attention for her own heartsick worry, Callie tapped Coop's shoulder.

"Catch me up." For a second, she saw him register pleasure at her presence, replaced with worry lines deepening into a frown.

"Nothing so far. The chief says when children are missing, it's routine to inform the FBI, so no doubt agents will be arriving soon." He gently steered her away from the others. "If something happened to her, this is going to be a nightmare of cops and Feds and reporters. Some girls say Harriet was bragging about having a date yesterday. Maybe she snuck into town. At this point I'd be happy if it was sex and not—" He didn't need to finish the sentence.

The screaming and vomiting, when it began, was contagious and continuous.

Everyone ran toward the sound. Teachers and cops ushered students away. In a clearing mottled with morning sun, Harriet's head tilted up toward the sheltering trees, her long hair fastidiously arranged like emanating rays, her curvaceous figure nestled onto a blanket, her youthful full breasts gleaming in the early morning light. The cloth under her was soft and decorative, shot through with blue threads almost the same color as her balletically parted legs. Only her face was missing, a crater of blood and bone and brains. A metal baseball bat lay across her neck like a guillotine that had not completed its work. Someone spent some time humiliating her after her death. And possibly before.

Callie had to look away. "Why so violent? So different from Stella?"

The chief, who was directing officers to tape off the area and photograph the scene, seemed irked by this question. "Can't assume it's the same killer."

In the century-plus history of the school, no student had ever been murdered on school grounds.

Coop spoke so quietly only she could hear. "Don't argue with him. It'll just make him dig his heels in." The very tiny tightening around his mouth and eyes showed how hard it was for him to keep his own commentary in check. "We need to be strong right now."

"I know." Callie was an old hand at appearing calm in crises. It was how she survived the first two decades of her life.

As Coop stopped to comfort student after student, Callie looked for Detective Belanger. By lucky coincidence, he was with the officers assigned the task of finding an on-campus headquarters for the investigation. "You can set up in admin." She led them to her office, still full of Dr. Chen's academic materials. "Detective Belanger, tell me the truth. What do you think happened here?"

The young man avoided her eyes as he set up the police department laptop. "Dunno."

"Speculate. Same killer as Stella's?"

He sighed. "We can't know yet, but…"

"But?"

"This county has seen only a handful of homicides in the past decade, mostly crimes of passion with witnesses. What are the chances that two teenage girls—friends—were killed by two *different* mystery killers?"

She suddenly remembered a detail from the night before. "Is there a chance that Dr. Chen's notes about Stella are on the cloud?"

The young detective glanced mindfully at the other cops, now too engaged in setting up to hear their conversation. "Nobody's said anything. I've been wondering the same thing myself. The doc was so careful. I find it hard to believe he didn't keep some kind of backup records."

Callie lowered her voice even further. "I think he meant to tell us the password that first night but now he has no memory of it."

Belanger's eyes lit up. "Thanks for telling me."

Within moments, the chief bustled into the room with FBI agents in tow. Callie answered what she could but since she hadn't been on campus, they quickly lost interest in her and sent her on her way.

Feeling the extreme grief and fear across the campus, Coop and Callie organized an assembly at the gym. It was a gritty affair. Everyone said all the right things, but nothing felt better afterward. Both the police chief and the mayor spoke, mouthing patently false concern about the students. Several asked if the school would close and Coop answered truthfully that he didn't know yet. Coop phoned Harriet's father, her only living relative. Reaching him was a major undertaking; he was in prison on a drug offense. He asked very little and didn't cry. Coop ended the call by promising to box Harriet's things and keep them until the father could come for them, which might be several years. He turned to Callie after he hung up. "He didn't seem to care."

Recalling her years in juvie, Callie considered the options. "Maybe he's numbed by prison or couldn't show emotion for fear of being bullied by inmates later." She felt like weeping at how light a mark Harriet left on the world. Everyone was shocked now but in years, maybe just months, her death would become a terrible story of a tragedy that happened to others and her life would be largely forgotten. "This is so unfair." Callie's finger went to her dove necklace. She wanted nothing more than to climb into Coop's arms, but neither of them could spare even an hour that morning.

When Callie called Dorothy to give her a heads up, she got the machine. Most likely, Stella's mother had already heard through the Flambert grapevine and wasn't ready to talk. Callie exhaled, both relieved she didn't have yet another duty right now and guilty for feeling relieved. Nonetheless, the heightened anxiety of being torn in all directions haunted her waking hours.

Coop, always aware of Callie's needs, found a local Cooper grad to cover her classes so they could handle a campus overrun with police and FBI together. A permanent replacement would come later, when he had adequate time for interviews and other proper hiring practices. Callie fidgeted at her desk in the Flambert office and tried to focus on the center for at least a few hours, including an upcoming meeting Lawrence arranged with Mohawk elders. Meadow, apparently seeking an excuse to see Elton, arrived with papers Callie didn't actually need. Meadow had a thousand theories about the murder, ranging from aliens to mobsters, none of them useful.

Her conversation did, however, confirm both murders were general knowledge.

Phoebe shushed the young woman as she negotiated with a contractor on the phone. She consulted Callie from time to time as if things were normal. *Remind me. What is normal, again?*

Worried that gossip or TV news would get to Dr. Chen before she could, Callie connected to a video chat. He seemed awake and cognitively able, unlike the last time she'd seen him. And well-informed.

He held up a file folder. "Printouts of the forensics for Harriet. The investigators messaged me a few minutes ago."

"What else can you tell me?"

"Nothing official."

"Of course, but …"

"This time we have a fragment of DNA. Doesn't match anything in the system and isn't enough for a description of the killer—can't even identify gender—but it will serve well as a comparison if the police catch somebody."

Callie quelled a growing excitement and kept her voice neutral. "Same as Stella's killer?"

"Stella's killer left no DNA, not even a hair. If it's the same killer, something spooked them this time and they weren't as careful."

Callie again broached the question of the password the doctor mentioned the night of his attack, but he still had no memory about that. She promised to visit him soon and disconnected.

That evening, she caught up with Shauni at the school gym. "What a cluster."

The soccer coach sat in her office, working on a practice roster. "I need to do *something* til we can start up practice again." She rose to hug Callie. "The team's been dropping by. Everyone wants to know if they're in danger. And whether the killer was somebody at school."

"What do you think?"

"Dunno. When Stella died, I had no clue, but … Harriet's killer had to be someone in good enough shape to bludgeon her." Shauni demonstrated, wielding an invisible bat, swinging her arms up together and then swiftly down toward her desk. "Unfortunately, that rules out nobody on my team."

An unwanted scenario jumped into Callie's mind. A deceptive flirt, perhaps Harriet's first lover, caressing her as they removed her clothing piece by piece, promising gentle lovemaking. Then doing heaven knows what, telling her to close her eyes, and striking her dead. Not like the cruel, agonizing poison for Stella. *What made killing Harriet so urgent? Fingers crossed she went unconscious after the first hit.* Callie closed her eyes, leaning back in the chair. "I hope to heaven it wasn't a student."

Shauni brought Callie's attention back with a rap on her desk. "Was it a guy? Was she raped? The girls want to know that, too, though most of them won't ask outright."

"We won't know until the autopsy is completed." Callie sighed. "And then I don't know what the cops will make public." She made a mental note to quiz Detective Belanger on this point. Long after Callie left Shauni and headed to Flambert, the question continued to haunt her. ***Was it a guy?***

Callie slept in her new bedroom in the Flambert apartment. Though she hated to be away from Coop, the yellow tape all over campus was disconcerting, and center tasks demanded her attention. After a restless night slid into morning, she sipped her umpteenth coffee in the downstairs office with Phoebe and Elton.

The first interruption was a call from Hazel announcing that Mohammed was going to the mountain, by which she meant that she and Callie and Coop were taking Stella's things to Dorothy rather than waiting for her to come to the school. "It's from the Quran," she'd chuckled. "Gotta admire a religion that commands people to read."

Before Callie could protest she wasn't sure how thoughtful it was to bandy about words from another culture's holy book, Elton, who had apparently been eavesdropping, sneered and muttered just loudly enough to be heard, "Racist." He'd become hypersensitive about any perceived bigotry since he started dating Meadow.

How nice it would be if he paid this much attention to his work. Callie continued on the phone with Hazel. "Do you really need me?" The thought of another task quickened Callie's pulse, and not in a good way.

"Yes, dear. The center can live without you for a morning. The acting vice principal needs to be in on this." Hazel spoke gently but Callie heard the determination.

Callie stalled. "Maybe Dorothy'll be more comfortable if we wait and meet at her home."

"I doubt it. She lives in one of those motels. Week-to-week rental. Did you read Barbara Ehrenreich's *Nickled and Dimed?* You think your life is stressed? Those places are—"

"I'm familiar with—"

Hazel's rant couldn't be stopped. "You and Phoebe just rented a place and signed a lease, correct? If you miss a payment, the landlord can't evict you without a legal process. But in those so-called motels, if you can't pay, they can put you on the sidewalk the next day, possibly confiscate your belongings."

"I know. It wasn't that long ago for me." Callie snapped her fingers. "I could secretly buy her a little house."

Hazel sizzled with sarcasm. "I'm sure an anonymous windfall for Dorothy would go over well with the council where half the members are looking for any excuse to get rid of her."

Callie sighed. "Okay."

Elton's voice startled her. "You can buy me a house." *You wish.*

Interruptions continued the whole morning. Her center work felt nonlinear and disjointed as she stopped for numerous calls from concerned parents asking if their daughters were safe. Although she insisted that the girls were in no danger, she knew they remained skeptical, so did she and the fibbing was eating her up inside. She texted Detective Belanger without success. Finally, she left Phoebe and Elton working in the office and returned to the school, seeking a direct report from the investigators. They had no news to share. Nor did the many students she questioned, cajoled, consoled or sat with in their classrooms and dorms.

Just after lights out, Coop and Callie held hands on their adopted mid-quad bench with its illusion of privacy despite the bustling school around them. With their phones on mute and their bare feet nestled in the autumn grass, they joined every other night creature immersed in croaking frogs. They sat silently for a few moments, watching the rooms go dark.

Hazel's proposal didn't appeal to Coop. "Dorothy might feel like we're ganging up on her."

Callie thought of herself as a champion, but a distress over the murders left her rash and unkind. She made a face he would hate if he could see it in the dark. "Flambert's in the dark ages—that council meeting was a perfect example. The members were mesmerized by irrelevant and unattainable promises. Small minds. Stupid judgments. No wonder she feels overwhelmed."

"Please don't generalize about my town."

Callie flushed. "Sorry."

Later, as she climbed into Coop's bed next to her already slumbering beau, Callie remembered to check her cell. A text from Nora read: **Call plz. Things seriously FU.** Callie crept into the living room to avoid waking Coop. She tried Nora a few times without success, so when the young woman finally answered, Callie was startled, expecting voice mail again.

"Holy shit, Callie, you're never up this late. Whassup?"

"Did you get my message about Harriet?"

"It's horrible. Everything is horrible." Nora sniffled. "Can I come home?"

"Always. Never ask—just come." Callie could hear Coop stirring, as if news of his daughter magically wakened him.

"Dad is so mad about Arthur. And Arthur is mad about you and Dad interfering. We had a huge fight and right now I'm just walking around Manhattan."

Callie pictured the long dark residential blocks of the

Lower East Side, threats lurking everywhere. "Come right now. I'll send a car."

"He isn't what I thought." Nora was almost inaudible.

"Arthur?"

"Yes, Arthur. He's what Coop said." Nora's voice rose. "Worse."

"What is it?"

"I . . ."

"You can tell me. No judgment."

"It's just that ..."

"Nora, I'm here for you. What is it?"

"Callie, he hit me."

Callie felt a pain behind her eyes. "Come home right now."

"I feel so ... betrayed."

"Of course you do. Honey, know that we're on your side but I gotta get off right now and hire a car to bring you here."

"Thanks, Callie."

As they disconnected, Callie squelched the inner voice yelling that she was already overcommitted. Instead, she focused on Nora's transportation, calling a car service in Manhattan that would get Nora to the school in a few hours.

After an hour or so, she woke Coop up. "Nora's on her way."

His eyes popped opened. "What happened?" He was up in a shot while she explained. "I'm calling the police."

Callie raised two hands in a gentle pushback. "Wait 'til we know the whole story." She followed him into the kitchen on alert, as if she could wrestle the phone from him. He'd apparently reconsidered and instead dialed Nora's cell. Getting no answer, he paced, dialing again every few minutes, swearing each time he got voicemail, shrugging off Callie's remonstrances.

She Googled New York sexual abuse laws.

Seeing the website over her shoulder catapulted Coop into action. "Gotta call Craig."

"At this hour? It's the middle of the night."

"That criminal should go to jail." He didn't phone the lawyer but instead commanded Siri to play a particularly raucous song and to crank up the volume.

Callie spoke to the machine, "Siri, turn down the volume." Then to her partner, "Coop, try not to wake up the whole campus."

He grabbed a beer. "Get off my back."

She tensed the toes in her slippers—a trick she learned in her youth to redirect ill-timed anger—and concentrated on the computer screen. "We both want Arthur to pay, right?" *Not each other.*

He stood absolutely still for a moment, staring at her. As if he literally returned to reality in that silence, he put the beer back and slumped into a chair. "Sorry. I want to smack someone. Not you of course, but—"

"I know the feeling." Callie put water on for tea. "Let's try not to do something stupid in the name of helping Nora. We don't want another round of her running back to him." She surveyed the spacious Cooper apartment with its eclectic mix of antiques and comfortable chairs, expensive art, and family photos, not finding answers in any of them. *Change the subject.* "And by the way—is running away the Cooper family method for dealing with conflict?"

"Pot. Kettle." A sheepish grin almost appeared as he settled into a chair to not read a book.

Callie leaned back into the desk chair and closed her eyes for a minute, somehow losing ninety. She awoke to Nora sipping tea, a red welt on her cheekbone. Callie, still half asleep, struggled to her feet, pushing away feelings of helplessness. "You'll need ice." Though she'd fought a few guys in her time, she'd never been hit by a lover and wasn't sure what would help.

Nora raised her voice as if irked to be interrupted. "—called me a little tramp so I slapped him."

Coop ran a hand through his unruly hair. "You threw the first punch?"

Callie could hear the tiny descant of pride under his

sternness. He'd thrown a few fists in his own youth and knew how useful it was to be known as a fighter.

"He slapped me back, much harder." Nora accepted a frozen bag. "When did you guys start eating frozen peas?"

The ski accident that first brought Callie to this apartment momentarily distracted her. "For when my shoulder acts up." Callie tried to shake off the fatigue skewing her perceptions.

"Oh, right. I guess my injury is kinda lame compared with yours." Nora held the package against her cheek.

Coop tensed. "This isn't a worst-victim competition. What do you want to do?" When Nora shrugged despondently, he jumped into the fray. "Ice cream? Action film?"

Nora brightened slightly. "Got strawberry?"

Her father rolled his eyes as if to remind her that he always kept a stash of her favorite. "X-Men?"

Great. Two teenagers. Tuning out Hugh Jackman, mutant hero, Callie dove for a comforting pillow on Coop's bed.

Uncharacteristically, Coop slept late. Callie wished she could stay snuggled against him but dragged herself to the kitchen in full martyrdom regalia, which at this moment consisted of a t-shirt and flip flops. The kitchen and living room were a disaster, strewn with remnants of late-night snacks and random debris. A backpack had overturned, spilling a disorganized heap of books and papers. The entire apartment reeked of buttered popcorn.

Callie gathered dishes and organized piles. *Now I'm Cinderella. Terrific.* After the bit of housekeeping, she showered, dressed, and collected Hazel in Flambert.

Hazel clutched the hand grip on the door, tense in her self-appointed job of judging their distance from the car in front. Callie turned on classic rock and sang along with gusto. A few minutes later Hazel gave up her traffic monitoring and together they butchered the greatest hits of several decades until Callie pulled into the mall parking lot.

The bright fall morning brought many shoppers to the mall, and it took a few minutes to find a parking place. Both women were sweating by the time they straggled into the extravagant air conditioning, which swept over them, carrying the scent of fries and coffee. A childhood memory arose for Callie—her mother feeding her in food courts because Cecile could hide the minor expenditures from her husband who seemed bent on keeping his wife underweight and depriving Callie of sustenance.

Hazel squinted at the map of restaurants and stores. "Fluorescent lights. Canned music. Now I remember why I hate malls."

Callie had endured her share of low wages in unhealthy environments. "Imagine working here." She and Hazel headed down a wide corridor.

Dorothy Kelly worked at a bead store displaying strings of everything from plastic to crystal and bins of individual gold, silver, glass, seed beads and charms. Artisan jewelry hung beside signs advertising classes. As Callie and Hazel entered, Dorothy greeted them warmly from behind the counter. "Thanks for coming."

Callie set the box of Stella's things on the counter, a rough contrast to the candle glass and prisms.

Hazel inspected an intricate necklace in the display case. "Is this Stella's work?"

Dorothy dimpled. "How'd you guess?"

"She uses—used—patterns and colors distinctively. This one is remarkable."

Dorothy opened the box and looked through the meager collection of notebooks, clothing, and personal items. Finally, she looked up. "It's not here."

CHAPTER 10

Hazel flicked grey curls off her face. "What isn't here?"

Dorothy clasped her hands, as if to keep from shaking. "Her diary. I've been putting off coming for it cuz … well, she bitched about me a lot."

Callie wrinkled her brow, certain she'd double-checked every drawer, closet, and locker. "I'll look for it again."

Hazel rounded the counter and put her hand over Dorothy's. "We try so hard to be good parents, to let them have their space, to respect their privacy. Then something happens and we wonder if we should have stolen a peek."

Dorothy shook her head. "But I did. I read her diary a few times. She thought I was …"

Hazel sighed. "Truth be told, I read Alexis's journals, too, when I could find them. Maybe every parent does. Didn't take long for her to encrypt it online so I couldn't get access."

"I just can't help …" Tears welled in Dorothy's eyes. "I want to read her words … even though I made her miserable. It'll keep her alive for me."

Callie perused the printed inventory of Stella's belongings. "The police got records from the phone company that showed her sending a text to a bunch of people. They thought it was a suicide note and now they think the killer wrote it. But they didn't find the actual phone. Did she keep it at home?"

Dorothy pulled out each garment from the box and searched the pockets, the third time through them after the police and Callie. "She usually had it with her. But the police didn't find it at my place, either."

Hazel and Callie took their leave after a little more general chatting. As they headed out of the bead shop, Callie asked one last question. "Do you think Stella was really being bullied or did the killer just make that up?"

"Dunno." Dorothy stuffed Stella's things back into the box and stowed it out of sight of customers. "In the diary, I wasn't the only one she crabbed about. Stella and Harriet were always on about this one or that one." She thought for a moment. "She'd write, 'Me and Harriet were laughing so hard at what happened to so-and-so. We put pix up.'"

Hazel stood as tall as her five foot two would allow. "Anyone in particular?"

Dorothy looked pained. "Can't remember. The only name I know for sure is Harriet."

Callie tapped a finger against the doorframe. "Put pix up?"

"That was in the diary a lot. Some website full of insults."

"A bullying website?" Callie felt ill.

Dorothy sighed. "Do you think Stella and Harriet bullied people and then those people came after them?"

Callie shrugged. "I don't know. Have you talked with the police about this?"

"Yeah, but they don't seem very open to suggestions from the victim's mother."

After they climbed back into the car Callie groaned. "I was just naïve enough to think cyber bullying would never reach Cooper."

Hazel consulted the internet on her own cell. "Schools don't agree on what to do about bullying. There's an article here—"

"I can't listen right now." Pulling out of the mall lot, Callie called Coop then Nora. No answers. Probably too hung over on sugar and CGI explosions. She dropped Hazel at her house and drove to the Flambert office. The morning had disappeared down a time-suck rabbit hole, but she knew Phoebe would be at the center site and with any luck had found a way to occupy

Elton's time at a distance from both of them. Fortunately, the office was empty so she could call Dr. Chen in peace. "Hello, it's Callie. Sorry to call you during lunch but it's the only time I have. How are you today?"

His voice sounded a bit stronger than the day before. "I'm slowly regaining my strength and my cognitive functioning. And my memory. But I still don't know what happened the night I was attacked. What have you learned?"

She heard him move his mouth away from the mouthpiece to chew. After apologizing again, she described the situation as he finished eating. "What do you think?"

"I heard a few rumors about a bullying website but didn't think they were credible." He sighed apologetically. "It's quite disturbing that I was wrong."

"What should I do?"

Dr. Chen thought for a second. "Start with the Cooper server. Ask tech support to examine it for bullying. If they find anything, you may want to inform the police."

Callie scribbled madly. *A guy in his 70s recovering from a brain injury is thinking more clearly than I am. Great.* At risk of further wasting his time, she asked her usual question. "Any new info about the murders?"

He answered too quickly. "Nothing."

"Was Harriet raped?"

"We know there was sexual activity, but we don't know whether it was consensual."

Callie rang off feeling waves of physical and psychic fatigue. She climbed the stairs to the top-floor apartment she shared with Phoebe, deciding to honor her bedroom with a well-earned nap. As she jiggled her key, she heard voices. Phoebe and a man. *Well, nap's out.* Back downstairs, Callie sat at her desk, cradling her head in her arms, as in grade school. "All I need is twenty winks." She wasn't aware she was speaking aloud.

"Well, girlfriend, don't sleep with your office door open then. I need my music." Elton had apparently returned and instantly dialed up his music to annoy-Callie volume. Even with the door to her office closed the bass thumped through to scramble her weary brain. She drove off to a quiet cul-de-sac. *A zillionaire sleeping in her little car. This has to be a first.*

A half hour later, stiff but less tired, she called Phoebe. "Is your gentleman caller gone?"

"Excuse me?"

"I didn't want to intrude." Callie suspected they needed some rules about roommate etiquette. Maybe the old sock-on-the-door thing.

"Oh, sorry." Phoebe seemed distracted. "I wasn't … I think you heard the radio." *Who has a radio anymore?* And then Phoebe's words came in a rush like a child making up a story. "I can barely hear anything because Elton is blasting his music two floors down. I'm surprised nobody's called the cops. I've just been sitting here trying to catch up on local property policies and …"

"I'm going to need time away from the center for a couple of days because of Harriet—" *So you can see your boyfriend in peace.*

"No problem. But we do need more roomie time. Late night gossip in pjs, the whole schmear."

"Sure. Movies and wine. That's a promise." Callie wasn't sure in which century, but maybe they'd have better movies then. And Phoebe would tell-all about the guy.

A call to the school's tech support consumed nearly the entire thirty-minute drive to the school. Beating through the undergrowth of jargon, Callie surmised that while they talked, the tech guy discovered the school server was linked to a site called Cuppa Cuper, full of slurs and disinformation and self-aggrandizement.

Whoever the website puppet master was, they actively encouraged malicious meanness between students. Too many students complied. At Callie's direction, the techs suspended computer privileges for everyone they could identify while making a backup of the site in case anyone who could still get in tried to delete anything. Her next call was to Alexis. "Could the school hire you as a consultant?"

"Let me check with my boss and get back to you." Alexis sounded hopeful. "Personally, I hope the town will want to stop bullies anywhere, but you never know what the mayor thinks is in our interest."

Leaving her car in the school lot, Callie dashed to admin. At Coop's office door she knocked, as always.

"Enter!" The bellowing was not a good sign. She crossed the threshold cautiously.

"What did I do?"

Coop clicked furiously at his keyboard, swearing audibly. "Did you suspend computer privileges for Juanita Jesus?"

"Yes, a couple of minutes ago. Why?"

"Her father just called, threatening to sue, picket the place, and report us to any agency he could think of."

"You've soothed angry parents before. It's my job to punish kids who violate school rules." Her cheeks burned with anger and humiliation at his questioning her judgment before discussing the issue.

He slammed his palm on the desk. "JJ's an intern this semester on an archeological dig that we approved. She couldn't have—"

"But ... really?" Callie sat with a dull thud, sinking into antique upholstery. "Wait, how did the stepfather find out?"

"He was trying to register her for classes for the spring semester." Coop scowled at Callie. "He couldn't get in, so he called tech support. Callie, this is no way to run things."

"We just let the bullies run rampant until we develop a protocol? I don't think so."

Coop headed out.

"Oh, no." Callie jumped between Coop and the door. "You stay right here, mister. Someone is hacking our system. You don't like what I did? Freaking fine. What are we going to do about it?" Less than a foot separated them, requiring her to crane her neck to see into his eyes; she had no intention of losing this particular staring contest. He could easily move her by force, but he wouldn't. He was stuck, glowering down as she barred the door. She was unprepared for his next move. He laughed. Loudly. Then she laughed. They embraced, they kissed, they lost the world for a moment.

He released her. "Okay, Callie. Let's go see what the tech guy knows."

A head-spinning three hours later, Callie's main emotion was gratitude that the school had employees who loved technology. Apparently, a sophisticated computer geek—which did not rule out a Cooper student—created the stealth website, Cuppa Cuper, and launched it with a slew of targeted insults. It was evident, she heard the computer whiz say, that many students were accessing the site as a hub for gossip, much of it deeply destructive.

The web masters covered their tracks but most of the students who participated weren't tech savvy enough to hide their identities, though they used fake names. The techs easily identified the frequent posters. Stella and Harriet were top contributors, singling out everyone they didn't like for detrimental judgments. Someone the techs couldn't identify retaliated with a campaign against them that was even more personal and horrifying. Callie felt sick and sad in turn. Then mad as hell.

Coop stayed in the computer center to oversee the destruction of the website and the complex efforts to track down its originators. Callie returned to mundane chores in Dr. Chen's office, hoping to focus elsewhere. She had almost succeeded when the phone rang. "Calinda Franklin here."

"Hi Callie, it's Alexis. What can I do to help?" Callie outlined the situation and supplied the tech department number. Alexis's voice softened at Callie's obvious distress. "I'll do what I can."

Callie checked her notes. "One more thing. How well do you know Meadow Goodleaf?"

Alexis hmmm'd. "Not well. Lousy taste in guys. Why?"

Callie's eyebrows shot up. "Why do you say that?"

"She went out with some guy her senior year, a tech whiz who promised her the world, took her virginity and what little money she had, then disappeared. She seemed so lost, Shauni and I begged Craig to hire her after graduation."

Callie took notes.

Alexis sighed. "What does this have to do with the bullies?"

"Maybe nothing."

"She always seemed more like a professional victim than a bully. But I wouldn't put it past her boyfriend. She told us he rewarded her for being mean."

"Rewarded?"

Alexis hesitated. "Meet me and Shauni at Hazel's later. Not a good idea to talk about this at work."

Callie sorted through a pile of mail, yelping when she came to a letter from the Mohawk Council. Trying to read the letter while dialing her lawyer's office slowed both.

Meadow answered with an upbeat lilt. "Landers and White, may I help you?"

"Callie here. Put me through to Lawrence, please."

"Hi Callie. He's in with Phoebe. Do you want me to interrupt them?"

Callie tried to remember why Phoebe was meeting with Lawrence. "Sure. Thanks."

"Please hold."

During the wait, Callie reminded herself that she'd asked Phoebe to handle things on her own during the school crisis. Still, she had to admit she felt left out.

Lawrence's velvety voice came on the line. "Hi, Callie. How are you? Phoebe tells me you're slammed out there at Cooper. We're—"

Callie directed her agitation to the matter at hand. "Did you get the letter from the Mohawk elders?"

"Haven't looked at the mail yet. Hang on a sec."

Callie heard him yell for Meadow. *Don't these lawyers have an intercom? Or at least a hold button?* She heard Phoebe's voice and then Meadow's before Lawrence returned to the phone.

"Callie, I need to study this but at first glance it doesn't look good. Seems they've found evidence of a treaty or land deed giving the Mohawk Nation prior claim to the center's land."

Callie heard Phoebe exclaim something fairly salty.

Lawrence apparently covered the receiver to speak to someone at his end. When he came back, he sounded resigned. "Let me look into this."

Callie massaged her temple. *Yet another thing to try not thinking about.* The rest of her tasks should have been enough distraction but focusing on work proved imperfect. At the end of the afternoon, she texted Coop that she was leaving for the night and drove to Flambert. She pulled up behind a rental van in front of Hazel's, her mood ironically elevated by the news station reminding her that the world was rife with worse troubles than her own.

Shauni and Alexis tumbled out of the house, talking at once. Callie considered each with pleasure. Shauni was athletic, green eyes gleaming, caramel skin browned by the sun. Alexis, short and round with a mop of black curls so like her mother's, looked serious and professional in work clothes. They dragged her into the house proclaiming that Hazel's cooking would cure all ills.

As always, Craig and Hazel greeted her like family, yet everyone seemed distracted despite a delicious meal. Callie wondered if she was projecting. Afterward, Craig excused himself to return to work and Hazel waved Callie, Alexis, and Shauni off into the living room while she cleared up.

Callie quizzed Alexis. "What did you mean about the boyfriend rewarding Meadow?"

"Gross sexual stuff. You don't wanna to know. I don't even want to know, and I know." Alexis flushed and exchanged glances with Shauni.

Callie felt a headache hover. "*Ugh.* What did you find out about the website?"

"This perp had chops. The website was on a discount hosting service, with obviously fake contact information. I did a standard search, but the designers anticipated that and covered their tracks. Tell you the truth, these people are good. I want to meet them before they go to jail."

Shauni giggled. "Alexis'll be like one of those movie detectives. Her interrogation will be so brilliant she'll catch all the hackers."

Alexis shrugged off the compliment but shot her partner a winking smile. "I didn't figure it out alone. The school tech guy was a lot of help. We spent hours following the breadcrumbs—I'll spare you the technical steps. The upshot is that it was uploaded right here at the Flambert public library."

Callie felt unfamiliar optimism. "Can we find out who set it up?"

"Don't know."

Hazel fluttered in with a tray of sloshing coffee cups and fresh-baked cookies. "I need to prep for class. I'll be up in my study if you need me."

"Thanks, Mom." Alexis took over serving.

Callie wrapped her hand around a warm cup, welcome against the creeping chill of the fall evening. "Tell me about Meadow."

Shauni handed over a Cooper yearbook from the previous year. "We weren't close—until the crazy boyfriend. I don't know why she chose me for the big share."

"Because she knows she can count on you." Alexis clinked her cup against her girlfriend's.

Shauni shook her head. "Something else."

Callie leafed through the yearbook. "She was pretty isolated. She's not in a single picture from a club or a chorus. And it looks like she fulfilled her community service requirement by working with her reservation—admirable enough, but she reads as kind of a loner."

"Definitely." Shauni leaned forward as if to make sure Callie got the point. "She wasn't always like that. She transferred in junior year. At first, she was everybody's BFF. Then she wasn't. I don't know what changed but ..."

Callie felt her head throb. "Spit it out. What?"

"Something was way off." Shauni looked at Alexis. "She was always moaning about being dissed, but nobody ever went after her on Cuppa Cuper. Her own posts were super mean, like she hated the school and everybody in it. Said we were all racists. Since lots of us aren't white, that was a big fail."

"Why didn't you come to Coop and me about it back then?"

With a sideways frown at Alexis, Shauni continued, "She used a screen name, so I wasn't totally sure it was her. Maybe she's like a little kid who slugs you to get attention."

Alexis shrugged. "Or maybe she's a sociopath."

Shauni took back the yearbook and flipped pages until she found a note from Meadow tucked between the pages.

Meadow's handwriting was atrocious. Callie struggled to read the words. **To the one person who helped when things were darkest. Thanks forever, M.** Callie stopped squinting and looked up. "This could be about the bad boyfriend."

"I once asked how she met him. She said she was lonely at school so she hitched a ride into town and went to a bar."

"And they believed she was over twenty-one?"

Alexis shrugged. "Most students have fake IDs."

Callie groaned. "I can never unhear that."

"I'm sure Coop knows. Anyway, I asked why she went to the bar by herself." Shauni spoke hurriedly, eager to get the story out. "She kinda implied she had no friends. Not anymore. When I asked what that meant, she didn't say. I think she came to me 'cause she saw me with Alexis and figured we both had secrets."

"Saw you with Alexis? Where?"

"Okay, we were there at the bar."

"At the bar?"

"God, Callie, don't get distracted by irrelevance. The Main Street Bar & Grill. We were there for the grill. Hamburgers. Fries."

Alexis snorted. "It's not like Flambert has a gay bar. By then, we were already out to our friends and family but most kids at the school didn't know. She thought she had us."

Shauni pushed forward. "We never met Clunk, or whatever his name was."

"Chip? Skunk?" Alexis smirked.

"I heard him on the phone with her a couple times, since she always put it on speaker. He said he'd 'get them.' Maybe that was his biker boy defense of her honor."

Callie finished her coffee and stood to leave. "Do you think Daryl might recognize the boyfriend? He remembered Stella's. Sort of."

"The bartender at Main Street? Maybe."

Alexis and Shauni each started to speak, each deferred to the other and then chortled. Shauni was the first to jump in. "Maybe you should let us ask him. I mean, you're great and all but you're—"

Alexis interrupted. "From another generation." She lit the tinder under the logs already laid neatly in the fireplace. All eyes went to the small flame that jumped into existence.

Over thirty and over the hill. Who'd a thought? "Sure." Callie covered the twinge of hurt expertly.

Hazel overheard as she joined them, offering another plate of desserts. "If Coop and Callie are old, Craig and I must be downright ancient. It's a wonder we can function." She pretended to limp across the floor with an invisible cane, creaking aloud.

Before the young women could respond, they were interrupted by the distinct sound of the front door opening and more than one set of feet stomping mud off their boots.

Shauni jumped up. "Who's that?" Shauni breathed more easily when the mysterious intruders turned out to be Craig accompanied by Nora.

Callie tried to take the bite out of her question to the young woman who'd ignored her all day. "Where've you been?"

"The library. The librarian's a girl I grew up with. We dyed each other's hair when we were fifteen." Nora snapped her fingers impishly. "We both rock this multiverse of the locks to this day."

"And?" Callie poured herself more coffee though she didn't drink it.

"Alexis sent me to butter her up and sleuth out computer use." Nora handed them each a set of printouts and made a beeline for the cookies.

"Sleuth out?" Shauni giggled.

"Butter up?" Alexis also giggled.

"Puttin' it in lingo the old folks understand." Nora chuckled when Callie opened her mouth to object. "I made Craig the printouts in case I broke any laws. I figured the rest of you would want copies."

Craig cleared his throat deliberately. "You're supposed to consult with your lawyer *before* you act. Not after." His eyes remained on the pages.

Callie scoffed. "So that's why you were all so distracted at dinner." *You're all amateurs at secret-keeping.*

Alexis considered the printout. "Paper copies. Soooooo 20th century." She flipped through them, nonetheless. "About forty people used the library computers the day the website was uploaded."

Hazel refilled coffee cups, offering sugar and milk. "I'm proud that our library's usually crowded. True, it's mostly with people who use the computers, but they're surrounded by books they might read someday."

Callie couldn't bear the small talk. "Well? Who was it?"

Alexis scowled and took each page as her stepfather finished reading. "We can identify users with library cards, but not those logged in as guests. Likely our website designer was a guest."

"Can't we ask the library staff working there that day whether they remember someone working on a website?" Callie wanted to do something.

"The bullies probably uploaded it off a thumb drive. That wouldn't register as unusual use." Alexis returned to the pages, absently jiggling her leg. "People upload personal websites and resumes and stuff all the time."

Shauni gently touched her partner's leg to calm her and changed the subject. "Thanks for assigning me to your old cabin. We're moving there tonight so gotta go soon. Nice digs for a hockey coach. I thought the new English teacher would get it."

Callie stood to stir the fire. "She got the one next to yours, also vacant."

"Coach's?"

Callie preferred to view Shauni's predecessor as The Murdering Rapist. Now that he was convicted and in prison, the title was a clean statement of fact. "You're the coach now, right? Pretty sure you'll be happier in my old place than you would be in his."

"True, thanks. So, um, what's the policy on significant others sharing your cabin?" She grinned as Alexis patted her shoulder.

Callie looked up a policy manual on her phone. "Since I spent half my time when I lived on campus at Coop's, I'd be a hypocrite to say Alexis can't stay with you, wouldn't I? And fortunately, it's not against the rules."

"We're not even the first gay faculty couple." Shauni made a face, as if she regretted not being the undisputed trail blazer.

"Um . . ."

"I'm not outing anyone. Everyone knows the physics and a math teacher have been an item for decades." Shauni flipped through the manual without looking at it. "Tweedledee and Tweedledata—nice guys. Not *very* out. They've lived across the road from one another for thirty years. That horrid website shows them holding hands, but I think it was photoshopped."

Callie asked the question that had lurked through the conversation. "Do you think Stella and Harriet were killed because they were bullies or someone thought they were gay?"

The fire crackled as they all fell silent for a moment.

Hazel rubbed her temples. "I hope the press doesn't think of that."

"Mom, stop worrying." Alexis teased, knowing her mother would always worry.

"Not a small consideration." Callie shuddered, remembering the onslaught of reporters and cameras in the past. "Even the dumbest reporter will connect some dots and paint our school as dangerous. Again. It's bad enough they've been out at the school trying to get dirt about Harriet since the murder."

Hazel said, "This could be a disaster."

Callie itched for escape so changed the subject. "You're moving tonight?"

"Yeah. We went out there earlier and moved all the stuff we don't want into Cooper storage. Then Hazel gave us so much new shit, we had to rent a van. Picked it up just before you got here. Alexis will drive; Craig insists on riding shotgun." Shauni yanked a set of car keys from her pocket. "I'll follow in his sports car."

"Craig, you helped pack?" Callie imagined the portly lawyer, in his 60s and no athlete, hefting boxes. "Is that healthy?"

The lawyer looked up from his consideration of documents. "Don't sound so skeptical."

"I'm hardly in a position to judge. I was a fish out of water when I arrived at the school." Callie recalled her first day, half sliding along that snowy road in footwear inappropriate for mid-January. "I need to go. Nora, do you have a way home?" She really didn't want to drive back and forth to the school again tonight. *But it's what you do for family.*

"Yeah. I have Coop's truck. I should go, too." Nora hugged everyone in the room and accompanied Callie to the sidewalk, lingering for a moment in the chilly evening air. "I shoulda worn a hoodie or somethin'."

Callie noted the t-shirt but had another agenda before she let Nora go. "I'd like to know what you and Coop talked about after I went to bed." Silence. "If you want to tell me."

Nora nodded, either in assent or as a token of deciding to share. "He's upset I had sex with Arthur."

"Yeah."

"But for the first time in years, he didn't blow up and walk out. I attribute that to you." Nora rubbed her hands for warmth.

"I can't take credit." Callie shook her head regretfully. "I, too, am perfectly capable of running away, as you well know."

"You and Coop are made for each other." Nora grinned

slyly. "If you can manage to be in the same place at the same time." Nora jumped up and down, rubbing the goosebumps on her bare arms, without becoming at all breathless. The walking culture of New York City apparently had improved her fitness. "Shauni and Alexis talked with me for hours. They don't judge." She looked sideways at Callie. "Course, they were younger than me when they got together."

"Coop was younger than you when he met your mother."

"Ew. Don't like to think of my parents in bed."

Callie scanned Nora's eyes. "The point isn't sex, it's Arthur. If you'd picked somebody your age and single, your dad would be okay. Not happy, perhaps. But okay."

Nora pulled down the brim of her baseball cap. "You yourself said you can't help who you fall in love with."

"Love, maybe not. But you *can* help who you have sex with. A married man who hits on his interns and abused you is a poor risk."

Nora kicked the pavement. Callie wondered if she'd blown it. *Have I become a preachy adult? Yikes.*

Finally, Nora nodded. "Alexis said the same."

Callie offered her palm for a high five. A gushier person would probably hug Nora.

Nora, gushier than most, threw her arms around Callie. "I don't believe that thing about generations. I've always considered you a friend first and Coop's girlfriend second." She pretended to pout. "Course, I'd be happier calling you stepmom."

"Good try at changing the subject." *Jane Austen wasn't kidding when she said we're all fools in love.* "Are you still stuck on Arthur?"

Nora didn't hesitate. "Yes."

"He seduced you, slapped you, and he's a cheat. That didn't poison anything?" Callie had left guys for less. But she wasn't in love with any of them.

"I seduced him. I hit him first. And he doesn't love his wife."

The words sounded like a chant. Also like a bad TV series.

"Phoebe says the whole art world knows about his proclivities for young girls."

Nora grimaced, her cheeks rosy from either exertion or embarrassment. "Phoebe's been flirting with Craig. Why should I trust her?"

"What? Who says?"

"Alexis overheard her mom arguing with Craig about it."

"I'll talk to Phoebe."

"And say what? The Flambert gossip machine has her in their crosshairs?"

"If need be." Callie's cell rang. Nora rolled her eyes and headed toward the truck. *This'd better be important.* Callie looked at the screen, surprised her lawyer was still working this late. "Hi Lawrence, what's up?"

"I finally got through to one of the elders on the Mohawk Council just now. Oddly, they just saw the documents for the first time when we did." He paused. "But until they know the status of the land, they are going for an injunction to stop the construction of the center."

Callie wanted to punch something but a nearby tree would hurt her hand. "Haven't done it yet?"

"Right. That's the good news if you can call it that. I went to law school with their attorney. She's smart and competent."

"What can we do? Or—"

"Not sure. To me, the documents look fishy, especially because they're just surfacing now and the elders had nothing to do with it. I've called in an expert." Lawrence sounded like he wanted to be reassuring, but knew he wasn't. "He's coming the day after tomorrow. I need you and Phoebe to be there."

Callie rang off and called Coop. "You'll never believe this."

Before he could speak, Alexis came out of the house. "I forgot to tell you something important."

"Sorry Coop, I'll call you back."

Alexis's story was short and precise. When she and Shauni had moved items from their cabin to Cooper storage earlier that day, they had a brainstorm. As they entered the outbuilding,

Alexis remembered that the school tech expert said the Cuppa Cuper designer needed a transmitter "or something" on school grounds. She and Shauni surveyed what they could see throughout the building, organized but packed, trying to spot an electronic item that was out of place. "We didn't move anything because we didn't want to, y'know, disturb evidence. But think about it. The building's on top of a hill—a perfect location to cover the whole campus with no dead spots."

Callie felt like pulling her hair out. "Why didn't you call me then?"

"I called the tech guys. They said it was a long shot and they didn't have time to look."

"Or when I called you or when I came over or when …"

"I forgot, okay? There's a lot going on." Alexis suddenly seemed like the very young woman she was instead of the mature adult she usually impersonated.

Callie led the way back into Hazel and Craig's living room and dialed Coop again, putting him on speaker.

Callie talked, Coop listened. Craig talked, Callie listened. Coop groaned in frustration.

"I don't want to call the police without actual evidence."

"What do they say about the website?"

"They're treating it as a prank. Apparently bullying as a serious crime hasn't seeped into the Flambert PD consciousness yet. Let me talk with Craig for a sec."

Craig took the phone off speaker and carried it into another room. When he returned, he was no longer on the phone. "Coop, with my approval, authorizes a thorough search of the storage building tomorrow. Nora will let you in. Alexis will use her expertise and Shauni will video everything on her phone. Understood?"

Everyone nodded. Callie knew the men were trying to take some tasks off her plate but couldn't agree. "But as Vice Principal, shouldn't I be in the loop?"

They all said their goodnights with that question unresolved.

Callie found Phoebe still up when she got to their

apartment and, shedding her outerwear, flopped down next to her on their couch. "Did you hear from Lawrence?"

"Uh huh," Phoebe growled. "But we're not stopping the center until the court tells us to. Jillian's got lawyers ready to fight an injunction if it happens."

"I can't sanction opposing Native American rights." Callie looked out the window at the intense array of stars over the mountains, too aware of who was here first. "If their claim has merit, we're looking for new land."

Phoebe hastened to agree. "Of course. But Lawrence says the papers are weird. He's surprised that the tribal elders agree. They told Lawrence they'd drop everything if it turned out to be a hoax. Both sides are being eminently reasonable. Even so, this whole thing could still turn into a PR nightmare."

Callie had a fleeting moment of gratitude that Phoebe and not, say, Elton, was her eyes and ears on the center. Still, she needed to know about Phoebe and Craig. "I have to ask you about something."

Phoebe rubbed her eyes. "Can it wait til tomorrow? I'm wiped out."

Callie agreed to postpone what would no doubt be a fraught and lengthy talk.

Phoebe was already up and gone when Callie woke up the next morning. After tending to the most urgent center planning matters, Callie drove to the school and joined the search team at the storage building. Although a small squad of police and FBI remained on campus, the storage building was far from the crime scene and the women were able to avoid them. Nora led the expedition. Snapping on all the lights and armed with flashlights for all the nooks and shadows, the search party scoured every corner, every oddly shaped item, every box, barrel, desk, and computer as Shauni videoed every move.

Shauni climbed on a ladder and surveyed the room. "This reminds me of the scene at the end of Indiana Jones. Endless boxes."

Alexis pushed her hair out of her eyes, so like her mother. "Some other Cooper buildings were empty over the summer.

Maybe it's hidden somewhere else."

Moving yet another desk, Nora groaned. "Dude, I gotta get this place in better order."

Callie stretched her aching back, surveying what resembled a bargain basement junk sale. "Copy that."

What seemed a century later, a piercing whistle from Alexis brought them all running to a jumble of mismatched cables and remotes. "Don't touch. I think that's it!" She pointed to a black box, unremarkable except for a tiny light. After Shauni recorded the find and then took still photos of it from several angles, Alexis grabbed it with the edge of her shirt and lifted it into a plastic bag she'd stuffed into her pocket. "Gotcha."

Callie was skeptical but didn't want to wreck the moment.

Coop texted the group, offering to feed the searchers plus Craig and Hazel while they discussed their next steps. Callie invited Phoebe to join them.

Craig arrived at Coop's place in his own car, explaining that Hazel was slightly delayed because she was baking and didn't want them to wait for her to start dinner. He hurried up the stairs to the private apartment and took charge of the electronic gizmo while Alexis sent everyone and the tech department the video and photos and the three young people offered alternate theories about bullies and secret websites. Phoebe was the next to arrive, sharing a shorthand report on the center with anyone who would listen. A few minutes later, Coop invited them all to the table. Everyone commenced eating as if it were a new experience.

Coop murmured to Callie, "Like a pack of wolves." When everyone was settled, he addressed the group. "I'm hopeful that identifying the bullies will get us closer to identifying the murderer." That set off more discussion of why people became bullies, how much sympathy to have for them, and appropriate jail sentence time.

Nora helped clear dishes saying over her shoulder, "If Stella and Harriet were bullies maybe they created the website?"

Callie struggled to explain the unfinished jigsaw puzzle in

her head. "No one thinks Stella and Harriet had enough technical know-how. But they were constantly sticking their noses where they didn't belong. Maybe the killer created the website to keep tabs on them. *And Stella sealed her fate by writing about it in her diary.*

Responding to a knock, Coop moved to the door and swung it open with a cheerful welcome.

Hazel pushed past him carrying two pies. Spying first Phoebe and then Craig, she slammed them down and squared her shoulders, speaking only to Craig. "We have to go."

Everyone froze. Craig raised two open palms. "Sorry?" The furrow between his eyebrows deepened.

"You should be." Hazel rarely snapped. This was an exception.

Alexis popped to her feet. "Mom, calm down."

"I'm perfectly calm. Craig and I need to go, that's all. Enjoy the pies." Dwarfed by Coop, she nonetheless broadcast warrior woman vibes.

Coop put an arm around her, evoking their years of consoling one another in tough times. "When you said you were bringing dessert, I thought you meant to stay."

If the expression *looked daggers* could be actualized, Hazel demonstrated it as she shook off Coop's arm. "Circumstances have changed."

"She did mean to stay. She does. We will." Craig didn't rise from the table. "Whatever it is can wait."

Hazel sent her husband a cold laser beam of a stare and then stomped into Coop's bedroom. Now Craig rose and followed. Alexis knocked over her chair racing to join them, slamming the door behind her. Raised voices seeped into the dining room.

Phoebe lifted a questioning palm. "What just happened?"

Nobody spoke. Was Phoebe an excellent liar—as Callie could be—or completely innocent? Glances shot around the table. Finally, Shauni leaned toward Phoebe. "Are you sleeping with Craig?"

Phoebe surveyed the assemblage, her mouth slightly

agape. "Craig? Don't be ridiculous. I would never do that to Hazel. How could you even think that? Plus he is way older than I am." Then, perhaps realizing the enormity of the accusation, she choked and teared up.

Callie wanted to squeeze her eyes shut, stick her fingers in her ears, and *la la la* until they all disappeared. She couldn't handle her life falling to pieces right now. But who would be the grownup? Coop? He looked confused and stricken. Shauni continued to stare at Phoebe.

Coop knocked at the bedroom door. "Okay in there?"

Tears puddled in Phoebe's eyes. "Really. I'm not having an affair with Craig. I don't date married men. Or guys twice my age. Anymore."

"Arthur's twice my age." Nora's offering was as irksome as it was tangential.

Commotion ensued on the other side of the door, then Alexis appeared. Hazel followed, clutching her daughter's arm, eyes planted firmly on the floorboards, mouth pressed in a straight line as the two of them left the apartment. Shauni grabbed her jacket and followed them out.

"Apologies for the untimely exit." Craig shook Coop's hand. "I will untangle this."

CHAPTER 11

Nora headed up the stairs to her room, already talking on her cell. "Dude, why'd you leave?" Callie, not for the first time, wished she could summon Callie clones—one to comfort Hazel, one to commiserate with Coop, another to accost Phoebe or sympathize with her, whichever she deserved. This would be determined by divining rod or crystal ball. Oh yeah, and a fourth to tell Nora it was her turn to do the dishes after this fiasco of a working dinner.

Coop pointed with his head. "You two need to talk."

"Sorry?" Phoebe sat numbly, like a forest fire witness who stares at charred stumps still seeing green branches.

Callie kissed Coop and ushered Phoebe out into the night.

"My car." Phoebe tripped over her own feet and grabbed Callie to keep from falling.

Callie guided Phoebe toward her own vehicle. "Get it tomorrow. Let me drive you."

"I didn't do it." Phoebe slid into Callie's passenger seat.

Callie waited for Phoebe to put on a seat belt. *Safety first. Yeah, right.* As she steered the hybrid onto the road, the symphony of crickets and frogs through the open windows calmed nobody. Callie turned the radio to bland oldies.

Phoebe punched the off button. "Say something, please."

"We'll hash this out back at the apartment over junk food and chick flicks." Callie hoped she sounded unconcerned about the rift between her two best friends.

"Why would Hazel even think I…" Phoebe sobbed. "I've never been anything but honest with her." She continued to alternate tears with strings of oaths for the entire 30-minute drive.

Despite the many weeping girls whom she'd comforted as a teacher, Callie always felt inadequate to deal with other women's tears. "It'll be okay." *It probably won't, whatever "it" is.* Callie eased the car into the parking lot of an all-night market and made a marathon run through the heart attack aisle. One thing she'd learned from fistfights in juvie was that nothing calms like carbs.

After parking in front of their place, she steered Phoebe up the stairs, ordering her into pajamas. She called Coop while Phoebe was in the bathroom. "What the hell happened?"

"Craig's mystified. As best he can tell, Elton started the rumor and told Meadow, who told everyone in the entire universe. The stories got to Hazel so many times from different sources she started to believe them." Coop sounded even more angry than Callie felt. "That guy is a menace. I suggested Craig fire Meadow, but he won't hear of it."

"He's always fair, even when everyone else is small-minded and mean." Callie poured cola over ice. She considered adding rum but mournfully admitted to herself that she needed to keep a clear focus. "Hazel, too. She usually cautions everyone against listening to gossipers and naysayers. Why does she believe this?"

Coop sighed into the phone. "Gossip is almost never about her. She doesn't have any experience with being the target of ugly rumors."

Was that true of Stella? Harriet? They talked about other students, so did others target them? Tucking her phone between her ear and shoulder, Callie assembled a platter of the most disgusting treats known to humankind. "Phoebe hasn't said much yet. Do you believe Craig?"

"Dunno. Hazel can always smell a rat. Something's going on in that office. Not sure what."

She hung up, longing for his arms and his bed.

Phoebe lumbered into the room in geometric-patterned designer robe and slippers, which tonight failed to compliment her face swollen from crying. She pitched face first onto the couch. "Sleepless in Seattle."

Au contraire. Sleep sounds pretty good about now. Callie searched the streaming services and selected the film. "Do you want to talk?"

"Not really." Phoebe reached for a concoction of sugar and chemicals. "I know how it looks. I've had affairs with married men, even men Craig's age. And yeah, I'm attracted to him. That Samuel L. Jackson look gets me every time."

Callie offered the so-called pastry, with its shelf life of a thousand years. "Perhaps some things are better left unsaid."

Phoebe surveyed the riot of sugar and preservatives offered. "I'm attracted to Coop, too. I'll say it. I like men. I like smart, accomplished men like Coop and Craig. But I'd never go after the guy of a friend—and let's face it, neither man would ever pick me over the woman they already have. I'm lusty, not crazy."

"Why does Elton think you're after Craig?"

"Elton?" Phoebe's eyes narrowed. "He knows better. He'll do anything to get me fired. He never liked me, but now that I'm his direct supervisor, he's working overtime to make me look bad. Especially to Jillian." Phoebe stabbed a cream puff with a plastic fork, watching the innards ooze onto the plate.

"Why would Jillian care who you have sex with?"

Phoebe licked her fingers and scooped up the cream with her fork. "Good question. She never did before, even when it was her colleagues. Maybe she doesn't care, and he just wants me to think she does. Or maybe she thinks it's a bigger deal in a small town."

"She knew about your affair with her partner?" Callie continued talking, raising her voice to be heard as she hurried into her bedroom and changed into a sleep shirt, setting an alarm for the morning meeting with Lawrence.

"Elton says everyone knew—probably including the guy's wife."

Callie stuck her head out the bedroom door and wagged a finger. "Elton says, Elton says. Consider your source."

"Yeah. Besides, how would he know?" Phoebe broke tines off the plastic forks, creating makeshift toothpicks. Then she skewered various pieces making a tiny sugar man.

Callie flopped into a chair, carefully selecting one treat as her very own. "About the affair? He was at the switchboard. If everyone knows, I bet he's the reason."

"Do you think Voodoo works?" Phoebe squashed the sugar man with a spoon.

Callie grabbed a spoon to join the destruction. "I think Voodoo is a religion that has nothing to do with how much fun this is. Make another one."

Amid the cheerful ambience of the rom-com, they boisterously built and smashed to smithereens tiny Eltons while repeating familiar movie dialogue and cooing over favorite moments. Callie wrestled through the situation at hand. She'd survived juvenile detention and years of abject poverty because she was sharp and tough, and mostly because she could read people. But she wavered on whether to believe Phoebe.

Phoebe, by contrast, seemed confident that Callie believed her. "Thanks. You're a godsend. I think I can sleep now. Leave the mess. I'll clean up in the morning."

Callie stood by her door, ready for this night to be over. "We need to be at Lawrence's office when it opens."

Sleepily, Phoebe nodded and stumbled into her room.

Six hours later the alarm jolted Callie into the next day, unprepared and resentful. Phoebe was already gone. True to her word, she'd washed dishes and disposed of debris. Callie was not appeased, cursing aloud, "We have a fucking meeting. Where the hell are you?"

She tried her roommate's cell without success, thrust herself into the shower, and arrived at Lawrence and Craig's office as it opened. To her surprise, so did Phoebe.

Phoebe looked the worse for their sugar orgy. "What? You said to be at the meeting. I'm at the meeting."

Callie forced a smile. "Yup."

Lawrence, his key in the lock, sniffed as if smelling the hostility in the air. "Meadow will be here momentarily. I texted her to bring us coffee. We'll need it."

Phoebe rubbed her eyes. "And donuts? I'm starved."

Lawrence smiled. "You're always starved. She knows that."

Callie settled into Lawrence's most comfortable chair. *How does Meadow know? Elton. Phoebe. Meadow. What the …? Coffee would be good about now.*

Magically, Meadow appeared with coffee and assorted pastries of a much higher quality than last night's fare, though it was still too much sugar for Callie.

Lawrence handed out printouts. "Meadow, please sit in on this meeting." Meadow reddened faintly.

Phoebe bristled. "The receptionist?"

Lawrence blinked. "The Native American expert."

"Being a Mohawk from the rez doesn't make me an expert." Meadow sounded more hesitant than offended.

Callie could see that Lawrence was up to something. "We need all the help we can get. You're a smart Cooper girl. That's enough."

Meadow stood in the doorway as if wavering, then after a moment took a seat.

While the women read through the documents in front of them, Lawrence called the tribal attorney. Callie half-listened to the conversation which consisted mainly of Lawrence saying yes and thank you. He absently straightened his tie and pulled the cuffs of his shirt out from under his jacket sleeve. It wasn't like him to be disheveled, though a crooked tie hardly qualified. But it suggested he'd dressed hastily. Why? He was Mister Overprepared most of the time. The printouts were reiterations of what he'd told Callie earlier—the document, the law, the email from the tribal elders.

As Lawrence hung up, a young man appeared at the office door. "There was nobody at reception and I heard voices—"

Meadow jumped to her feet. "Oh, sorry, I—"

Lawrence offered a hand. "You must be Mr. Brant, I'm

Lawrence White, the attorney for the women's center project. Everyone, this is Hale Brant, the investigator I hired. These are …" He continued the introductions and offered coffee. Meadow hovered by the door. Lawrence waved her back to her seat.

"This won't take long." Brant flicked back waist-length black braids as he opened his briefcase. "I've compared your document with several others of the period." He laid out photocopies of verified nineteenth-century letters and declarations. "Further chemical tests are required, but I suspect this document is forged. An excellent forgery, though. A good lawyer might make a convincing argument that it's real."

Callie groaned. "Perfect." Phoebe shot her a *shut up* look.

"The tribe isn't interested in jumping to conclusions." Lawrence's pen was poised over his yellow pad. "But they're hiring their own investigator."

Brant pointed to discrepancies in language use and formation of letters. "Full disclosure. I'm Mohawk and I'd like nothing better than to claim more land as Kanien'gehaga under treaty. But historically speaking, it doesn't make sense. Most of this area was sold to white farmers just after the Revolutionary War. I'd be surprised if my ancestors managed to keep this particular piece of land. It's too far east."

"Maybe the French burning all the villages to the ground soured the deal," Meadow barked at the others, in a only-I-care-about-the-downtrodden voice.

Brant grinned. "You're right. The settlers terrorized our people. But that was in 1666. Long before the war."

"But not before *my* ancestors arrived in chains." Lawrence spoke mildly but his point silenced the room for a moment.

Phoebe had already consumed a cinnamon roll and was working on a cheese Danish. "You're saying right now we don't need an additional expert?"

"You can hire anyone you want to, of course. At this point I think it would be a waste of time and money." Brant shook hands all around and promised to keep them informed.

Callie waited until she heard him leave the building to

confront Meadow. "Do you know him?"

Phoebe winked. "I'd like to know him. Cute."

Lawrence looked uncomfortable at Phoebe's joke. "Meadow found him for us. He has a great reputation."

"He's originally from Ontario." Meadow gathered food trash. "An internationally known expert on Native American affairs." Tilting her head to Phoebe, she opened the door. "And he's like my twelfth cousin sixteen times removed or something. Careful who you flirt with."

Phoebe raised both hands defensively.

Lawrence looked directly at Meadow. "Everything said during this meeting is confidential. Nothing may be repeated outside of this room without my permission. To anyone. Not even Elton. Do you understand?"

The color in Meadow's face rose as she nodded and departed, closing the door behind her.

Callie paced, wishing for more coffee but reluctant to accept the jitters that went with overconsumption. "I'm against violating a treaty, not just because the optics are bad but because it's wrong."

Lawrence swallowed the last of his brew. "I suggest you let Mr. Brant finish his research before you decide to fall on your righteousness sword."

Callie tried to connect dots that seemed too far apart. "Who benefits from Hazel fighting Phoebe or having trouble with Craig? Who benefits from the center being distracted by the Mohawk documents?"

Lawrence nodded. "Wish I knew."

Phoebe neatly slid the papers into her briefcase and sat back. "Alright, then. Let's talk about me and Craig."

Callie rolled stiff shoulders. *How can it feel like a long day when it's not lunch yet?* "Talk about Craig? Doesn't that violate something, like partnership privilege or the blue line or something?"

"Not funny." Phoebe brushed powdered sugar off her slacks. "Hazel thinks I'm a slut who's after her husband. Alexis probably hates me, too. Maybe I should resign from the center and go back to New York."

Callie rubbed her eyes. "And let Elton win?" *Two students were murdered and we're talking about Elton's stupid fantasies?*

Lawrence cleared his throat. "Are you after Hazel's husband?"

Phoebe dropped a pastry, splattering confectioner's sugar across her clothing. "No, of course not. How could you think that?" Phoebe and Lawrence stared at one another, exchanging something Callie couldn't identify. "What does Craig say?"

Lawrence flicked fingers as if shooing away an invisible fly. "He denies any involvement."

Callie looked at each in turn. "Phoebe says no. Craig says no. Why are we talking about this?" *Two girls are dead.*

Phoebe straightened her spine, raising her chin. "Small town gossip. Favorite son and don't forget world famous lawyer ruined by scarlet woman from the big city. Scarlet lady represents the women's center. Presto, the ski resort gets the contract."

"Melodrama suits you. Wait. No. Horror. That's what suits you. Add a vampire or a zombie or something and some historical event and you've got a best seller." Callie wanted to go for a run. *To, say, Mexico or Australia.*

Lawrence cleared his throat, perhaps to remind them they were in his office. "I wish I could say Phoebe was overstating the problem, but pernicious rumors could negatively affect your support on the council."

Callie knew he was right. As an outsider who had won the heart of Harold Cooper, hitherto the town's most eligible bachelor, she, too, sometimes felt the sting of soap opera scenarios. "And by extension, their relationship unsettled the standing of the school." *Will I be an outsider forever?*

"I'll kill Elton." Phoebe paced around the room, running her finger along the rows of law books none of which justified murder.

"Perhaps we should start with something less drastic." Lawrence rarely joked, so both women halted for a second. He turned to Phoebe. "How do you know that Elton started the rumor?"

Phoebe sighed. "Meadow asked me about it. How else would she know?"

"She asked you here, at work?" Lawrence narrowed his eyes.

"Worse, just as she was asking me, Hazel came out of Craig's office and overheard her. It was one of those perfect storms. If Meadow had planned it, it couldn't have been more awful."

Lawrence didn't seem pleased. "What did you do?"

"I was so shocked by the question that I didn't say anything right away." Phoebe blotted the confectioner's sugar with a napkin, helping not at all.

"Interesting theory that Meadow heard it from Elton. Not evidence." Lawrence handed Phoebe a tissue.

"Let's ask Meadow." Callie bounded toward the door, a puppy after a flying Frisbee. She shouted down the hall. "Meadow!"

Lawrence reached for the receiver on his desk, glaring at Callie. "I have an intercom. Could we retain some amount of decorum, please?"

Meadow arrived in seconds. "What's up?"

Lawrence, Phoebe, and Callie, sometimes speaking simultaneously, sometimes in tandem, were finally able to ask clearly enough to elicit an answer. "Oh my God, is that what you thought?" Meadow's dark eyes became pools of innocence. "I asked if you were meeting with Craig. Not sleeping with Craig."

Phoebe's usually melodious voice rose, shrill and aggressive, an out-of-kilter aria. "Why? I never meet with Craig—or sleep with Craig, for that matter. Lawrence is the center's lawyer. My business is always with him."

"Dunno. Maybe Lawrence was out of the office?"

Suddenly, Callie knew what she had to do.

CHAPTER 12

Callie excused herself from the meeting and dialed Hazel, trotting out to the street where she could be assured of privacy. When she heard Hazel's greeting, she plunged in. "It was a big mistake. You misunderstood what Meadow said." Callie pulled out her most persuasive arguments. Hazel resisted. After a while they had both repeated themselves to the point of distraction.

Hazel's resistance was waning. "I guess I owe Phoebe an apology. It's just that Craig's been so distant lately. And he has phone calls that stop abruptly when I come into the room." Hazel choked a bit, as if biting back tears. "I was so sure he'd never cheat on me."

Callie paced the sidewalk in the freezing cold. "He wouldn't. Craig is the most loyal person in the world. And he adores you."

Hazel continued as if she hadn't heard. "We've only been together a few years. My first husband, Alexis' father, left when we were so young, we never had to deal with the yearnings of old age."

"The earnings?"

"Yearnings. You know. When men get past a certain age and want to know they're attractive, so they go after young women to get back their youth."

"Is that a thing?"

"My first husband..." Hazel sighed. "One thing I liked

about Craig when we met is that he seemed to appreciate me despite the gray hair and wrinkles and extra flesh."

"Hazel, listen to me. Try to stop freaking out and listen." Callie waited for some kind of confirmation.

"You sound like me."

"Craig isn't having an affair with Phoebe." Callie repeated those words in as many variations as she could muster.

Hazel muttered something about a recipe and then returned to the subject. "He disappears for hours, sometimes going all the way to New York City. When I ask him, he says it doesn't concern me. Doesn't that sound like an affair?"

Callie unlocked her car and started it up for some heat. "If it was anybody but Craig, I'd be suspicious, too. But not Craig."

Hazel clanked something and swore at it. "How would you know?"

Callie wanted to pound something, too. Heaven knew she'd done it on other occasions. "Craig praises you to everyone and anyone. You two always act as a team. I think you're on a path to living happily ever after."

Hazel's clenched jaw came through in her tone. "We were until your friend showed up."

Callie tried counting to ten and got to about three. "She's your friend, too. Phoebe is not interested in Craig. Period. End."

Hazel sniffed. "I guess you'd know if Phoebe was seeing someone."

Callie wondered. She hadn't really accepted Phoebe's explanation of voices in their apartment. "Hazel, we have to deal with two murders, a corrupt town council, and my ridiculous coworker—"

"You think Phoebe is ridiculous?"

"What?"

"That was supposed to be a joke. I know you meant Elton. I understand you don't think I'm funny right now. Oh dear, I owe everyone an apology. Oy. This is exactly the kind of thing I tell other people not to do. Jump to conclusions. But put to the test, I failed—"

"For heaven sakes, it wasn't a test, it was a mistake. Turns out you're human. Who knew?" Hearing Hazel giggle gave Callie permission to say goodbye.

Phoebe exited the office moments later, ready for their daily jaunt to the construction site. On the drive, Callie wanted to repeat the conversation with Hazel to assuage Phoebe's hurt feelings but felt strongly they needed to resolve it between themselves without her mediation. Instead, she downloaded the stresses in her own life—her ongoing sorrow over the murders, the bullying, the women's center, her job as vice principal. Phoebe said nothing. They parked next to several vans and pickups of the construction workers, who were hard at work, at least for now.

While they were still in the car changing into work boots, Phoebe broke her silence. "I didn't hear wrong."

"Sorry?"

"Meadow. She said sleeping, not meeting. My hearing is very good."

"Maybe she misspoke. Meant meeting, said sleeping?"

"Maybe. Weird slip."

Callie handed Phoebe a hardhat. "Ignore Meadow. Talk this out with Hazel."

Phoebe headed for the office trailer to check in with the foreman. Callie followed, her misgivings rapidly supplanted by irritation at whatever misguided thing Elton was doing today.

* * *

Time progressed with yellow-red leaves underfoot, many trees now bare, and complaints about midterms and papers. The yellow tape and uniformed law enforcement on the Cooper campus disappeared, though Coop hired a security force of off-duty Flambert police to patrol the campus.

Callie continued to worry that unless the murders were solved, many of the girls would leave at the end of the semester. A few had left already. Routine calls to Detective Belanger and Dr. Chen yielded exactly nothing. Cooper School computer techs shut down the ugly website without discovering the perpetrators.

A school assembly on bullying elicited new stories and an outpouring of tears describing personal attacks about ethnicity, weight, disability, sexual orientation, and a myriad of other subjects. Apparently, Stella and Harriet didn't spare anyone, though they remained unidentified as the perpetrators to all but a handful of adults. Callie wondered how much to tell Stella's mother. And it still wasn't clear who had gone after the two of them. Was it retaliation? Threat? There didn't seem to be a pattern to any of this.

Callie invited each of the targeted girls to her office, offering them support, finding them counselors, devoting many hours to offsetting the damage from Cuppa Cuper. She found it wearying that these otherwise bright young people could be so senselessly cruel to one another and hoped fervently that the worst of it was past. *Best not to speak ill of the dead but what a temptation.*

The police seemed stalled on the investigations of the murders but at least town gossip slowed to an occasional barb. The Phoebe/Craig rumors also seemed to die down, though Elton continued to drop innuendos about Phoebe's sex life.

Center construction continued since Brant's initial findings convinced the Mohawk Council to delay seeking an injunction, though they went on with their own investigation. Nonetheless, the threat of a forced work stoppage hovered over Callie like an armed drone. In her nightmares, the center was on fire or in a deep crater or clear cut like a forest set upon by an evil corporation.

Equally threatening to Callie's equilibrium, Nora seemed always on the verge of returning to Arthur, requiring somebody—usually Callie—to talk her off the ledge.

"I should be happy." Callie curled up in Coop's bed, her cheek against his chest. "So many things are going well. But it all seems so precarious, like a house of cards."

"Should I be offended that you're in my arms and not blissful?" He twirled a strand of her hair in his finger and kissed her.

"Mmmmm." Her hands followed the map of his body, her own muscles tightening in response.

When they first met, their desire for one another expressed itself as verbal sparring across a table, but once they touched, there was no going back. Even now, his strong hands kindled a breathless alchemy of warmth and weightlessness. Kissing those early frogs hadn't been a prelude to kissing Coop. They had been an alien language from a barren planet several galaxies away.

Much later she murmured into his ear, "I'm not cynical about this."

"Our house is made of bricks. No cards. No big bad wolf."

She giggled. "Mixed metaphors confuse me."

Sleep followed.

* * *

Callie worked in Dr. Chen's office each morning and met Phoebe at the job site at lunch, often bringing Coop's gourmet leftovers as a peace offering for beginning the workday at its halfway point. The male construction workers at first bristled about women bosses but grew to accept Phoebe as one of their own, perhaps because she could swing a hammer with the best of them. They were colder with Callie. Everyone understood she was The Money, so she heard a lot of "Yes ma'ams" even when she was pretty sure they wanted to say something else.

At least she wasn't Elton, who managed to create a commotion at least once a week by misreading specifications, ordering wrong items, entering the site without a hard hat causing unplanned delays, or making small talk with someone trying to do precise work. Phoebe sent him to consult or update Jillian whenever possible.

Now and then Callie or Phoebe or both would meet with Elton, attempting to create systems that would avoid future mishaps. He was either too arrogant or too careless to take any of their gentle remonstrances to heart. His catalogue of excuses included blaming them ("You weren't clear" or the perennial favorite, "That's not what you said"). He'd also pretend he wasn't computer savvy though each of them had seen him deal with complex online systems when it suited him or when he was trying to impress Jillian.

Callie wanted to complain to Jillian during their regular video meetings, but Phoebe warned it was best to let it go. "She's more likely to condemn you than him. You don't want her to quit this job. Elton would go, but I'd go with him. Worse, Jillian might stop in mid-mission and leave you hanging."

* * *

Snow fell over the Thanksgiving weekend, slowing the progress on construction. Dr. Chen returned from rehab, a little shaky but able to work part time, still putting in some hours at the forensics lab. It helped free Callie up to get to the construction site a little earlier a few days a week.

Now that the temperatures were routinely below freezing, the hockey team began to practice on the skating rink outside the gym. Some days Callie would time her own workout to cross paths with Shauni as practice was letting out. One day, Shauni waved Callie over. As the players yelled "Night, coach," she fell into step with Callie. "Bad news. Our bullies are back."

"What?"

"They've started a new website, even viler and more disgusting than the last one. I just heard about it at practice." Anticipating Callie's next question, Shauni nodded. "Yeah, I already called Alexis."

Ordinarily, Callie would resent outsiders knowing school business since it almost inevitably led to new smears, but Alexis was not only Hazel's daughter and Shauni's girlfriend, she was also now on retainer as a tech expert.

Callie punched speed dial for Coop's number and handed Shauni the phone. "Tell Coop."

Shauni repeated what little she knew ending with, "The girls say the site blames the school for not solving the murders. Especially you and Callie. Because of Stella and Harriet's deaths, the girls don't know if they're safe. And they say Callie fighting with the town council just makes it worse, and that the cops don't want to help. Some students are talking about staying home after winter break."

Callie could feel the conspiracy theory forming. *Who does it serve to undermine the school and the center?* She almost missed Shauni's next sentence to Coop.

"No, they don't feel safer with the rent-a-cops." The mostly young men Coop hired seemed to be more interested in watching the students than in watching out for them.

Taking the phone back and saying good night, Callie continued her run, beginning to braid the pieces of the puzzle together and not happily. *Is there a fox in this hen house?*

CHAPTER 13

Every stressful part of Callie's life converged one Monday in December. Sunday had been almost idyllic. A bright sun illuminated powdery snow and shards of prisms greeted Callie and Coop as they donned snowshoes and hiked for miles up a mountain trail to a favorite meadow by a brook, now solid ice. When they stopped for lunch, they built a fire. They talked about of literature and love and theater and film; not one word about murder, bullying, or lawsuits. They returned to his place, reluctant to re-enter real life, extending their blissful ignorance far into the night.

When her alarm went off only a few hours later that Monday morning, Callie turned on her phone for the first time since the morning before. It buzzed with eleven messages from Phoebe. The house phone rang, waking Coop. Nora complained loudly about it, yelling down the stairs from her room. Everyone seemed instantly on edge.

Instead of listening to the messages or reading the texts, Callie called Phoebe. "What's up?"

"Did you get my messages? My texts? My smoke signals?" Phoebe talked faster than her usual New York clip.

"Smoke signals? Really? Can we cut the racism?"

"Shut up, Callie. Somebody's sabotaged the center! Lots of damage. Tools missing. The foreman called the cops. They're at the site now. On top of that, Jillian's planning to come from the city herself. On the train. Hell must have frozen over because she never takes public transportation. I hate to think what this means."

Never had the expression *no rest for the wicked* repeated itself so often in Callie's head. "I'll be at the site as soon as I get dressed. Can you handle Jillian by yourself? You've done it before."

"Not this time." Phoebe's voice shook. "I think I'm about to get fired."

After the women said their goodbyes, Coop brought Callie a cup of coffee, his face revealing that his call had been on the same subject. "What a crappy way to start the week. You look awful."

"Thanks"

"I mean you only twist your hair in times of crisis." He gently tugged her hand away from her head and squeezed it.

"I need to go to the site." Callie felt far too weary to handle whatever awaited her but hoped she could rise to the occasion when she got there.

He frowned. "The cops didn't give me a lot of details. They wanted me to know about it, though, since the construction site is so close to the school." He insisted on driving her and grilled her for Phoebe's details. When they arrived, he spoke with the police. He knew the officers and Callie suspected the men were happier to talk to him than with the two outsider women in charge.

The whole area was in shambles. Previously constructed walls were down or askew, creating unnaturally split lumber in odd piles. The door to the temporary tool shed hung open, revealing mangled and missing equipment.

Callie felt as if the vandals had challenged her to a fist fight and whipped out hidden chains and mace. She found Phoebe and the foreman going over an itemized list of damages. She could see it was extensive. "Broad strokes, please."

The foreman named an astronomical number of work hours to replace the losses. She nodded approval of the overtime and he called out orders to the workers while his assistant dialed the insurance company.

Elton clambered over a row of debris to alight at Phoebe's side. "Jillian's super pissed."

Callie pulled out her cell. "I'll talk to her."

"You can't. She's in a meeting and then is going right to the train." He smirked and yanked the list of damages from the foreman's hand. "Zowie. This will really piss her off more." Without further comment to the women, he tossed the list and ambled off toward the men sorting the mess.

Pale under a bright hard hat, Phoebe sat on the edge of a damaged floor, slumping like a deflated hot air balloon. "Elton no doubt suggested to Jillian that I somehow caused this through my ineptitude or negligence."

Callie found a thermos of coffee and offered a cup. "Why would he say that?"

Phoebe raised a hand long enough to refuse the hot drink. "He wants Jillian to get rid of me so he can take over."

"I'm the money and I'd never agree." Callie drank the coffee herself. "What do the cops think?"

"I have no idea. I've been a step behind all morning. I think he's turned them all against me."

Callie swept a glance around the area where workers stood in small groups as cops strung yellow tape. Nobody seemed interested in either woman, but nobody seemed hostile either. "Now is no time for paranoia. Come sit in Coop's truck and warm up."

Phoebe hauled herself to her feet, following Callie like a forlorn baby animal. "Who would want to smash up the center?"

"Garden variety women-haters? Teenage vandals? Enemies on the city council? I'm afraid the list is fairly long." Happy that Coop had left his keys in the ignition, Callie turned over the engine and cranked the heat. Maybe Phoebe would stop trembling if she warmed up.

"I'm no good in situations like this." Phoebe sniffed, a tear escaping.

"Have you been in a lot of situations like this?"

"Not exactly. But I've been wrongly accused before. Then

I screw up and everything I do makes me look more guilty."

"Like the Craig thing." Callie watched Coop through the window, wondering what he would say. He rarely revealed his own emotions but was a master at handling others' feelings.

Phoebe hugged herself, still trembling and ghostlike. "Not just that. I…" she wiped her cheek with a gloved finger.

Callie had learned from Coop that it was best to wait, though her inclination was to barrel forward. After a few minutes of silence punctuated by sniffles and sobs, her patience ran out. "What else?"

Before Phoebe could answer, Coop knocked on the window. Callie rolled it down. "We're in the middle—"

"The police want to question both of you. I talked them into meeting at my office since it's closer than the police station." He cocked his head toward the officers behind him. "They also want Elton."

Callie put her hand out for his keys. "I'll drive Phoebe. You ride with Elton.

Coop assented, no doubt knowing that Callie expected him to curb Elton's false narrative. Callie wondered if Elton would be different with a man than he was with his female colleagues.

With little time to tease out Phoebe's story, directness seemed the best option. "What has you so upset? The center can be repaired. It's only money and I have that."

Phoebe looked out at the snow-covered countryside but apparently saw far beyond. "Did I ever tell you about what happened to me in middle school?"

"Middle school?"

"I was fourteen. Fat. Braces. Acne. Every bad thing you can think of."

Callie considered a retort comparing teenage angst to juvenile detention where she'd spent her teen years, but let it go.

"Some girls in gym class decided to make me the object of their entertainment. At first, they'd come near me and drop little remarks about my weight or my zits. But the attacks didn't stop there."

"Is this why you never want to hear about bullying?"

"Kinda."

"How did it escalate?" Callie kept her eyes on the road, trying to gauge Phoebe's state of mind by the sound of her labored breathing.

"They stuffed me in my locker but that got them in trouble. They thought I ratted them out. I didn't. They got really mad and went to war. They dumped soda on my homework, ripped off the buttons on my skirt when I was in the shower, left disgusting things in my locker." Now her words crowded one another, as if tumbling out of prison.

"I'm so sorry, Phoebe. But what does that have to do with today?" Callie hoped she sounded less impatient than she felt.

"I'm not finished."

"Sorry."

"Then stuff disappeared from lockers. Cash. Jewelry. Musical instruments. And wouldn't you know it, they ended up in my locker, mangled and destroyed. And mysteriously, the gym teacher knew to look there. I was charged with malicious mischief but got probation. The school hushed it up."

"Private school worried about public image?" *Sounds familiar.*

Phoebe sighed. "No. Public school in a fancy middle-class suburb. They didn't want my misdeeds to reflect poorly on kids applying to college. They suspended me and hushed it up. Still, all the kids knew what happened—or, I mean, what didn't. They knew the wrong version, the lies. I did nothing but eat cake and cry for weeks. Finally, my mom moved me to a different school."

"Reasonable solution."

"Not really." Phoebe sighed again. "I was completely powerless against those petty criminals. Never got to defend myself. Left behind everything—including my few friends who couldn't decide what to believe. Needless to say, we're not still in touch."

Callie patted Phoebe's shoulder. "That won't happen

here.”

“Thanks.” Phoebe blew her nose. “But if they look into my record, this time I’ll probably lose my job and go to jail. And I thought it couldn’t get worse.”

“No one will think you caused this sabotage.” Callie parked in the Cooper garage, wondering if she should encourage Phoebe to wash her face before she met with the cops.

“Elton will convince Jillian, then Jillian will convince the cops. I’m screwed.”

“This time you have a friend who knows who to believe. Two, if you count Coop.”

Soon they were ranged around Coop’s spacious office. While the assembled group waited for Craig to arrive, Elton took center stage. “It had to be an inside job, right?” He paced, offering one B-movie plot after another, apparently for the benefit of the police, wanting to dazzle them with some New York City swagger. They seemed unconvinced by his theories.

Callie figured the faux brilliant-amateur-detective act probably worked somewhere on someone but was confident Coop wasn’t buying it any more than she was. She hoped he could dissuade the police in case they started to fall for this nonsense. Phoebe looked ready to kill.

Craig arrived, serving as lawyer for everyone including Phoebe and Elton, and supervised the several hours of questioning. Apparently, the sabotage occurred a few hours before the crew arrived. At the time, Elton was in bed with Meadow, which he made sure everyone understood. Nora could verify Callie and Coop’s alibi since she’d complained about the phone. Phoebe was vague about where she was during that time, though she claimed she’d spoken with a barista.

The police seemed ready to haul Phoebe into the station as the only one without an alibi but eventually left, disgruntled by Craig’s insistence that they follow the law and delay arresting anyone until they had evidence. Finally, Callie’s day drew to a close. She fell onto Coop’s bed, still wearing clothes.

The new day brought almost no respite. At breakfast Coop seemed more taciturn than usual.

"Why the long face?" Callie poured coffee for both.

"You're so convinced of Phoebe's innocence that you won't see evidence against her, no matter how convincing."

Callie felt ill. "You think she would sabotage the center?"

"I don't know. But unlike you, I won't make any assumptions until the investigation is complete." His dark eyes burned into her, increasing her queasiness.

"She's one of the most honest people I know."

"Except when she isn't."

Callie was on her feet. "What do you mean?"

"Maybe she really does have designs on Craig. She's done it before, right?"

Callie's volume rose with her ire. "What?"

"Maybe she needs an excuse to leave town." The picture of control, he continued to sit and speak quietly. "To build a love nest somewhere."

"She doesn't even have a boyfriend."

"Hazel's not given to flights of fancy. And she thinks Phoebe's still after Craig. She says Phoebe's at the office far more often than the center job requires."

Callie heard her voice climb to a screech. "Craig? This was settled weeks ago. Phoebe's not interested. They both said so. And if she wants to leave, she can just leave. She doesn't need to destroy my property."

"I'm speculating. Consider that maybe she's not completely innocent. I trust Hazel."

"And I trust Phoebe. I can't have you talking this way about her." Callie grabbed her backpack and slammed the apartment door behind her, barely hearing him call her name.

* * *

Phoebe's ID appeared on Callie's ringing cell. "Just got off the phone with Jillian. The good news is I didn't get fired." Phoebe didn't sound relieved. "I wanted to talk to her face-to-face, but

I guess her meetings ran long so she put off her trip til today. You know she's too impatient to wait until she gets here. Heaven knows how much more garbage Elton has fed her with all his texts and Insta photos in the meantime."

"Do you want me to come into Flambert?" Callie, who was not a praying woman, prayed for Phoebe to say no.

"Not right now. Jillian may want to meet with you when she arrives. I'll call you either way." Phoebe rang off.

Before settling in with the enormous pile of paperwork Dr. Chen had delegated to her, Callie called Alexis. "Where are we with the new bully site?"

"It's down. We haven't caught the person who put it up, though. Give us a few days."

Callie wanted someone to be on her side. She was too mad at Coop to call him for comfort and couldn't expect anything from Phoebe at the moment. She dialed Hazel.

"Hello, Callie." The musicality of Hazel's voice always comforted.

Callie wished she could forget everything and curl up in front of Hazel's fire with a cup of tea and some heady conversation about art. But not today. "Heard about the center?"

"Yes. Just a few minutes ago." Hazel sounded ready for action. "It's disgusting."

Callie gripped the phone. "From Craig?"

"Of course not. He doesn't talk about clients, even clients I know and love. Dorothy called me."

"Why?

"She asked if I thought the sabotage was related to the murders."

"I've been wondering the same thing."

"A theory going around is that Phoebe and Craig started their affair long ago, and that the murders didn't start until Phoebe got here."

Callie broke a pencil. "And she murdered two young women and started a sophisticated website and sabotaged a women's center for—"

Hazel's voice was cold. "Women have done worse for love. Dorothy says Phoebe has a record."

"Surely you don't believe she did this? You know her. She's no—"

"I can't talk about this right now." And Hazel was gone.

A few hours later the camel's back hit capacity. Lawrence called saying, "Callie, the Mohawks have filed for an injunction. They'll probably get a construction delay of at least a few weeks." Weariness blanketed his voice.

Callie was confused. "Why now? I thought Brant said they accepted his view that the documents were false."

"They got an anonymous message saying Brant wasn't to be trusted."

Callie groaned. "And they believed it? I thought he had *bona fides* six ways to Sunday."

Lawrence hissed in a breath as if he, too, was having trouble breathing. "He does. They have their own investigation to verify everything. Their lawyer told me that until the veracity of the documents is established, stopping construction was the most prudent path."

"We can't even repair the damages?"

"I'm afraid not. The foreman has been instructed to send the men home. I'm not sure what this means for the future of the center." A few more exchanges and he, too, took hung up leaving her deserted.

Callie pressed fingers against her eyes. She'd been alone before, she could do it again. She grabbed her backpack, climbed into her car, and drove away.

CHAPTER 14

Callie was several hours from Cooper School, on an obscure shore of Lake Ontario, when she realized that she'd left her phone on her desk. *Blessing or curse? Not a lot of reception around here anyway.* The grey, icy water stretched silently to the horizon; jagged rocks and black trees offering no solace. Winter meant the sun was already finding its way to oblivion.

Callie had never before considered the Virginia Woolf solution—filling her pockets with stones and marching into the water. Her usual response to adversity was anger, not despair. When she witnessed her mother's murder by her stepfather at age eleven, she'd shot the bastard.

"We promised not to run away from one another."

She started at Coop's voice, until she realized it was only in her head. Tears welled up. *Damn. Suck it up.* Years in juvie taught her a walled, uncaring affect, a key survival skill through years of abject poverty. She wanted that back. Petulantly, she yelled out the window at the lake, "No crying."

Poverty didn't turn out to be the biggest challenge. Managing her stepfather's fortune was harder. How could that be? How many times had she wished for an extra hundred or even a twenty to stave off a bill collector? Now she had millions.

She could practically hear Aunt Sophie's sweet reedy voice chiding her. "Nobody promised easy." Sophie's dying directive to be a teacher had guided her to Cooper School, to Coop, to a life that promised meaning. And love.

Shut up, Sophie. Hard is too hard. No guidebooks. No blueprints. Virginia Woolf said you had to have money and a room to write. But Virginia hadn't found a reason to live, had she? Money and a room didn't seem to be doing the trick.

Callie shut off her engine and got out of the car. The wind stung her face and sliced through her down parka like a steel blade. Dusk obscured the horizon and reduced the world to land and lake. In this weather no wildlife lurked by the shore to hear her shouted curses. She was completely alone.

She scooped up a frozen rock, stuffing it into her pocket, breathing audibly. Then, stepping forward, she yanked the stone out again, and slung it toward Lake Ontario. She didn't hear whether it hit ice or open water. *Can't even do that right.* She'd tried about a dozen times when she saw the headlights.

The officer driving the car that pulled next to her appeared to be about Nora's age. How old did someone have to be to get into the police academy? Or the highway patrol academy. *Is there a highway patrol academy?* He rolled down the window, holding up a badge. "This park is closed, ma'am. You can't stay here."

"Sorry, officer. I didn't know."

His partner had a hint of grey at the temples. "The park season is posted at the entrance." He wasn't buying that she'd missed the only sign for miles.

Right. In English and French, she recalled. "Yes, sir. I'll follow you out, so I don't get lost." *Let's create a common myth so we all save face.*

"Just a minute, ma'am." The driver aimed a flashlight at her license plate and entered it into his tablet. Instead of finding her crime free except the current loitering, he responded to something on his screen. "Stay out of your car ma'am." He picked up his cell as his partner got out and joined her.

Great. The Flambert police must have put her on a watch list or whatever they call it. They'd probably arrest her for skipping town. Would the police be familiar with Virginia

Woolf? Maybe she'd plead temporary insanity.

As the grey-templed cop approached, she briefly considered fleeing into the woods, knowing that even an excellent marksman had difficulty hitting a moving target in the twilight. But if she got away, she'd probably freeze to death. Not up to Virginia Woolf standards of romantic ends.

"I'm freezing, sir. Can I get in the car?" She shivered, not entirely for effect, and headed to her car.

"Ma'am, please sit here." He opened the back door of the police car.

She hesitated, knowing better than to argue without a lawyer present. "Do I need an attorney?" Maybe whatever she'd done was so horrible, Lawrence couldn't help her. Maybe Coop could bake a cake with a file. Maybe he was too pissed off.

"Not to my knowledge." The driver thumbed some numbers on his phone. "Ma'am, you were reported missing."

She slid into the car, her body welcoming the heat, her mind ambivalent. "I've only been gone a few hours." *On TV they always wait 24 hours.*

"You're wanted in…" he looked at his phone, "Flambert."

"I don't understand. Who reported me missing?"

"I can't say, ma'am."

After a quick discussion between the two officers, the older partner offered to follow the squad car in her hybrid to their nearby town. Like Flambert, their city hall doubled as a police station and a post office. But this town was even smaller, sporting only one other public building—a grocery/hardware store.

"I'm famished. Can we stop at the store?" Callie decided to treat the entire encounter as a social event until they told her she was arrested.

The two officers exchanged glances. The older partner shrugged. He stayed beside her as she chose a plastic-wrapped sandwich and a bag of chips, refusing her offer to treat him and his partner. Plunking money on the counter, she glanced at the TV screen above the clerk's head, shocked to recognize Flambert on the screen. "Could you turn that up?"

The unkempt teenager behind the counter raised his eyelids just enough to gaze through her.

"The TV. That's my hometown." *For now.*

The clerk looked to the cop for approval. The office nodded.

The voice of the announcer grated as the volume rose. "—job action. The union claims the company locked them out unfairly. The company CEO could not be reached for comment."

A photo of Callie appeared on the screen. The cops and the clerk stared.

"—construction of the controversial Miriam Cooper Women's Center. The lockout has put nearly 200 people out of work during the holidays. The attorney for the center cites yesterday's early morning vandalism as the cause for what he calls a temporary closing—" Live footage of Lawrence appeared. The report continued.

Callie whirled toward the door, forgetting she didn't have her car keys. "I have to get home."

"Yes, ma'am." The police officer didn't seem surprised.

"I'm not under arrest?"

"No. But you are wanted in Flambert. You the owner of the center or something?"

"Or something." Callie flipped her hand face up for her keys. "Can you tell the Flambert police I'm on my way home? I don't have my phone."

"I'll escort you."

"Not necessary."

"If I'm with you, you can go over the speed limit." The cop had evidently never had the opportunity to make this offer before and seemed eager.

"Oh. Right. That's wonderful. Will you marry me?" She watched the consternation on his face.

"Um, I'm spoken for." He reddened.

"So am I." *So am I.*

The trip home was fast but uneventful. The small-town cop operated his lights and sirens the entire way, which Callie found alternately annoying and endearing. At the Flambert city limits, the escort made a U-turn and left with lights off and siren silent.

Callie drove to Craig and Lawrence's office, noticing Coop's truck parked in front as she got out. Might as well face all the music at once.

At the reception desk she caught Meadow's eye and pointed to Lawrence's office, still moving.

Meadow nodded. "They're waiting for you." She stopped Callie long enough to hand her the phone she'd left in Dr. Chen's office. "Coop said to make sure you got this."

Entering, Callie suddenly felt small. At five seven, her muscular build usually put her at an advantage, but not with Lawrence, Craig, and Coop, who were all over six feet. "Please be seated, gentlemen." Aware that her bravado contained not one iota of truth, she felt a frisson of triumph when each found a chair. *The old Callie is still around.*

Lawrence quickly filled her in on the current crisis. The union stated that they hadn't caused either the vandalism or the injunction and thus the workers should be paid for lost time. The attorney for the Mohawks asked that all work cease until their investigation was completed which could be weeks or months.

"Don't the Mohawks want us to clean up the mess? That gives everyone a job, at least temporarily." Callie fastened her attention on Lawrence to avoid the fury she imagined in Coop's eyes.

"I'll argue that in court first thing tomorrow. The judge's up for reelection in the spring and two-hundred votes around here is nothing to sneeze at." Lawrence made notes on a legal pad.

Craig cleared his throat, which was his signal for introducing unpleasantness. "What if the judge says no?"

Callie spoke next. "Options?"

"Fight the union or pay workers to sit at home." Lawrence's long slender fingers drew each choice in the air as an abstract shape.

"What do you advise?"

Coop stirred in his chair without a word. Callie hadn't looked at him since she arrived. *He must be furious.* Now she had no choice but to go on the offensive. "Why are you here?"

His raised chin was the only tell for a deep emotion. His voice remained calm. "You couldn't be found. Craig asked me to—"

"Speak for me?" Her glare traveled to Craig. "Harold Cooper isn't my husband, you know. Or my business partner. What gives you the right?"

Craig, graceful despite his girth, drew himself up like a ballet dancer ready to leap. "I asked him for ideas about where you went."

"She's here. I'm done." Coop was out the door before Callie could apologize.

Lawrence drummed his slender fingers. "As one of the largest employers around here, anything you do will get press. Weigh that against the financials."

Torn between a desire to be responsible and a longing to hand it all over to Lawrence and chase Coop down the road, Callie slouched like a teenager. "Which are?"

"If the work stoppage goes on for, say, two weeks, I estimate it will cost this." He handed her a printout of calculations.

Callie barely glanced at the total, which was more than her annual earnings only a year earlier. "Call the union and say we'll try to get them back to work but otherwise will pay while they're out."

Craig shook his head. "Not sure that's a great idea."

"I'm sure it sucks but it's what I want."

Lawrence exchanged a glance with Craig. "You're certainly not a typical capitalist."

"What you call a typical capitalist often earns her money by exploiting workers. My wealth came from a criminal stepfather, so I'm not motivated to be exploitive. Besides, I can't risk the women's center getting a reputation of screwing anybody, especially men." Proud of her high ground, she swept her hair off her shoulders. She was eager to share her insight with Hazel and Phoebe. If either was speaking to her.

Craig rose to his feet. "Fancy words, Callie. But even you need to save for a rainy day."

"Thanks for your advice." Realizing her words could be read as ungrateful, she jumped to explain. "It's just that…"

"Yes?"

"As far as I'm concerned, this *is* the rainy day."

"Of course." He nodded and escaped, mumbling something about getting back to his own work.

Lawrence handed Callie the relevant documents, his further explanation interrupted by a buzzing intercom. "What?"

Callie wondered briefly whether Meadow's arrogant disregard of her boss' wishes was transmitted from her boyfriend.

"Put her on." Lawrence swiveled away from Callie as if that could magically create phone privacy. "Callie's here." A few cryptic remarks later, he hung up. "Phoebe's in the lobby, on her way in."

Callie hoped this meeting, at least, wouldn't be contentious.

Phoebe swept in, followed by Meadow with water and pastries. The young woman clearly knew what Phoebe liked. Phoebe lunged for Callie, clutching her like a small child who missed her mother all day at nursery school. "I heard you were lost."

"More psychically than physically." Callie took one of the waters. "But I'm back——in every sense."

Lawrence glanced at the elegant designer clock on his wall. "What's the latest from the police?"

"These aren't garden variety vandals." Phoebe carefully divided a sweet in two and ate half, though Callie knew she'd shortly take the other half.

Callie addressed the lawyer. "Lawrence, why don't you call the chief yourself?" *That's what Coop would do.* Callie tried to shut out forebodings of the coming storm at home.

"They'll be less guarded with Phoebe, and we'll get more

information." He smiled at Phoebe. "Phoebe's our secret weapon."

"Thanks." Phoebe flushed. "I asked Officer Belanger, who's the only one who will tell us anything at all. He says they didn't find any forensics that would identify a culprit."

Callie grimaced. "Are they giving up?"

"They wouldn't say so, but I'm pretty sure they have so many other crimes to solve, this one will go on the back burner." Phoebe took the other half right on cue.

Lawrence smoothed his perfect hair. "Other crimes?"

"Oh, you know. Rescue the cat lady's cat. Find out who's stealing the grocer's empty bottles. Chase down truants. Solve some murders. Uncover some bullies." Phoebe gulped water between listing the offenses.

Lawrence buzzed Meadow. "I'll call our investigator."

Callie patted Phoebe's arm. "Let's go back to our place." *So I can avoid Coop awhile longer.*

Phoebe shook her head. "Gotta talk to Lawrence about strategy in case I get fired."

Knowing the unlikelihood of that scenario, Callie concluded that Phoebe had her eye on the remaining treats. "Sure."

"Besides, how is it *our* apartment? You haven't slept there in weeks. Why don't you admit you're living at Coop's?"

"After today, I might not be." Suddenly ravenous, Callie grabbed a pastry and another water as she left the office. For a second or two, she saw the kaleidoscope of pieces she'd been jugging fall into a pattern. The murders, the attack on Dr. Chen, the bullying website, the vandalism.

In the lobby, Meadow handed her a phone slip with a terse note in Coop's handwriting. "Come home."

Meadow seemed a bit too interested in the note. "What are you going to do?" Meadow's association with Elton suggested she had an ulterior motive. She might be recording a podcast or reporting for a tabloid for all Callie knew.

"Gotta go."

Once outside the office and in her car, Callie drove to

Hazel's, not Coop's. *Right now I can't deal with recriminations.*

Hazel apparently had seen the car lights and opened the door before Callie could knock. "You need to stop running away when you're stressed. I thought we agreed you'd come to me."

Callie wished apologizing didn't feel so false. "I'm sorry. I'm here now."

"Where'd you go?" Hazel led Callie into the kitchen, setting a kettle on the stove and waving to a kitchen chair.

"A stone's throw away." *I'm hilarious.* "I'm glad you're speaking to me."

Hazel sat across from Callie, for once not bustling about. "You and I are both so passionate—we have to expect blowups from time to time. Ask Craig." Her musical laugh followed. "We have bigger fish to fry, though."

"Now we're cooking?" Callie knew it was a lame joke and looked around at Hazel's kitchen, orderly in spite of boasting every kitchen tool known to humankind.

Hazel screwed up her face instead of groaning. "Craig thinks the vandalism has to be an inside job."

"One of the workers? Why? A jealous wife who thinks Phoebe's after her husband?"

"Watch it." Hazel took a deep breath.

Knowing she'd overstepped, Callie hurried on. "My point is that anyone could get in—and out of—the site during non-work hours. There's no security because it's out in the country. The only neighbor is the Cooper School and if someone there did it, I'd be shocked. Everyone at school seems enthusiastic about the center. Miriam was loved by students and staff alike." Callie waited through a moment of silence. "Sometimes I'm jealous, too."

Hazel shook her grey curls. "We have these great loyal men and yet we suffer from human weakness."

Callie sidestepped the unspoken invitation for more confidences about Coop. "So do they."

Hazel laughed, "Ain't it the truth."

"Nobody would think twice about some big vehicle driving

along the road—if anyone saw it." Callie frowned.

"Alexis says the current police chief never solves anything unless the criminal walks up and introduces himself."

"We have two murders that prove that." Callie stuffed her hands in her pockets to keep Hazel from noticing how fidgety she was. "However, he did get out some kind of alert to find me today."

"That was Coop. He didn't say anything to me, but I think he was afraid you'd run away. He and Craig planted themselves in the chief's office until the guy sent out the alert just to get rid of them."

Coop had long ago forgiven Callie's indiscretion during the time she fled Flambert and returned to her hometown, but if it happened again, he'd be devastated. For a moment she felt his heartbreak. "Wow."

Hazel poked Callie. "Put Coop out of his misery and marry him, for heaven sakes."

"I'm not sure the offer still stands."

"Oh pshaw." Hazel rose as the tea kettle whistled.

A small revelation isn't a betrayal, is it? "He's really mad at me." Callie thought about texting him to explain where she was and rejected the impulse.

"I refer you to my earlier comment about necessary blowups."

The doorbell interrupted them. *I hope to hell it isn't Coop. Is this what love does?*

Dorothy Kelly was at the door. Hazel invited her in and within a few minutes, the three women sat together, drinking tea and sampling Hazel's baked goods.

"Stella once told me you assigned someone to paint her portrait, but it disappeared."

Hazel narrowed her eyes, as she always did whenever she was sorting through memories. "Yes, now I remember. Last year I divided the class into pairs and they drew portraits of one another. The girl who drew Stella was exceptionally skilled. The picture was stolen from the art room not long after. The artist was devastated because she wanted it for her portfolio. To be honest, I suspected Stella took it."

Dorothy dropped her spoon on the table loudly. "Stella wasn't a thief."

Callie wondered how many parents assumed their children were honest despite evidence to the contrary, but decided it was no time to join the conversation. She handed Dorothy a tissue.

Dorothy shook her head. "I heard that the picture turned up on that horrid website."

Hazel sent a note to her daughter on her tablet. A response came immediately, which she showed Dorothy. "Alexis says a version of that picture was there, but horribly distorted and manipulated. Do you want to see it?"

"I don't think so. Was there a similar picture of Harriet?" Dorothy choked a bit as she spoke, crumbling a cookie without eating it.

"No, and Stella's portrait was the only one stolen." As Dorothy sniffled and Callie surreptitiously checked her messages, Hazel assembled a plate of vegetables and humus, realizing it was far too late in the day to keep soothing with sweets.

"Try to eat something." Hazel was confident of the curative power of food. "The artist graduated and is now at Rhode Island School of Design, but someone emailed her the URL. She called me in hysterics and asked me to apologize to you. I decided not to say anything because they've taken the website down and I didn't want to give you any more pain. I'm surprised anyone saw it."

Dorothy considered for a long moment. "I can't remember who told me."

The pattern that had evaded Callie just got a little clearer again, it was almost in focus now. "When was the painting stolen?"

"Last semester."

Dorothy pulled her sweater close. "Long before Stella—"

"Talk about a long con." *Dots! Now is the time to connect.*

The doorbell again. Certain that this time it really was

Coop, Callie rose to answer. Facing the music seemed appropriate. All of them were surprised to see Meadow. "Hi Callie. I'm uh … I have some papers for Craig." Meadow tossed pink braids, tightly plaited, over her shoulder as if summoning energy to barge in.

Callie was wary. "Isn't he still at the office?"

"No, he left a while ago. He needs this stuff."

Hazel joined Callie. "He's upstairs in his study. I'll take the papers to him."

Meadow managed to slither by both of them and move toward the staircase. "It's no trouble." She stopped when she spied Dorothy in the dining room. "Oh, Mrs. Kelly. I was so sad to hear about Stella."

Dorothy offered a wan smile and a brief thanks.

Meadow never seemed to know when to leave well enough alone. "I'm sorry about the picture on the website—"

Dorothy raised her voice. "Hazel said nobody saw it."

Hazel wrenched the papers from Meadow's hands. "You need to leave."

Callie grabbed her own coat. "I'll drive you."

Meadow acquiesced and followed Callie to the car. "Can you take me to Elton's place?"

"You mean my office?"

For a second, Meadow looked puzzled, but her expression resolved into acknowledgment. "Oh, yeah, but he's probably upstairs. Done with work for the day."

They said very little to one another after that. Meadow dialed Elton and related the events to him in the most melodramatic terms possible while still remaining more or less within the boundaries of truth. She seemed to fixate on Dorothy snapping at her and not wanting to talk. Callie glanced at her phone and saw six messages. Unwilling to pursue them while in Meadow's presence, she pressed the accelerator a tad harder.

Elton was waiting outside the office when they arrived, wearing a bright red pair of earmuffs that clashed with his hair. He folded Meadow into his arms and glared at Callie. "You thought it was a good idea to expose my girlfriend to Dorothy Kelly?"

Callie knew from daily experience that trying to correct Elton's distortions was useless. Without saying a word or even glaring back, she pulled the car door closed and left them both on the sidewalk as she drove toward Cooper School. She turned on her phone, which had been in her pocket since Meadow gave it to her. The first message was from Coop asking where she was and five were from Nora wondering whether she was okay. She called Nora first.

"Oh, Callie. I heard you were gone. After the last time—"

"Where are you right now?" Callie wondered if Coop could overhear the conversation.

"In admin. Going home for dinner in a minute."

"Where's Coop?"

Nora sounded like she was walking outside. "At home cooking, of course. Where are you?"

"Needed to clear my head."

"That's what Dad said. But that's what he told me the first time."

Nora saying 'Dad' instead of Coop always signaled she was emotionally fragile. They chatted long enough for Callie to believe Nora had calmed down. "I'm almost there."

"Probably should warn you that Dad's on the warpath."

"Tell me something I don't know." Callie tried to sound jolly. "And given our current circumstances, we should probably avoid the term warpath." Callie disconnected. Dragging herself from the parking garage to Coop's place she repeated silently that she was an adult, she could handle anything, and if that failed, she had a great left hook. *None of this is comforting.*

The scent of some exotic dish reached her as she climbed the stairs from the common room full of girls studying. All hopes of arriving quietly were dashed in the chorus of greetings from students. Coop opened the door to the apartment before she got to the top of the stairs. She could tell from the streaked apron that he'd been cooking for a while, his normal practice when he was upset. "About time."

"I've had a terrible day. Can we put off you yelling at me until after dinner?" *By about a century or two?*

"I don't yell." He moved to his creation on the stove. The table was set and Nora was grating cheese.

He was right, of course. He rarely raised his voice. And he was wrong. He was an expert at quiet yelling, if you define yelling as saying whatever will make the other person feel deservedly guilty. Callie dropped her backpack, hung her jacket, and poured herself a glass of wine. She drank it and poured another.

"You two need to talk. I'm going to eat in front of my TV upstairs." Nora loaded a plate and tore up to the third floor studio closing the door against irrational adults.

Coop turned up the radio to mask their discussion if Nora should decide to eavesdrop, as she often did. He served two plates and re-filled his own wine glass. He was not a habitual drinker and a second glass of wine was rare, as it was for her.

She stared at the elegant food as neither of them lifted a fork. "I know you're really mad at me. You have every right. I promised not to run away but at the first sign of adversity, I broke my promise. I didn't know what else to do. Running's not just my first line of defense, it's apparently my only one." Callie debated whether to mention Virginia Woolf.

"You seem to miss the salient issue." He set his napkin on the table. "I love you. I was terrified when I couldn't find you. Two people have been murdered, for fuck's sake. And everyone knows that you've been poking around. Yes, it made me immeasurably sad that you'd leave without checking in with me but—"

"We had a fight."

"I'm sure we'll have others." He held out his hand, waiting for her to take it or reject it.

She took it. She pulled him up from the table and burrowed into his chest. "I hate it when we fight."

"I do, too. But we're going to fight. You can't let that jettison you from the relationship." He held her close, breathing into her hair.

She could hear his heartbeat through his shirt. "It wasn't just that. It was … you know, everything."

"I know."

"I still trust Phoebe. I'm not going to change my mind."

"I know."

"I don't want to talk about this anymore."

"Me either." He raised her chin and kissed her. At first it was chaste and soft, but their inevitable chemistry and his tongue took over. He lifted her and carried her to the bedroom.

"Nora." Callie knew Nora had been present during other lovemaking, but they'd generally been discreet and waited for her to go to sleep.

"She's fine. I believe her words were, 'Dad, you need to get that woman into bed.'" He grinned and peeled Callie's clothing off.

She tugged at his belt, muffling a semi-hysterical giggle in a pillow. "Thank heavens we live in the twenty-first century."

As his kisses became ever more insistent, her responses intensified. She wondered whether the girls studying downstairs could hear the thuds as his shoes left his feet and hit the floor.

She didn't care.

CHAPTER 15

Despite her personal maelstrom, for the first time in weeks, Callie slept in. She heard Coop and Nora leave for work. The phone rang a couple of times. She let herself push it all away as she drifted back to sleep. Nothing could penetrate her fortress of fatigue. Someone pounding on the door awakened her shortly before noon. She threw on Coop's robe and pulled the door open, praying the visitor wasn't Dr. Chen. Worse, it was Meadow and Elton.

Elton sneered as he tromped into Coop's apartment. "Why are you still in bed?"

"Don't be rude, honey." Meadow surveyed Callie's robe with disdain. "We need your help."

Sure. On a cold day in hell. "Be right back. Help yourself to coffee and whatever food you can find."

Neither had been in Coop's place before and they seemed more interested in drooling over his antiques and art than in a hot beverage. Callie dressed, poured coffee, and prepared toast, hoping the two would state their business and leave. Instead, they settled in the living room waiting for her to serve them.

"Why are you here?"

Elton sipped coffee like a taster in a contest. "Hmmm. Not bad." As Meadow began to answer, he spoke over her. "Meadow is really freaked about what happened with Dorothy Kelly."

"Yes, it was a difficult situation." Callie set plates of toast in front of each of them and slathered her own with jam.

"Meadow didn't deserve that."

"Sorry?"

Meadow looked down at her feet. "I want Dorothy to apologize."

"For not wanting to talk about her daughter's murder?"

"Or we'll sue her for defamation of character. And it's a hate crime against a Native American." Elton bit into his toast as if demonstrating his ferociousness.

Callie tried to apply Coop's yelling-without-yelling skill. "What lawyer would bring that case to court?"

"Craig said he'd talk to Dorothy." Meadow's hand shook as she brought a cup to her lips.

I get it now. "You want money."

Elton's eyes flashed, suggesting she was a dull child who had just figured out basic arithmetic. "She caused my girlfriend terrible pain and suffering."

Meadow raised an empty hand. "She's on the city council. Surely she can afford a little."

What's that old blues line? A hand full of gimme and a mouth full of much obliged. Callie had no intention of explaining the realities of service in a small town and how little city council members were paid. "I need you to leave now."

Elton smirked. "And Hazel has money."

"I'm like totally traumatized ..." Meadow teared up and clutched Elton's hand. "Callie, you're my witness."

"You can't lie under oath." Apparently, Elton was the pair's legal expert.

"I witnessed a big nothing. If you don't leave, I'll throw you out." Callie held up her cell, pushing the autodial for Coop.

"Well, talk about uncooperative." Elton swigged his coffee, grabbing the toast in one hand and pulling Meadow with the other. "You'll hear from our lawyer." He slammed the door behind them.

Coop answered. "Good morning, my love."

"Oh Coop, you'll never believe the latest." She summarized the encounter while poking around in the refrigerator, seeking further sustenance. "Why would Craig represent them?"

"I'll speak with Craig. Your mission is to take the day off. You don't have a single meeting or project today. Lawrence is communicating with the Mohawk elders, the union, and the police. The center site is closed, the workers are being paid, and Dr. Chen can wait until tomorrow."

"I'll show you how grateful I am when you get home." She did her best to sound lascivious but was pretty sure she came off as cheesy. She unplugged the land line and turned off her cell, nestling back under the soft comforter on Coop's bed.

Her dreams were not peaceful. Hammers pounded, though they seemed to be in the middle of a frozen Lake Ontario. Elton and Meadow lurked behind random pieces of machinery and dark shadows. Now and then, Jillian appeared in some odd outfit, pronouncing it the latest in designer chic. Callie forced herself to waken. Unrested, she threw on workout clothes and dragged herself out, turning on her cell and sliding it into her pocket.

The crystal blue sky belied the icy cold afternoon, though the snowfall was still fairly light for upstate New York in December. Students in winter gear hurried across campus, pulling scarves tighter and stuffing gloved hands into pockets.

At the gym, Callie shed layers of outerwear, eager to do something to challenge her muscles. A call from Dorothy interrupted the preparations with one boxing glove tied on and the other at the ready. Stella's mother described a visit from Elton and Meadow similar to Callie's. "Do I need a lawyer?"

"Their so-called case is absurd, as in totally absurd. You don't have to speak to anyone just because they talk to you. I suspect a judge would laugh it out of court. But if you need an attorney, I'll find you a good one." Callie hung up and called Lawrence. "What the hell is going on?" Wrong tack, no doubt, but fatigue shredded every social filter.

"Pardon me?"

"Why is Craig representing Meadow and Elton against Dorothy? The whole idea is effing ridiculous."

Lawrence scoffed in annoyance but would never voice vulgarities. "Baloney." He then called on his polished manners. "Meadow and Elton may have overstated Craig's position."

"What? Okay, put him on."

"Craig took the train to the New York City early today and has been incommunicado ever since. He left specific instructions not to be disturbed."

Callie reluctantly untied the boxing glove and returned the unused pair to the shelf. "Isn't it a conflict of interest if he's on their side? I mean, they're accusing Hazel, too. Or something." Once again in winter wear, she jogged out of the gym toward Coop's office.

"Callie, I have no information. Let me get back to your labor case."

Callie dialed Hazel. "Why is Craig representing Meadow and Elton?" *Why am I focusing on this instead of, say, sabotage and murder?*

"How is he representing them?" Hazel spoke as if reasoning with a small child.

"Legally."

"Of course." Now she sounded annoyed. "Which case?"

"Against Dorothy. They want money for pain and suffering because we yelled at Meadow at your house and Dorothy wouldn't talk to Meadow. Which was Meadow's own fault for having no social skills, so I don't see how there is any legal case." Callie deliberately turned her head away as she passed students.

Hazel cleared her throat. "I can't ask him until he gets back."

"It's the twenty-first century. We're all connected twenty-four seven." Callie hated her own sanctimony.

"He said he needs space. Time." Hazel's voice was unsteady. "I think he's in New York with Phoebe."

"No. She's here. I talked to her ..." *When was that?*

"Lawrence told me Phoebe went to meet Jillian, but I think it's just a smoke screen."

Callie responded without thinking. "I thought Jillian was

supposed to come up here."

Hazel's tears were audible. "I have no idea what these people do. Listen, I need to get it together. I'm teaching this afternoon."

"Don't jump to conclusions. I'll call you as soon as I know something." Callie raced across campus to admin, bolted up the stairs past Nora's desk and into Coop's office, knocking but entering without waiting.

Coop was in conference with the new English teacher, the one who'd taken Callie's job. She didn't know the woman but recognized the materials in front of them. On Callie's first day, Coop's erudite explication of the curriculum made her wonder whether she was up to the job. How she longed to simplify her life to that one concern again. He frowned. "Callie, please wait in Nora's office."

She considered a tantrum that would effectively terrorize the teacher into self-banishment. Instead, she apologized and left. Nora wasn't at her desk, but her computer was on and her coffee cup half-full. Callie sank into a chair reserved for people who came too early for appointments, dialed Phoebe, and got voicemail. "Call me." Next, she tried Shauni. More voicemail.

Callie's phone hung in her hand like a revolver with an empty magazine. She usually welcomed solitude as a rare treat, but not now. She tried answering email, reading the book in her backpack, solving the metal-and-wood puzzles on Nora's desk, but couldn't focus. Would it be tacky to listen at the door? Just to gauge how long she might have to wait, of course. *Callie, get a serious grip.*

Nora appeared with a pile of student folders. "Hey Callie." The young woman inspected Callie's sweat-drenched workout clothing. "What's wrong?"

"Just about everything." Callie poured out her tale, half-aware that Nora's office was a public thoroughfare so any passing student might overhear. By now she was beyond caring.

Nora's eyebrows rose incrementally with each additional chapter. "All that just this morning? Hate to think what the afternoon will bring."

Callie frowned. "Please don't joke. I need help."

"What can I do?" Nora discarded her files and hugged Callie.

Coop and the English teacher chose that exact moment to appear. The teacher left as quickly as good manners allowed.

"Callie, Nora. My office." Coop reached for Callie's hand.

Nora brought them each a cup of coffee as Callie summarized her woes one more time. Coop grinned.

Callie fumed. "You think this is funny?"

"Look, Callie, not long ago we had capital crimes on school grounds. Now we have a frivolous lawsuit and a completely apocryphal affair. Neither impacts the students. You should consider laughing, too." He glanced at Nora, who smiled dutifully.

Callie shrank back into her chair fighting the urge to contradict him even though he was right. She took a minute to reassess. "Well why is Craig in New York?"

"He went to see his own attorneys about some personal business."

Nora slurped from her cup. "Dad, 'personal business' could mean anything. Maybe it really is Phoebe."

Callie quoted Shakespeare's *Julius Caesar*. "*Et tu, Brute?*"

"And maybe it's per-son-al." Coop glanced at the portrait of the school's founder above the cold fireplace. "I know you both love intrigue, but there's none here. Craig is not interested in Phoebe. He wouldn't betray Hazel." He tapped a pen on the desk. "He'd have to answer to me."

Callie's eyes strayed to the painting of Gwendolyn Cooper above the fireplace, the school's founder dwarfed by the scenery of upstate New York. She wondered if his great-great whatever grandmother Gwendolyn was Coop's muse the way her Aunt Sophie was hers. Two dead women advisors. *Could be worse.*

"Callie?" Nora'd apparently said something Callie missed. "Sorry?"

"Text from Phoebe. Listen" Nora imitated Phoebe's New York accent. "Jillian has arrived. Prepare for Armageddon.'"

Simultaneously Callie's phone buzzed with a message from Jillian, who rarely texted. "Prepare for my site visit." *Whatever that means.*

As Callie trotted down the steps of admin, she crossed paths with Shauni.

The young woman grinned. "Glad I found you. You left a crazy message. I gotta tell you something. In private."

"Come to Coop's."

As they arrived at the lower floor of the building, full of students studying or pretending to, Callie lowered her voice. "Sure, but first I need to call Hazel."

Waiting until they were safely inside the apartment, Shauni raised her voice. "Earth to Callie. What I tell you will help. Let me go first."

Callie took in that her attention was needed but wasn't ready to pay attention. "Do you want food?"

"No." Shauni draped her jacket over a chair.

"Talk."

Shauni focused on the floor. "I was so wrong about Phoebe. Both me and Alexis."

"And this is news how?"

Shauni traced a pattern in the tile on the countertop. "Have you noticed that she practically lives at the law office when not at work?"

"Craig's office." Callie set a plate of grapes between them. "And?"

"Not just Craig's."

Callie stopped, grapes halfway to her mouth. *This moment would be so much more meaningful if it were actually dawn.* "Lawrence."

"Well, she's hardly hanging out with Meadow and Elton." Shauni carefully cut a small group of grapes from the bunch.

"She's seeing Lawrence? Did she say so?"

Shauni shook her head vigorously. "No, of course not. I don't think she'll tell anyone before she tells you."

"You and Alexis accused her of going for Craig." Callie flipped a thumb toward the dining room table where the confrontation occurred all too recently. "You really hurt her."

Shauni popped a grape in her mouth. "I know. I owe her an apology."

"Big time. But Lawrence and Phoebe could have cleared it up so easily." Callie dug sock-covered toes into the silk rug at her feet.

"Maybe they had to get Craig's permission?"

Callie felt a pain behind her eyes. "Craig could have cleared it up so easily if he'd known."

"I'm guessing they don't want everybody in their business while they figure out how they feel. When I was first with Alexis, we didn't tell anyone for months."

"I didn't read your signs, either." Callie remembered seeing the girls together a few years earlier. "Romance isn't my forte."

Shauni lined up a few grapes on her palm and rolled them onto her tongue. "Alexis stopped by the office to drop something off. Meadow wasn't there."

"When she was at Hazel's?"

"Was she? Anyway, Alexis was about to leave when she saw them."

"Speed this up, for cripe's sake. Saw who?"

Shauni chortled. "Cripes?"

"Shauni. Don't make me kill you."

Shauni threw Callie an *as if* look, flexing her considerable muscles. "She saw Lawrence and Phoebe kissing. Serious. The type where the clothes will come off in about twenty seconds. Alexis skedaddled. Quietly so they'd never know she was there."

Callie's turn to make fun. "Skeddadled?"

Shauni winked conspiratorially. "Old fashioned expressions R us."

"Why didn't Phoebe tell me?"

"No idea." Shauni glanced at the time on her phone. "Gotta go to practice."

Callie left a message on Hazel's voicemail.

Day off now officially impossible and rolling fast toward

dinner time anyway, Callie showered, dressed, and drove to Flambert without a definite plan. She averted her eyes as she sped past the construction area, still crisscrossed with yellow tape. Driving around the country and then the town cleared her head not at all. She found herself in front of Craig and Lawrence's office. *No time like the present to catch up.*

The front door was unlocked but the reception area was dark. Lawrence must be working. Meadow was wrong about a lot of things but correctly pegged Callie's lawyer as a workaholic. Only an emergency ghost light illuminated the corridor to his office. Possibly everyone had gone, and Meadow had forgotten to lock up. Callie listened at Lawrence's door for client voices. Hearing none, she knocked and pushed the door open.

Big mistake.

Phoebe and Lawrence, both substantially disrobed, jerked apart on the couch. Not as quickly as Callie leapt away down the dark corridor.

"Wait, Callie." Phoebe slid her head around the door. "Don't go. Give us a sec."

"Um. . . er . . ." *Words fail now? Perfect.* "I can come back." *You say pahjahmas and I say peejamus. Let's call the whole thing off. But first, let's actually wear some pajamas.*

"Please wait." Lawrence's usual aplomb had fled.

"Okay, going to reception." Callie sat at Meadow's desk, idly straightening papers and pens scattered every which way. She clicked the mouse, hoping the computer was on and Meadow, like all office workers, had a game of solitaire or cute cat videos. The virtual desktop was neither shut down nor password-protected and as disorganized as Meadow's real one. Annoyed that her own legal records were so easily accessible, Callie clicked on several folders labeled with random words and numbers such as **House 123.** One took her to the bullying website. She groaned and called Alexis. "The website's back up again."

Alexis groaned, too. Callie heard the click of a keyboard. "No, it isn't. What url are you looking at? I'm getting a 404 error."

Callie, lacking tech knowledge, read aloud what she could. Alexis clicked some more and talked to herself in cyber lingo, finally returning to the phone. "Callie, that's not a live website. Meadow must've copied it when it was up. God knows why. Can you email it to me as an attachment? I can figure out when she saved it if that interests you."

That much Callie could do. Just as she hit Send she heard Phoebe call from Lawrence's office.

"We're decent now."

She recalled a Rita Hayworth line from the movie *Gilda*. Dressed but never decent. Something like that. But of course, these two were usually decent so it wasn't exactly appropriate. Just an amusing expression of embarrassment. *They won't find it funny.* As Callie crossed the office threshold, Lawrence and Phoebe, sitting as far apart as possible—he at his desk, she on an uncomfortable chair in the corner—spoke at the same time. Phoebe was the first to cede ground.

"I'm sorry you—" Lawrence's dark skin glistened above a well-pressed collar and conservative blue tie. Callie had never seen him sweat before.

Phoebe interrupted with a bright red face. "Sorry, not sorry, because I've been dying to tell you."

He tented his fingertips, a gesture that usually suggested he was the smartest person in the room and simply catching everyone else up. "Sorry you had to find out like—"

Callie slid into a chair. "Why didn't you at least tell Hazel? She's been so freaked out."

"Craig asked us not to tell anyone."

Callie struggled to circumvent the rabbit hole. "Craig knows? Why wouldn't he ...?"

The story went on much longer than needed since the two of them couldn't stop talking over one another, apologizing and then doing it again. Callie gathered that as a matter of ethics, Lawrence told Craig the first time he and Phoebe declared their feelings for one another, a couple months ago. Craig hadn't opposed the relationship and suggested that they immediately tell the client affected: Callie. But before they did, Alexis accused Craig of seeing Phoebe. He might have brushed that aside had not Hazel believed her daughter over her husband.

"He was seriously pissed." Phoebe rolled her shoulders as if releasing a great weight. "I really wanted to tell you that night, but I'd promised both of these guys—"

Lawrence straightened his already straight tie. "He asked us to wait."

"Why? Does everyone just love mystery?" Callie included herself in everyone.

"Whatever your judgment—or ours—about his choices, we honored them." Lawrence smiled. "That's why Phoebe said I was the radio when you overheard me at the apartment."

Phoebe crossed and uncrossed her legs. "And why we're here rather than his place or mine."

Callie sighed. "I understand that you didn't want to come to our place again, but why not his?"

Phoebe began to speak but Lawrence raised a hand and she demurred. "Too many prying eyes. I live across the street from the mayor. His wife, Council President Anjali Verma, is the most intrusive busybody I've ever met. If she saw us, not only would Hazel know but the local TV stations, too, and probably CNN." Lawrence sipped coffee that must be stone cold. "Meadow didn't come in today and Craig's out of town."

Unconsciously, Callie wrapped a strand of hair around her finger, remembering the first time she'd been with Coop. "Perfect for a tryst—if you'd only remembered to lock the door."

"Happy accident, right, honey?" Phoebe moved next to Lawrence.

Callie sighed. "Hate to burst your little bubble, but Alexis saw you two this morning before I did. By now Hazel probably knows."

"Sure hard to keep a secret in this town. It's a wonder Elton didn't figure it out." Phoebe pulled on her jacket. "I'll go see Hazel."

"She'll be at school for another hour." Callie felt torn. She wanted to get Phoebe alone for all the girlie details, but she also wanted to know about the lawsuit. "Lawrence, anything to report?"

Lawrence seemed relieved to leave the personal behind. "The court will rule on whether we can clean up the site before the Mohawk claim is decided." He glanced at his watch. "Probably not today, but it looks good. Even the Mohawks conceded that cleanup no matter what ultimately happens to the land will benefit everyone. They would be more than happy having you foot the cleanup bill." He looked from one woman to the other, seeing them on the edge of their chairs and barely paying him any attention, he was resigned to the inevitable exchange of confidences. "You two go."

〜

CHAPTER 16

Phoebe and Callie had each ordered cappuccino at a nearby coffee shop when Callie's phone vibrated. "Hey Callie." Alexis rushed to her point. "I'm not sure what this means but you know that website you sent me from Meadow's computer?"

"Yeah." *An hour ago. Not senile yet.*

"It isn't live, it never was."

"What difference does it make?" Callie tended to zone out when tech talk began.

Alexis seemed to search for common parlance. "The picture you sent was what they call a screenshot. Like a photograph of something on the internet. But it's not a screenshot of any site we took down. I kept records of them all in case we ever need evidence for a prosecutor." Data-infatuation and years working for the cops made Alexis meticulous.

"What does that mean?" Callie watched Phoebe open two packets of sweetener, spilling some of the white powder onto the bistro-type table.

Alexis continued. "Dunno. Maybe Meadow created her own version of the website for some reason. She's an artist, right? She took a bunch of my mother's classes. Maybe she was trying to help figure out who did it by analyzing the design style."

Callie wanted to give Meadow credit for thinking of

someone besides herself, and for joining the investigation but feared that Elton's influence made that unlikely. "Thanks, Alexis." Callie hung up and turned her attention to Phoebe. "Dying to hear the dish, but gotta call Lawrence." She laid out the website issues to the attorney, aware of Phoebe listening. He said he would look into it. "If I had a nickel for everything everyone said they'd do." Callie ordered another coffee.

Phoebe added pie to her order. With whipped cream. "Lawrence is super reliable. He'll fix it or fight it or whatever you need."

"Tell me everything." An hour later Callie had recaptured the warmth in her friendship with Phoebe and knew more about Lawrence than she really wanted.

"Satisfied?" Phoebe sounded more than a little self-righteous.

"I will be when Stella and Harriet's killers and the center saboteur are in jail. But, yeah, I'm happy for you. Lawrence is a great guy. I still wish Craig had told Hazel but I guess even perfect guys get mad sometimes."

As the sun set, Callie nosed her car out of Flambert along the half-hour drive to Cooper School. Blasting the radio, she successfully lifted her spirits by singing along with Beyoncé until she reached the construction site. The glint of dying sunlight off an unexpected yet familiar vehicle got her attention. She pulled her little car next to his SUV. "Elton?" She bellowed it, assuming he was doing something the court expressly forbade.

"What?" He was leaning against the far side of his car, smoking a cigarette. For a guy who bragged about his prowess at skiing and, well, all sports, he was awfully cavalier about his health.

She tamped down the desire to knock the thing out of his mouth and his teeth with it. "Why are you here?"

He sneered, blowing smoke toward her. "Someone has to do the professional thing."

"We've been ordered off this site. What professional 'thing' did you have in mind?"

With a laconic nod, he indicated the site. "We stay away.

That's just what they want. Then they can wreck the place for good."

Callie couldn't tell whether he was describing something real or imagined. "Can't do anything about it now. Time to go home." She was determined to stay until he departed.

"Home? What kind of home do you think I have? I live downstairs from that bitch, Phoebe. My girlfriend is having a nervous breakdown. I have to live in this godforsaken middle of nowhere until my aunt lets me move back to the city. All your fault." The glow of his cigarette threw a tiny light on his face, revealing a distorted frown.

"You could always get another job." Callie leaned back against her car.

"I do work other jobs sometimes. You think I'm a dilettante but sooner or later you'll know—" he broke off. "Anyway, I'm pretty sure the town's going to rescind their permission for this center and we'll all get to go to our real homes pretty soon."

Callie clenched a fist in the gloom. "How would you know?"

"Meadow heard it from someone on the council." He was a wiry creature who inhabited glitter bars and designer shirts. Callie was tough, toned, and (toward him) ruthless. Fortunately, he was smart enough to know when he was outmanned. He tossed his cigarette and climbed into his car, revving his engine. She waited until his taillights were dimes and then pinpricks on the road to Flambert.

Callie unearthed a flashlight and tried to assess whether anything had changed. Couldn't tell. Shutting the light off, she listened intently. If vandals roamed, they weren't evident. Finally, she drove the remaining few minutes to Cooper School.

Dinner with Coop and Nora and a subsequent lively game of Settlers of Catan was followed by the family (*family!*) reading separately but together in front of the fire. Immersed in a wonderful novel, she temporarily set aside the day.

A call from Hazel brought it all back. "Callie, did you hear about Phoebe and Lawrence?"

More than heard. "Yes, isn't it wonderful?"

"I'm glad it wasn't Phoebe. I like Phoebe. It broke my heart to think she'd … but Callie, then who is it?" Hazel's voice trembled.

"Who is what?"

"Who is Craig seeing in the city? Who's he having an affair with?"

Callie hadn't considered that possibility. "Hang on." She covered the mouthpiece and spoke to Coop. "Hazel still thinks Craig is having an affair."

Coop looked up from his book. "He isn't."

"How do you know?"

"I know."

Nora snorted. "Don't question the great man."

Callie offered him the phone. "Tell Hazel."

He leaned back, rubbing his temples as he spoke. "Hazel, please. You have nothing to worry about." He listened patiently, apparently to a plethora of damning evidence, finally leaving her with a promise that everything would be okay.

"Will it, Dad? I mean, it's great that you talked her off the ledge and all, but people always say that." Nora's eyes, as deep ebony as her father's, bore holes into him. "They always say everything will be okay. And it isn't."

Choosing to let them duke it out, Callie crept into the kitchen area and found things to clean. For once she resented the open layout of the apartment and considered disappearing into the bedroom. *What if I miss something?*

Coop added wood to the fire and stoked it as Nora explained more. "When Mom died, everybody said that. Everybody. And it wasn't okay. At all. I mean, not until Callie came." Nora sniffled.

Coop nodded. "People say things they think will comfort you. But you're not talking about your mother." He didn't break eye contact with his daughter. "Are you?"

"No."

"Arthur?" Coop laid his book aside.

"Yeah. He calls and texts and emails about every ten

minutes." A tear careened down Nora's cheek. "I told you I wouldn't answer, and I don't. I keep my word."

"I know." The Coopers had deep abiding trust in one another's integrity, which Callie had come to share.

"But it's not okay." More tears. "Dad, I love him." She dropped her head into her hands.

"You don't."

Muffled protestations erupted into a well-worn complaint. "Don't tell me how I feel."

Callie said the one thing she'd avoided all these weeks. "He belongs in jail."

Nora swung her head toward Callie. "He isn't a criminal."

"He hit you. He's harassing you. Those are illegal behaviors." Callie carried a glass of milk and plate of cookies to Nora. *Thank heavens Coop's unhappiness expresses itself in massive cooking and baking.*

"He can't stand to let me go because he loves me." Nora wailed for a few seconds and inhaled a few cookies, absent-mindedly brushing crumbs on the antique carpet.

"You and every other gallerina who crosses his path." Callie hated being cruel; this needed some full-frontal assault.

Nora shook her head. "He's changed. He's never felt this way about anyone else. And neither have I."

"Weren't we here a few months ago? How did we get back?" Coop poured himself a brandy, offering one to Callie, who declined.

Callie sat next to Nora. "Is there something new?"

"He left his wife." She sounded hopeful and defiant. "I heard it from somebody at the gallery."

Coop shook his head. "He jumped into bed with you while he was still married. He's likely to cheat on you next."

"My generation doesn't care about that stuff the way yours does." Nora dried her eyes on her sleeve. "I can tolerate polyamory."

Callie pressed a finger to a throbbing brow. "Until he tells someone else he's never felt that way before. And does it over and over ... like he's already done over and over."

"He won't. I'm his number one. I'm super sure. I need to give this thing a chance." Nora gazed earnestly at the two people she loved most in the world but were, clearly, hopeless old fogies.

"I forbid it."

Callie had never heard Coop use the word. *Scary.*

Nora set her plate on the side table. "I'm an adult. You can't stop me."

Coop knocked back the brandy and poured another. "You're acting like a child."

Callie gently loosened the glass from his hand and set it aside. "You're both acting like children."

He stood, began to speak, apparently thought better, and grabbed a jacket.

Callie planted herself at the door. "The hell? Yesterday you told me we can't walk out on one another anymore. So where are you going?"

Nora growled.

Coop stared down at Callie, every muscle tense in his athlete's body. She, too, tensed. He waited for his anger to settle. Minutes ticked by, all three of them in suspended animation. Finally, he reached for Callie, and she clung to him.

Nora fell back in her chair. "Great. You two have this and I'm *for-bidden?*" She dragged the final word out sarcastically.

Coop, his arm still circling Callie's waist, grinned. "Everything will be okay."

"Was that a joke?" Nora lobbed a cookie at him.

He shrugged. "Kind of."

"It was stupid. And insulting and …" Nora couldn't keep a straight face.

Coop dropped his jacket as he moved to her side. "Hilarious." He held her hand and the two laughed their private laugh.

Crisis averted, Callie re-hung the jacket and picked up the flyaway cookie.

Nora held onto Coop's hand. "Now you're saying I can go?"

"I wish you wouldn't. But you're right. It's your choice."

"I hit him first."

"I don't care."

Callie sighed. "We'll be here when he breaks your heart again."

"He might not." Nora stood.

Callie recognized the bravado from her own youth. "Right."

Nora's retort was perhaps a tad sharper than intended. "Everyone doesn't get a Coop."

"Everyone *deserves* a Coop." Callie smiled, too. "And nobody should settle for less."

Nora frowned. "But if you're in love, is it settling?"

Coop searched his daughter's face. "I'm not sure you know what love is yet." As she protested, he raised a hand. "I said I'm not sure. Time will tell whether this is the man who—"

"Completes me?" Nora groaned.

"Deserves you. Understands that you're a gift in his life."

"Is that what Callie is to you?"

Coop didn't hesitate. "Yes."

Nora headed toward her stairs. "And Mom? Another gift?"

"Yes."

"So maybe Arthur is my first gift. And I'll get another one later who suits my parents better."

The plural *parents* wrapped around Callie like a warm winter coat.

"I love you both but I'm going. I have to." Nora hugged each of them and ascended to her room. Within an hour, Nora had packed and left. Callie ached to soothe Coop but nothing seemed right.

As always, he knew what she was thinking. "Honey, you can't fix this. Neither of us can."

Not long after, Callie and Coop, spooned in bed, murmured to one another about the day, puzzling through each of the events, drifting toward sleep.

"Do you think the council could really stop us, like Elton said?"

Coop considered for a moment. "I'm not sure. Talk to Lawrence."

Callie reached for the phone.

"Tomorrow."

Callie glanced at the time and slid back under the covers, summarizing all the seemingly unrelated facts. "Two kids get murdered, causing a huge amount of distress for students and townies alike. Forensic evidence disappears when Dr. Chen is attacked so nobody can prove who did it, though they got DNA from Harriet's murder."

Coop caressed her. "And?"

"Two murders, especially the brutality of the second, have the council and the whole town buzzing that the center will bring more crime to the area. Exactly the opposite of our mission."

"In the early days of the school—long before my time—local luminaries and editorials suggested that a school for poor girls would bring nothing but trouble. For all these years, it's been a lie. Now——" Coop shook his head.

"The truth is the school is terrific both for the girls and for the community. That's a provable fact." Thanks to taking Dr. Chen's job, Callie had read many expert assessments of the school and studies of similar schools nationwide. "The center will be, too."

Coop agreed. "Flambert distrusts anyone who is different. The community loves Hazel because she's a local—"

Callie was afraid she knew what was coming. "But they don't like Craig because he's black."

Coop raised an eyebrow. "No. People of color have lived in Flambert for three generations. Craig is distrusted because he isn't considered a local. He moved here after he met Hazel. He retired from his New York City firm and hung out his shingle here to be near her. I think he believed that overseeing the rare legal problems of a girls' school and wills and adoptions for the town would be easy. Little did he know he'd end up dealing with major crimes."

Callie cleared her throat. "Rumors that Craig cheated feed

the notion that outsiders, which include me, by the way, are the root of all problems. I think someone has taken advantage of that. Think about it. Fake documents cause a court to delay construction just long enough to make construction more difficult as winter comes on. And create doubt that may not be justified but stays in peoples' minds anyway. Then vandals undo much of the progress on the center once we finally got it under construction. On top of all the uncertainty from the murders."

Coop narrowed his eyes. "You make it sound like a plan rather than local prejudice. Who would use murder, forgery, and vandalism to get what they wanted?"

Callie pushed herself out of bed. "The ski lodge. Can we prove it?"

Coop followed her out of bed and handed her a robe, perhaps accepting they'd be up for a while. "It's not ours to prove. Callie, please stay out of it."

"The police won't do anything. Who will?"

When the phone rang, they said, almost simultaneously, "Now what?"

* * *

On the other end of the phone, Jillian clipped through demands without taking a breath. Callie, phone wedged between her ear and shoulder, scribbled on a pad next to the bed, wishing she hadn't answered.

→ Inform Phoebe & Elton her majesty will arrive in the morning.

→ Find her a hotel. A nice one with a gym and a restaurant. Tonight. In the past, Jillian was content to stay in Flambert's not-fancy inn. No accounting for the escalation.

→ Get her an appointment with the mayor. And ...

"Gotta wait til morning." Callie slid her comment between an "and" and a "the."

Jillian seemed surprised that someone besides her was speaking. "Excuse me?"

"Flambert doesn't have a hotel like that. I'll have to check the B&Bs." Callie contented herself by drawing a devil, dramatically tearing it out of her notebook, and folding it into a paper airplane she aimed at Coop, who settled into reading a book while he waited for her to finish.

"Impossible."

Did Jillian mean that Callie was lying, that Flambert was ridiculous, or that it was beyond imagining that she could not get her way? *How does the song go? Impossible things are happening every day.* Coop drew a long tail on her cartoon and labeled it Designer Accessory. Callie bit her cheek in mirth. "What time will you arrive?" *Why doesn't she call Elton, her actual employee?*

The older woman seemed to have heard that thought. "Do you know where Elton is? He's not answering his phone. He needs to come down here so he can drive me. I thought the train would be okay, but I changed my mind."

"Sorry." *Not my brother's keeper. Certainly not Elton's.*

Vociferously frustrated, Jillian hung up.

Callie dialed Phoebe and got voicemail. *Because normal people are asleep right now.* She left a message. Then texted Elton.

"Can we go to sleep now?" Coop set his book on the nightstand and switched off the light.

"Not really sleepy anymore. You?" She nuzzled his bare chest.

He pulled her tight. "Now that you mention it, no."

* * *

The next morning, the fatigue from choosing sex instead of sleep hounded Callie as she struggled to interpret her notes.

Tired and grumpy as she was, Callie could nonetheless predict the next few minutes. Coop fed people when they were upset. Or when he was upset.

Coop presented her with an elaborate gourmet breakfast. They ate. He filled a handful of minutes putting the kitchen in order before he spoke. "Miriam would have made her stay."

"I did my best." Callie wished she could avoid barking.

He held up a dish dripping with soapsuds. "You're not the failure here. I am."

She covered the space between them, pulling his wet hands into hers. "Nobody failed. She's making her own mistakes. Like we did."

"God forbid." His hands slid away from hers.

"Miriam was a legend, partly because she encouraged students to trust their own instincts. Would she be different for her daughter?"

"She'd find a way to put Arthur Bement in prison and throw away the key." He swept trash into a garbage can.

No doubt Miriam would've ended world hunger and signed everlasting international peace treaties, too. "Coop, get your big brain back in gear and think logically. How can we convince Nora that he's a rat?"

"Beats me."

Callie waved a dishtowel like a flag. "Let's hire a detective to follow him. Phoebe says he's famous for philandering. A few photos of him with other girls might convince her."

He looked at her for a moment, considering. "Or she might be angry that we intruded."

"Fine." Callie added a note to her Jillian list.

"Callie, what are you up to?"

If only he couldn't read me so well. "Would you believe nothing?"

"No."

"Then don't ask." She winked.

"Don't ask, don't tell? Reminds me of a failed government policy. Failed." Without further discussion, he kissed her and left for work.

She took his response as tacit approval and called Phoebe. "Get my message?"

"Yeah. Jillian's coming. She's told us this how many times?" Phoebe yawned audibly. "How can I help?"

"Listen to this." Halfway through the Jillian list, they burst into exhausted giggling.

Phoebe—a fan of celebrity TV—ticked off more items. "Don't forget the trailer full of green M&Ms. And maybe a leopard."

"How about a gold porta potty." Callie silently saluted her late Aunt Sophie, who slept on cement floors in foreign countries to attend meetings of international women's rights organizations. Sophie could teach Jillian a thing or two.

After they divided tasks, Callie called the mayor's office, finding it surprisingly easy to make Jillian an appointment that afternoon. *The joys of small-town living.*

Callie had some time before she needed to shower, dress appropriately for Jillian, and drive the half hour to the office in Flambert. Hastily pulling on sweats, she headed outside. Callie chose a path into the woods, among the lightly frosted evergreens. Evergreens. Cool, steady, tall, able to withstand winter. So like Coop.

The run helped.

Not enough.

She wanted Nora to absorb the lessons of Callie's own profligate youth. Do not pass go, do not collect two hundred heartaches. Grow up happy. *Where did this come from, this attachment?* Callie'd spent most of her adult life on her own and been fine. Okay, that was a lie. Maybe not fine, but numb. Not like this. Not prickly and heart-achy.

The drive to Flambert was sufficient to blow away the dusting of snow that blanketed her car, and the streamed music buried her emotions. Predictably, neither Phoebe nor Jillian's cars were parked outside the office yet.

As she locked her car door, a vaguely familiar voice greeted her. "Hello, Ms. Franklin."

"Yes?" She spotted the speaker on the front porch.

"Mr…er … Brant, is it?"

The handsome young man with the waist-length hair and expensive brief case offered a hand. "Yes, ma'am. Sorry to show up like this but I've just come from a meeting of the elders and took a chance you'd see me."

"Should I call my lawyer?"

"Up to you, of course. This is urgent and confidential." He held open the storm door as Callie unlocked the office.

"Come in." She gestured toward the chair just inside the door to her office and texted Lawrence. **Mohawk investigator at center office. Jillian on her way. Please come.** She hung her coat and his jacket in the office closet, purely as a stalling tactic. "Can I get you something?"

Brant smiled, perhaps sympathetically. "I'd appreciate your full attention."

"Of course." Callie smiled. "I can do that so much more easily with coffee." The office, identical to Elton's apartment on the second floor and her shared apartment with Phoebe on the top floor, featured a kitchen adjacent to the front room. She dashed into it, deliberately stretching each brewing step, hoping Lawrence or someone, even Elton, would arrive. "How do you take yours?"

"Black, please." A metallic snap followed by rustling papers suggested he'd opened his briefcase.

When Callie heard Jillian come through the outside door, for the first time in their acquaintance, Callie wanted to hug her. Returning from the kitchen with a tray of steaming mugs, Callie saw the look of astonishment on the older woman's face when Brant rose to greet her.

"Who are you?" Jillian peeled off her expensive coat and held it out for the invisible valet.

Callie set the tray on the coffee table and rescued the coat before it fell, hanging it in the closet next to her own practical jacket. "Jillian Wilson, this is Mr. Brant, an investigator. Jillian is the center's architect."

"Call me Hale, if you want." His high cheekbones set off eyes as black as Coop's.

"Why are you here, Hale?" Jillian claimed the office couch as her personal territory.

He smiled. "I need to discuss something with Ms.——"

"Callie, please." *As long as we're on a first name basis.*

Jillian lounged. "If it's about the center, then I must be informed also."

Callie sighed, ready to dither about nothing, then she heard voices outside on the porch. "Our lawyer is here. We can start." *If it's really Lawrence and not, say, the mail carrier.*

Phoebe and Lawrence bustled in, cheeks red from the bracing wind. Only when they were all introduced and seated did Callie realize Elton was still missing.

Jillian was quicker, displaying a text. "Elton and Meadow are, um, detained. We won't wait for them." Apparently even Jillian understood that "detained" meant *in flagrante delicto.*

"Mr. Bra... Hale. Please begin." Callie thought of Nora and wondered if he worked as an independent contractor who could track down the bad deeds of an errant boyfriend.

Brant passed around copies of a document that purportedly indicated Mohawk claims on the center property. "My research proves, and the Mohawk Council agrees, that this so-called treaty is a forgery. Clever, but a forgery, nonetheless. They no longer wish to make a claim on the land."

Callie took a cleansing breath. "And your reputation?"

"I'm related to half of the elders. Nobody really believed the email but they had to do their due diligence." Everyone spoke at once, demanding clarification, celebrating, whispering thankful prayers.

"Thank you for coming in person but..." Callie wondered if he'd be upset if she hugged him. *First Jillian, now Brant. A thoroughly inappropriate day.*

"Yes, if that were the whole story I'd have called or emailed." He glanced around the room. "I suggest you take this forgery as a serious attack on your project. At first, I thought it might be similar to other false documents—that someone found it and made an honest mistake."

"Please clarify." Lawrence took notes on a legal pad.

"During times of activism, some young Mohawks or allies created false treaty documents and equally false corroborating letters in a misguided attempt to protect the land. They believe that Indians had been cheated by existing treaties, so they invented fairer ones. Their aim was either to return land to a tribe or to keep developers out. Using sophisticated methods to age paper and ink, some forgers created real works of art that had absolutely nothing to do with real treaties."

Phoebe leaned toward him, as if physical proximity would increase her understanding. "Why weren't they discovered at the time?"

He passed around several historical tracts supporting his thesis. "They seeded documents into libraries and even private collections. When they believed development was imminent, they'd make anonymous calls bringing attention to their inventions. Most such forgeries were from the 1960s. These days, only a few people are even aware of the practice."

Jillian pointed a finger at Brant, as if pinning him to an insect mounting board. "Some kid fifty years ago caused all this trouble. Aren't they dead now or in jail or a retirement home? Why do we care?"

Brant paused, sizing up each person in the room. "It's important to understand that activism never ceased. Both the U.S. and Canadian governments violate some of the genuine treaties and need to be called out if and when they do. But this document is not genuine. Our tests suggest that it was created just a few months ago."

Theories and conspiracies flooded Callie, each more absurd than the preceding. The obvious perpetrators were the ski resort backers. How to expose them? Organize picketing. Generate a front-page article in the New York Times, probably by magic. Sue everyone in sight. Hardly the time for coffee warmups, though that seemed to be Jillian's current demand, judging by her waving cup. Callie ignored it.

Unaffected by the hot drink drama, Lawrence studied the photocopies Brant provided, still note-taking industriously. "Does your research suggest who created this?"

Brant shook his head. "I can tell you it's a fake, but, so far, I have nothing indicating who created it. The Mohawk leadership was more interested in authentication than finger pointing."

Wrinkling her nose, Jillian got up and poured herself coffee. "Well, I want to point a damn finger. What kind of investigator do we need? Can you recommend someone?" She drowned her cup in cream and sugar.

Phoebe interrupted her boss. "Mr. Brant, can we hire you to continue this investigation?"

Brant sat quietly for a moment, then nodded. "I am available, but perhaps you'd like fresh eyes. I can recommend several good investigators."

"Lawrence, what do you think?" Callie would've hired Brant on the spot but learned to consult her attorney before signing a big check.

"Mr. Brant has a sterling reputation. However, you and I should discuss this privately before making a commitment." Lawrence stood, indicating that he was dismissing Brant, temporarily at least. Everyone followed suit, shaking his hand and thanking him.

Callie escorted Brant to the porch, speaking quietly. "Do you do all sorts of investigations?"

"Yes, though I specialize in historical documentation." He looked up at her from sidewalk level. "I don't interfere with police investigations, if you mean the murders."

"I wish I could hire you for that, but no. I need some help on a private matter I don't want to share with the others, not even my attorney." Wondering how that sounded, she flushed. "I mean, it's not illegal or anything."

"I'd be better equipped to help if I knew more." A smile played across his features, as if he assumed that cloak-and-dagger was not her specialty.

Little do you know. "I can't explain right now. Can you meet me later?"

"Certainly." He handed her his business card and departed.

Returning to the office, Callie found Jillian holding court, simultaneously making pronouncements to the room and snarling into the phone. "Handwriting analysis … yes, for legal purposes. What other purposes …"

Feigning ignorance of Jillian's need for an audience, Phoebe sat at her desk, Lawrence at her side, perusing the documents.

Elton arrived with Meadow in tow, and without removing his coat, made a beeline to his desk. Someone had left a coffee cup there. Callie was pretty sure it was hers. He grimaced and dramatically held the cup away from him with two fingers, carrying it to the kitchen.

Meadow shrugged her jacket onto the chair next to Lawrence. "I thought you might need me here." She removed a steno notebook from a tote bag decorated with Mohawk symbols.

"Thanks for your consideration, Meadow, but please return to our office and answer the phones." Lawrence picked up her jacket to help her back into it.

"I came with Elton. I don't have a ride."

Phoebe and Callie exchanged *smack her* glances.

Lawrence's calm was unbroken. "I have faith in your ability to walk six blocks."

Elton interrupted. "She's my girlfriend."

If Jillian had not intervened, Callie might have done something she regretted.

"What does that have to do with the price of eggs in China?" Jillian's stare could wither a hundred-year-old fir. "For the purposes of this meeting, she's Lawrence's secretary and he doesn't need her here, he needs her there."

Elton wrinkled his brow, apparently expecting a mere association with him would elucidate Meadow's need for kid glove-ness. "She's my fiancé and—"

"I don't care if she's the Queen of Sheba. She's out." Jillian tapped a stylishly clad foot until Meadow grabbed her things and left.

"That's really not fair." Elton slumped into his desk chair, lacking only a rock-band t-shirt to fully embody a petulant teenager.

Callie took this in. For the first time since she'd met Jillian, the architect wasn't mindlessly defending her nephew. *What further joy can this day bring?*

"What time is my meeting with the mayor?" Jillian seemed sure that she was chairing the meeting, regardless of anyone's title.

Callie glanced at the wall clock. "About an hour. Why are you meeting with him?"

"The delays on the center are unconscionable. I'm sure he'll see my point." Jillian turned her back on the assembled group and furiously took notes on her phone, occasionally offering commentary aloud.

Callie was eager to let this imperious New York City architect loose on Flambert's unsuspecting elected officials. As Jillian enumerated the details of the vandalism and the forgery, using Brant's report for ammunition, Lawrence clicked on Phoebe's laptop, creating a legal request to lift the injunction and let the center resume construction. Phoebe crowded in next to Callie at her desk, going over the remaining items on the Jillian list. The only bump in otherwise cordial proceedings occurred when Callie proposed hiring Brant.

Elton immediately broke his sullen silence. "Meadow says nobody in the Mohawk community trusts Brant."

"That's patently absurd." Lawrence's retort was unusually sharp.

"When Lawrence first hired him, I Googled him and called a bunch of his references." Phoebe sat back in satisfaction, as if she'd just checkmated Elton's beleaguered king.

"Don't say I didn't warn you." Elton set his jaw and rose to accompany his aunt to the mayor's office.

Jillian waved him off. "Help Phoebe. Lawrence, come with me. We'll attack on two fronts. You submit the motion to the court while I'm next door intimidating the mayor."

By now everyone knew Elton was out of favor, apparently even Elton.

CHAPTER 17

Crossing her fingers that Lawrence would curb Jillian, Callie took advantage of this free time and exchanged texts with Brant. He directed her to The Eagle Feather, a bar mainly for tourists, thus the hokey name, but also frequented by young people from a nearby reservation. After a vague excuse about needing fresh air, she left the office on foot.

Minutes later, she peered through the poorly lighted saloon, alive with the clatter of colliding pool balls and beer swishing from a tap. Feeling decidedly overdressed in her Jillian-appropriate attire, she hurried to a wooden booth in the back where Brant nursed a coke.

"Thanks for meeting me, Mr. Brant." She eyed his attire.

He'd traded the sports coat and tie for a brown tee and bright red hoodie. "Hale. Hope this is okay."

In truth, she found working-class bars far more comfortable than the snooty environs of her own office but didn't consider this a good time to trade confidences. "Hale, then. I'm glad to get out of the office."

Mindful that she needed input from Lawrence before signing a contract, she mentioned the murders of Stella and Harriett and the attack on Dr. Chen. "It's possible that the forgery is related to those crimes."

"I won't draw any inferences unless I find evidence." He paused as if wondering how much to say. "But in my experience, small towns don't have a lot of crime. The chances that everything is somehow related are high but that doesn't mean I can prove it."

Callie sighed. Although she rarely drank alcohol at four in the afternoon, she ordered a beer.

"You wanted to discuss another matter?" His careful manner suggested that if she said no, he would wipe it from his memory.

"It's about my, well," she searched his face for qualities she could trust, "she's sort of my stepdaughter."

Flipping his long hair out of the way, he pulled a small device from his briefcase. "Do you mind if I record our conversation?" He waited until she shrugged. "I will, of course, keep everything confidential."

"You're not a lawyer, though, right? That means if a court compelled you to share your findings, you'd have to tell the truth." So much of her understanding of the system derived from Law & Order reruns.

"I'm not a lawyer, no, but my business depends on my discretion."

Dismissing Elton's insistence that Hale was untrustworthy, she plunged into her story.

Brant listened attentively. "Do you want evidence that Arthur's cheating on Nora, that he's abusing her, or something else?"

"Dunno. I guess whatever you can find." She could almost hear both Nora and Coop telling her to butt out.

"Before we go on, I want you to think about this." He leaned against the gleaming wooden back of the booth, as if searching for the exact right words. "Sometimes people have me investigate family members but don't like what I find."

"I want her to leave him. She thinks she's in love and that it's mutual. If I can prove it's not—"

"Evidence doesn't usually impress young people in love." Signaling for another coke, he suggested Callie take a few moments to think it through.

Callie's mother, the ultimate cautionary tale about bad relationships, swam up from pools of blood she could never forget. "My stepfather murdered my mother when I was eleven. I shot him. Nothing you can show me would be more traumatic." *Why did I tell him that?* Few people outside her inner circle had any idea.

He nodded. "I caught that."

"You did not."

"Not the details, of course, but I can tell you've survived some rough times."

"That sounds like an insult."

"Believe me, Callie, it's a compliment. It means my instinct says I can trust you."

"All this time I was worried whether I could trust you." She smiled.

He returned the smile before focusing on the matters at hand. "Does anyone else read your email?"

"No." *They'd better not, or else.*

"I'll send you a contract as an attachment. I suggest you have your lawyer look at it. I want you to know what you're getting into. Unlike forgery, personal behavior requires far more intrusion and a lot of time watching and waiting which I will bill for. And my fees are higher for this kind of investigation."

"Why do you keep trying to talk me out of this?"

"I don't need the work, though I'll be glad to take your money." He shifted in his seat, pushing up the sleeves of his hoodie to reveal a tribal tattoo. "You're a nice woman. Do you really want to turn over the rocks in your own family?"

More insulted by 'nice' than 'rough,' she swallowed a swig of the beer. "I want the evidence. Whether I'll share it is another question."

He paused a minute, black eyes piercing her. "Alright, then." Business concluded, he ordered a beer and hamburger, inviting her to join him.

Drawn to his handsome face and easy confidence, she considered staying. Before Coop, she'd have drunk him under the table and dragged him to a hotel. *But this is After Coop.* She demurred.

Her cell sounded as she left the bar, signaling that this day was not yet done. "Hazel."

"Callie, I know I'm being overly needy, but could you come over?"

"Of course. Needy? How?" She picked up the pace to a trot.

"Craig isn't back from New York." Hazel's voice broke. "I'm worried he wants to divorce me."

"I'll be right there." She called Phoebe as she raced toward Hazel's. "Text me whatever you know whenever you know it. I'm…" *How much to say?* "…going to be tied up for a few hours."

Hazel yanked open the door as soon as Callie's foot hit the porch. Backlit by the house lamps, the older woman appeared in silhouette, literally a shadow of herself. "Oh, Callie." Hazel fell into her friend's arms.

Callie steered her inside, dropping her jacket en route. "Let's have a drink."

"I've already had a few." Hazel pointed to a bottle of sherry and a half-filled glass.

"How about some food?" Callie headed toward Hazel's kitchen.

Hazel slumped at the table, her fist around the sherry glass. "Stew on the stove. Help yourself. I'm not hungry."

Callie summoned a nineteenth century schoolmarm manner. "I'll dish it up and you'll take it."

Protests followed by placemats and silverware followed in turn by threats of force-feeding finally resulted in a substantially more sober state for Hazel. Callie substituted tea for alcohol and settled her friend in a comfortable chair by the living room fire.

Hazel acquiesced to Callie's ministrations, pulling a hand-knitted Afghan over her as if the fire could never be warm enough. "I can't stand that this is happening again."

"Again?"

"My first husband, Joel, ran off with his secretary. An embarrassing cliché. After child support ended, he unplugged from us completely." Hazel pulled at her grey curls.

"You never hear from him?"

"His wife sends 'our house to yours' Christmas cards because she knows I'm Jewish."

Callie raised an eyebrow. "How old was Alexis when her father left?"

"Three."

"Does she remember Joel?"

"Not really. He calls on her birthday when he remembers." Hazel closed her eyes as if to shut out her life. "She's much closer to Craig even though she was a teen when I started seeing him."

Callie considered calling Alexis. Or Craig. Or Coop. But for now, she was the one here. "How did you meet Craig?"

"I met him at a charity event while he was still working in New York. I found out later he moved up here because of me but I was still married so I didn't think of him that way. Then I hired him as my divorce attorney." Hazel shook her head. "Another cliché."

"I thought he did corporate law." Callie continued the questioning to keep Hazel talking.

"Small town lawyers do everything."

Callie poked the fire. "Did you start seeing him then?"

"No, of course not, though I was smitten. He was the most honest man I'd ever met. And he fell for me, too. But neither of us said a word." The tears returned. "We were too ethical."

Callie handed Hazel a tissue. "So how?"

"I ran into him at the same charity event where we first met some years later. Next thing I knew, we were dating."

Callie giggled. "Next thing you knew? Dating befell you— like a branch falls on your car?"

Hazel shot Callie a *not funny* look. "Like a miracle. He's younger than me, you know. Maybe he's finally found someone his own age."

"He married you. You're still more or less newlyweds. Alexis was happy, you were happy, he was happy. Good for everyone including me." Callie hoped grinning might be contagious, like yawning.

Hazel frowned. "How? I didn't even know you then."

"When Coop hired me to teach, I inherited your cabin. Took me awhile to get used to the gold and purple bathroom." Callie hoped Hazel would shift to discussing her innovative home décor. Hopes quickly receded.

"Maybe he's sick of me. I can be really annoying."

"Who can't?" Callie shrugged. "Craig's still crazy about you."

"Says you."

"Says Coop, who wouldn't lie about something that important." *Or much of anything.* Her phone pinged, indicating a new text. And again. And again.

"Would you shut that infernal thing off?" Hazel headed for the sherry bottle, but Callie intervened.

"Sorry, but I have to be available." *Jeez. That sounded too Jillian-esque for comfort.*

Hazel frowned. "Well, fine. Then let me drink. It will dull the noise." She whimpered but didn't fight when Callie moved the bottle out of her reach. "I'm tired."

Callie glanced at her phone. Three texts from Coop. "I'll help you upstairs."

"Put me to bed like a child? No thank you." Hazel wove toward the stairwell, unsteady more from distress than alcohol.

Callie clicked through the messages. The third read: **On my way from NYC w Craig.**

"Sober up. Your husband's coming." Callie steered Hazel toward the bathroom. "Wash your face. I'll make coffee."

"If he's coming to break up with me, he can deal with puffy eyes." Hazel followed Callie into the kitchen. "Decaf, dear. I'm not in my 30s anymore." As the coffeemaker gurgled and spit, Hazel surreptitiously washed her face and straightened her disheveled clothing.

Callie texted Coop. **ETA?**

At station. Five min?

Throwing on a clean crisp apron, Hazel surveyed the kitchen like a general marshalling troops. "Heat up the stew, dear. The men will be hungry."

"Did we just lose a century? They can warm up their own food." *And apologize, too.*

"Callie."

"Alright, alright." Callie turned the flame on low. "Do you want Alexis here?"

"No. Yes. I don't know." Hazel set out colorful Italian ceramic bowls. "Somewhere I have a … yes, here it is." She extracted a baguette from her full refrigerator, wrapped it in foil and threw it in the oven.

Callie texted Alexis.

"Those girls never answer their phone, but they text all day long." Hazel continued to slam flatware and dishware onto the table. "I told them, 'Call me or don't bother to communicate.'"

Callie doubted she'd said anything of the sort. *Mothers and daughters. Me and my mom. Stella and Dorothy. Harriet and …*

As if on cue, a text from Alexis appeared on Callie's cell. **OMW.**

Coop and Craig arrived. The greetings were awkward all around. As the Landers withdrew into the living room, Callie could hear low murmuring and possibly crying from both.

Coop drew Callie into the kitchen, hugging her close and whispered something about getting home soon.

"Nothing would make me happier. Not even kidding. But don't we have to pick up the pieces here?" Callie leaned against the counter, wishing they were horizontal.

"No pieces."

"Okay Mister Man of Few Words, spit it out. What do you know?"

He grinned an annoying Cheshire Cat grin. "Not mine to tell." Responding to a timer, he pulled the bread out of the oven.

"You are the most maddening—"

"Sexy, brilliant man you've ever met." He flashed her a boyish grin.

Hazel's voice crossed several rooms. "Callie, come out

here."

Callie and Coop found Hazel and Craig curled together on the living room couch. Coop, always the practical resident of upstate New York, refreshed the fire.

Hazel clung to Craig. "He wasn't having an affair."

Craig laughed, pushing her grey curls off her face and kissing her. "Who besides you wants a portly middle-aged black man?"

Hazel raised a brow. "You're saying you would have an affair if someone asked?"

"Of course not. Oh, maybe Kamala Harris."

She kissed his cheek. "I knew it was a younger woman."

Callie leaned against the door jamb and ahem-ed. "Repeating. What's—"

Craig nodded. "I'm retiring."

"Sorry?" Callie was trying to piece together a story—any story—that made sense when Alexis and Shauni burst in, creating their usual chaos.

When the coats were hung, stew served, wine poured, and eyes dried, Craig addressed them as they ate. "I apologize, especially to Hazel, for making everyone nervous. I've been thinking for about a year about retiring so we'll have more time to play while we're still relatively young."

Callie hoped she'd feel young in her fifties. Relatively.

Hazel reached for him across the antique lace tablecloth. "You're not nearly old enough to retire. No wonder I didn't think of it."

Craig kissed her offered hand. "Black men tend to die young. I don't want to lose any time with you. I'll keep up my license so I can continue as the legal attorney for Cooper School and a few others but—"

Alexis leaned back in the oak dining chair and surveyed her stepfather with narrowed eyes. "Why the secrecy?"

"Some delicate business arrangements. Lawrence will take over most of my clients, but I had other loose ends to tie up and people to inform. I don't want anyone to panic when I make the announcement public." He stood to refill wine glasses.

Shauni, ever the crusader, pulled herself up, shaking her auburn curls. "Why not tell Hazel?"

"I wrote her a note. I was on my way back when I found the note in my briefcase."

Hazel laughed. "How absurdly Shakespearian."

Alexis laughed the same laugh as her mother. "I woulda said Soup Opera-ish." She punctuated the word "soup" so everyone would groan appropriately.

Like any satisfactory journey's end, the evening grew into a major celebration, rife with happy stories of comparable missed opportunities and coincidences. Oiled with Châteauneuf-du-Pape and Belgian chocolates, everyone stayed too late. When Hazel's fatigue finally caught up with her, she insisted that nobody was in any shape to drive and assigned bedrooms.

"Mom, don't you want some time with your handsome husband?" Alexis winked.

"Didn't you hear? We're retiring. We'll have lots of time." Hazel shooed everyone upstairs.

Finally alone with Coop in the guest bedroom Hazel designated, Callie wanted embarrassingly noisy lovemaking. Instead, she caught him up on the day's events, summarizing Hale Brant's findings about the treaty, and skipping how attractive she found the investigator. Reluctantly, she revealed hiring Brant to spy on Nora. As usual, he said nothing at first. She braced herself for anger or aloofness.

"Good idea." He slid into bed next to her and caressed her.

"You're just saying that to get into my pants."

"Honey, you have no pants at the moment." He kissed her neck.

Callie put a hand over his insistent lips. "Really. Tell me what you think."

"Tomorrow, I'll write you a 500-word essay approving your every move. Tonight, we have better things to do." He turned off both of their phones.

"Seriously. Do you approve?"

"I'm struggling with the ethics, but yes." He stroked her

hair.

"Okay, good." She kissed him. "So ... what were you saying about my pants?"

In a house full of lovemaking couples, nobody paid much attention to anyone else—until bleary eyed and hungover they all met at the breakfast table. Coffee'd and breakfasted, everyone headed toward their respective work.

Coop drove Callie to her office in contented silence, listening to the local news on the radio.

"Construction on the Miriam Cooper Women's Center resumes today after a judge ruled yesterday ..."

Wondering why Lawrence hadn't called her, Callie discovered that her phone was still off. Clicking it on, she squeezed Coop's arm. "Good start for today."

He pulled up to her office. "Let's hope it doesn't go downhill from here."

She frowned playfully. "Right. Rain on my parade."

"Hey, I work with teenagers. I have reasons to be cynical." He kissed her.

Callie raced up the two flights to her apartment, hoping she had a clean change of clothes. Inside, she found Phoebe's door closed and noisily signaled her presence.

Phoebe came out, whispering and fastening a bathrobe. "Let Lawrence sleep." She opened the refrigerator, hanging on the door as if waiting would create breakfast with no input from her. "What's up?"

"I sent you eighty-three million texts."

"Oh right, Hazel. Craig. Nice." Phoebe tousled already tousled hair. "I need coffee." She measured grounds into their machine.

In her own room, Callie sorted through the sorry pile of discarded clothing from the last week—or two—and found nothing presentable. She returned to Phoebe. "Got anything I can borrow? Jillian will notice if I'm wearing yesterday's outfit."

"It will swim on you but sure, the blue dress. Help yourself." Phoebe giggled. "No, wait. I'll get it."

In college, when they brought men into their shared space, they'd yell "Man on" in lieu of a sock on the doorknob. Callie whispered "Man on" more for herself than Phoebe.

In the next half hour, the two women dressed, woke Lawrence unintentionally, and each answered several 'urgent' texts and calls from Jillian.

"And it's not even nine." Phoebe headed down the stairs to the office, pausing briefly at Elton's door on the second floor to bang and yell, "Meeting in five."

Jillian on. To Callie's surprise, Hale Brant arrived with Jillian. Apparently, they'd breakfasted together. Nobody could say Jillian wasn't efficient. Sometimes Callie had to remind herself that Jillian was the architect, not the administrator of the project. *Someone should probably remind Jillian.*

Jillian occupied the office couch as if it were a throne. "The mayor says the ski resort isn't behind the attacks. Of course, he also thinks George W. Bush was the country's greatest president—so much for his judgment. The point is that Hale is our only hope. Explain."

As Hale described his procedures, Callie mused that she liked him better in blue jeans than today's designer suit. *We all dress for Jillian.*

Elton joined the meeting mid-explanation and, as was his habit, disrupted the proceedings. He demanded that Hale start again from the beginning. Before Jillian could retort, Lawrence arrived. Hale quickly summarized his findings. He now had concrete proof that the papers were false. The judge had agreed and lifted the injunction.

"The workers will return to the job site today." Lawrence handed Phoebe her coat. "I'll accompany you to finish the paperwork at court."

"Small town lawyers sure give full service." Jillian laughed at her own joke. No one responded, though Callie and Phoebe telegraphed their invisible eye rolling.

Lawrence smiled without teeth, more grimace-like than he probably intended. "Yes, ma'am." He and Phoebe departed.

Callie was grateful for Hale's presence, an antidote to the

looney twins, Jillian and Elton.

Elton picked at every word Hale delivered, causing the meeting to drag on at least an hour longer than necessary. Finally, Jillian took charge again. "Mr. Brant bills us by the hour, Elton. Let's wrap up."

Elton's entire face flushed to match his hair, always moussed to stand up on its own. As the door closed behind Brant, Elton stood, feet apart, warrior pose. "Aunt Jillian, you're making a terrible mistake. Like I said, Meadow says you can't trust this guy. I don't think you should let him poke around in our business."

Jillian's ample body bristled with ire. "Do you think I wouldn't check him out? I ran a security check. I have dozens of recommendations from law firms I trust. I don't know where your ... Meadow gets her information but she's off the mark." Jillian gathered her things. "Callie, please take me to my hotel, if you can call it that."

"I'll take you." Elton moved between Jillian and Callie, reaching for his jacket.

Jillian waved her hand at the notes and disheveled papers on Elton's desk. "You have hours of filing and phone calls." Jillian crooked her finger at Callie.

"No." Elton seemed a cross between a schoolyard pugilist and a kicked puppy.

Jillian stood, both taller and wider than Elton. "What am I paying you for? You're an assistant. Assist."

"But—"

Callie imagined him protesting long after the door closed. To Callie's surprise, Jillian neither disparaged Callie's choice of cars nor commented on the backseat disarray of her mobile second office.

Callie nosed her car into traffic which, in Flambert, was about four cars. She waited for Jillian's usual lambasting of Flambert's limited amenities—she frequently claimed that the council had cryogenically frozen the town during the least attractive part of the 1990s.

But Jillian had a different agenda. "Be honest, Callie. What do you think of Meadow?"

Thin ice. "Uhm. Don't know her very well. She never took any of my classes."

"Is she good for Elton?"

Callie wanted to retort that it was the wrong question. "I don't know."

"Could you be any more noncommittal?" Jillian adjusted the heat in the car and changed the setting on the radio.

Callie felt any answer was a trap. "I just … I hardly know her."

"I don't like it when people I love are sleeping with people who I distrust." Jillian's pronouncement held a tiny undertone of sadness.

I know what you mean.

"I'm going to split them up before she manipulates him anymore. I'm sure she's after him for his money. My money."

Callie sighed, thinking of Nora and Arthur. "Maybe your choice for him isn't the same as his."

"Callie, you're not getting it."

"Okay." *Jillian's entitled to her own opinion, however off the mark.*

"Meadow's a con artist. She can't make art worth a hill of beans, but she can wreak havoc. She's—"

Callie half-expected her to say "the devil" until she remembered that Jillian was very literal.

"A criminal."

"Maybe she's just crazy."

Jillian flung a gloved hand in the air dismissively. "Crazy doesn't make you a bad artist. Dishonesty does. Me, I don't believe in talent. The artists I admire work like mad and are true to their own visions. Some of them have been called crazy. And half the Flambert City Council thinks you belong in a funny farm. And me, too."

Callie reminded herself that Jillian was a world-famous architect, and for all her overweening nature, an old friend of Coop's. *Maybe she's on to something.* "Did you tell Elton?"

"I will." Jillian swung open the car door in front of her

hotel. "I'm going to stay here in Flambert for a couple of days. I'll be in touch."

Callie recognized that she had been dismissed and unlike Elton, accepted it gladly. Her next stop was Dr. Chen's office at the police lab.

The doctor greeted her warmly. "You know I can't discuss an ongoing investigation."

"I came about a Cooper school question. You said awhile back that you'd heard rumors of the bullying website but didn't think they were credible." Dr. Chen nodded. "How did you hear about them? I'm sorry if this taxes your memory."

The doctor's face crinkled with a gentle smile. "You are kind to be concerned but I remember everything now except the exact moment of my attack. I even have a vague sense that someone I knew came to the door of the lab that night."

Callie was relieved that he seemed to have regained his nuanced intelligence with his memories. "Do the doctors think you'll remember at some point?"

"No one knows. But I do remember who first told me about the website. It was Meadow Goodleaf. I don't generally ignore student complaints, but she had so many and so few of them turned out to have any merit, that I think I filed it in the back of my mind as something I should look into if I got some time."

Thinking about her own recent encounter with Meadow led Callie to the next question. "What kind of complaints?"

"I think they were about mistreatment, but you'd have to look at her file." He grinned. "At the best of times I don't remember the details from every student file."

As she left the lab, her phone pinged with a text from Hale. **Can we meet?**

Wow, that was fast. Arthur must be a real scumbag.

∞

CHAPTER 18

The Eagle Feather served a lovely healthy menu that included corn cakes and wild rice with cranberries. Callie wasn't at all hungry but made a mental note to return when she was.

Brant was at the same booth as before. "Welcome to my Flambert office." He pronounced the town name with the hard "rt" as locals did. "We can have a private conversation here."

"I appreciate your discretion. What have you found out about Arthur Bement?"

"I'm still working on that. This is something else." His eyes turned somber.

Callie quelled the impatience she felt. "And?"

"When the anonymous emails about me began to surface, I had a tech whiz trace where they originated."

"And?"

"Callie, the messages came from Meadow. They originated on her computer at the law office." Brant opened a folder, prepared to show her some kind of technological map.

Callie waved it away. "I believe you. Surely you don't think Craig or Lawrence…"

Brant opened another file. "I spoke confidentially with each of them, and they were as surprised as I was."

She almost whispered, "And you're sure they're telling the truth?"

His face was impassive, but his tone was confident. "It's

my job to know who's lying. They had my technician examine her computer and theirs as well. I'm inclined to trust them."

Callie blinked. "Me, too."

"I have more bad news."

Callie shook her head. "Hit me."

"Meadow created the bullying website."

"What? I saw it on her computer, but I thought—"

Brant interrupted. "I know. For some reason, she left a screenshot on her desktop. She very cleverly covered the actual work on the website, but my guy is cleverer. My next step, commissioned by Craig and Lawrence, was to investigate Meadow herself."

Callie nodded. "Of course."

"Meadow Goodleaf, at least the one we know, didn't exist until about six years ago."

Callie leapt to the obvious conclusion. "It's an alias!" She paused. "Do you know her real identity?"

"The fingerprints on her desk belong to a woman named Valerie Anderson."

"Is she even Mohawk?"

His answer was quick. "No."

Callie considered several possible scenarios. "Did she create this alias just to get into Cooper School?"

"Possibly. She apparently believes she has been maligned as a bad artist and was seeking validation from Hazel. But…"

"But?"

"Art was just her hobby. She has a record. Mostly cybercrimes but she's also suspected of much worse."

Callie shook her head. ""But she went to Cooper for at least two years. Who's a criminal mastermind at age fourteen?"

He sat back. "Valerie Anderson is 31. She either has unnatural genes or had expensive plastic surgery. I suspect Ms. Anderson found an underground cosmetic surgeon to make her younger and more," he made air quotes, "Mowhawkish, whatever that means to her."

"I feel like an idiot. I thought she was broke and kind of …"

"Flighty?" He nodded. "She got away with a lot over the years with that act. Meadow has a bank account of $127. Valerie Anderson has a corporate accountant."

Callie pressed her hands on the tabletop until her knuckles were white. "Please get to the *much worse* part."

"She's a registered business owner who runs a website design company. The feds suspect her of using it as a cover for a crime syndicate. A little cyber spying here, a little capital crime there." He stopped to let her catch up.

Callie swallowed. "Website."

"Yes, she's a pro. She may not be an artist but she's an expert."

"Hazel never loved Meadow's work. Said it was derivative, not original. Meado-er-Valerie must have really hated Stella, who was naturally talented." Callie closed her eyes briefly to shut out reality. "Did she murder Stella and Harriet?"

"Personally? Probably not. If the deaths were her doing, she assigned them to one of her goons."

Callie considered. "She'd send someone to poison Stella out of jealousy? And to pulverize Harriet? Wouldn't those be big risks, even for someone as self-centered as Meadow, Valerie, whatever her name is. And what about Dr. Chen's attack?"

Brant nodded. "I'm not sure the murders are Valerie's."

"But you said yourself that it's unlikely that a town the size of Flambert would have two different crime sprees simultaneously." Callie hoped she didn't sound whiney. "How could she be a criminal mastermind? She's petulant and braggy. She weeps feverishly over perceived slights. She threatens frivolous lawsuits."

"I wonder if some of that was meant to make her seem younger. She's a much better actor than painter." He offered a wry smile.

Callie began to see the pattern that had been evading her. "Who paid for the bullying website and the emails?"

Hale showed a printout of the forensic accounting. "The website paid for itself. Users had to pay to play. This doesn't explain why she started it, but it may have been a long game to make the school look bad. It certainly had the effect of undermining life at Cooper, judging from your own experience meeting with students. Her arrogance was never more evident than when she re-started it after it was discovered and taken down. I suspect she believes she is better at covering her cyber tracks than she is."

"That story about her being bullied at Cooper was—"

"Probably fabricated."

"And the emails?"

"As you may have guessed, she was hired by the ski resort."

Callie thought back to their overblown display at the council meeting. "I knew those guys were no good. What did Craig do when he saw her?"

"She hasn't been to work today and the authorities want him to keep quiet for now." He pushed the printout toward her. "As you can imagine, the police are looking for her."

"Did she also sabotage the center site for the ski resort?"

Hale pointed to some lines on the printout. "We think these are payments for the destruction but can't prove it without more evidence. We've traced these payments to the ski resort, and we think the CEO will turn on her rather than go to jail himself."

Callie's mind kept returning to Stella and Harriet. "Why a murder-for-hire of girls she knew?"

He slid his files into his briefcase. "Callie, I deal in facts. I know her identity, her record, and the list of crimes the police would like to charge her with. I can prove she designed the website and who paid for the complaints against me." Brant leaned slightly forward and met her eyes directly as if to emphasize his point. "I have no evidence about the murders. Her organization works for pay. Who would pay for her to play out her emotions?"

Callie was still sorting through all the new information. "Who else knows about this?"

"The authorities know but as I mentioned, are keeping it

under wraps until they arrest her. Craig and Lawrence are the only others. They asked me to tell you. They expect you'll want to bring a lawsuit against the ski resort."

"I do." Seeing him raise a warning figure, she flushed. "I'll wait until she's in custody." *The woman is a menace. No telling what she'll do in the meantime.*

Callie headed to the center, focused on making sure security precautions were in place. Cleanup and rebuilding were well underway when she arrived. Despite her worries, Callie grinned at the familiar sounds of hammering and drilling, breathing in the sweet perfume of sawdust.

Jillian was on site, looking just as elegant in a hard hat and boots as she had in the couture she wore earlier. She gestured for Callie to join her conversation with the foreman. Jillian had tucked away her customary imperious manner in favor of a completely believable façade of good-old-boyism. The three of them discussed repairs, with both Callie and Jillian dismissing any suggestion to cut corners on the rebuild. The foreman seemed relieved that they wanted him to continue with the quality work already underway.

"I've hired some guys to patrol at night." Jillian didn't seem to think she should have informed Callie in advance, despite the bills. "I hope we can prevent any further incidents."

She toured the site with Callie in tow, their breath visible in the air as she reiterated plans to incorporate the natural landscape into her design. Callie half-listened as she checked for locks on the tool sheds and other security measures.

When a light snow began to fall, the workers ignored it. But Jillian headed to her car, continuing their one-sided conversation. "By the way, do you know where Elton is today? I had to drive myself out here."

"No, I haven't seen him since we left the office." Callie didn't add that she generally avoided him.

Jillian seemed worried. "He won't answer my calls or texts." She closed the door of her car and drove toward Flambert.

* * *

At the end of the workday when most people had left, a pickup slowed off the road and crunched onto the snow and gravel in the parking area. For a moment, Callie thought it might be Coop. *Wishful thinking. That truck looks nothing like his.* The shadowy figure who opened the door materialized into Detective George Belanger.

"What brings you here?" She handed him a hard hat.

The detective tucked the hat under his arm and indicated that she should walk with him. "Let's talk."

Callie hesitated. *Anyone could be the murderer-saboteur.* He led her to a spot in plain sight but out of earshot of the remaining workers who were busy wrapping things up for the day.

"The chief isn't happy that you hired that Indian guy to investigate the murders."

Callie wrinkled her brow. "I didn't."

Belanger was belligerent. "Then why is he questioning Dr. Chen?"

"I really don't know. Did you ask him?" Callie glanced around, wondering where Jillian's patrol was. Belanger seemed like legit police but what if he wasn't?

"Your architect hired me to watch the site at night. At first it seemed like just another easy free-lance job. I can really use the money. But now that my chief thinks you're messing with him, I'm out." Belanger turned toward his car.

Callie raised a hand. "Wait. I'm not. I hired Brant to investigate something completely unrelated to either the murders or the damage to this site."

"That's not what the chief believes. He says this conflicts with my professional duties. Sorry, Callie but I ain't getting' fired. I coulda texted you but I came all the way out here to tell you in person because I want you to understand. When my boss says to quit, I quit." Belanger drove away without saying goodbye.

Great. Now I guess I'm the patrol.

One by one, everyone left until only two cars remained in the parking lot—hers and the foreman's. *Could it be him? But why would he kill anybody?*

"I saw the detective leave. He probably got the same anonymous text I got saying you hired Hale Brant to monkey with the cops' investigation."

Callie nodded, backing away from the man and wishing not for the first time that she had a weapon.

The foreman seemed unaware of her nervousness but got no closer, apparently intent on finishing his workday. "I'd stay but my wife works second shift, so I have to get home for the kids. Are you gonna be okay? Use the trailer if you need. Here are keys."

What's wrong with you, Callie? He's a perfectly nice man. "Thanks. I'll be fine."

As soon as his car pulled out, she got out her phone to call Coop. Apparently, she'd left her phone on, roaming as it did out here in the middle of nowhere, and it now had no juice left. She rummaged in her car for a charger that she couldn't find. *Damn. No calls, no texts, no flashlight.*

Darkness crept up on the site. No electricity yet. During the day they powered their tools with a generator run out of the foreman's trailer. She should have insisted that they hang lights overnight but until now hadn't seen a need for them. She went to the trailer door with the foreman's keys, figuring he had a flashlight and possibly even a charger inside. The keys didn't work. She noticed they were labeled with the name of his daughter and concluded he'd accidentally given her the wrong keys. *Is this really an accident?*

The dilemma was this: go to Cooper School, just a few miles away, and get help but take the chance that in her absence the site-wrecker would return. Or stay with no resources until morning.

No contest. She pulled her car out of the parking lot, intending to drive like she was in the Indiana 500 and return with supplies. Gluing her eyes to both the road in front and the rearview mirror lest she should encounter another motorist or a deer, she tore down the road. In moments, she noticed car lights turning into the center site parking lot. *Get help or go back?* No contest again. She went back. At walking distance from the parking lot, she cut her lights and engine and jogged toward the site, hoping to find a big branch since nothing in her car was remotely like a weapon. Her progress was slightly hampered by jogging on grass in order to keep her footfalls quiet.

During the minutes it took to reach the site, she heard the unmistakable cracking of a sledgehammer against wood. Then two people arguing.

First, Elton complaining. "This is overkill. Every time we do something else, we have a higher chance of getting caught."

Meadow crabbed back. "Everything is in place for us to disappear tonight. New identities, a new bank account, a new car. They paid us a lot. But the center got fixed and we were contracted to wreck it. We need to do this so they don't come after us for the money."

He smacked something. Maybe the car. "It's useless. That woman is made of money. She'll just fix it again."

Callie crept into a position where she could see them in the twilight but was fairly certain they couldn't see her. Meadow had buzzed her hair to about an inch long and dyed it blonde. Elton sported a black mustache on his lip, the kind you buy at a Halloween store.

"I could burn it down."

"Do not start a forest fire."

"Oh, who are you, now? Smokey the Bear?" she said wielding the sledgehammer like someone twice her size.

Elton did nothing. "There. Do you feel better? Let's go."

"Feel better? Oh, tell me you didn't get pleasure from fucking those girls and then killing them." The voice of the woman formerly known as Meadow rose to a screech.

He embraced her, apparently trying to calm her.

"Ew, don't kiss me with that thing on your face."

Elton hissed. "Those girls? That's what I got paid for.

That's what you paid me for. You."

Callie could hear a garbled voice over a device she concluded was a police scanner.

Meadow/Valerie stopped her wonton destruction, dropping the hammer and turning up the scanner. "Did they say my name?"

Elton picked up the hammer and threw it in their SUV. "Did you delete everything off the computer and wipe down your office like we said?"

In that question, Callie could hear the man who had managed to get in and out of Stella's without leaving a trace.

"No time. I went there today to do all that but Brant and some tech guy were already there."

Elton bellowed like a mad bull. "You waited til today?"

Callie looked around for a way she could distract them and disable their car until she could get help. *Two against one. Not great odds.* She picked up a rock and threw it as hard as she could beyond them.

Elton, ever alert, heard the thud. "What was that?"

Meadow, still kicking at the construction site like a woman mad at the world, looked at him as if he were a five-year-old. "What? It's the woods. It's probably a chipmunk or something."

Callie threw another rock, aiming for the same exact spot.

Elton was evidently spooked. "Who's there? Val, we have to go."

"Gimme five more minutes."

Five minutes was enough for Callie. She raced back toward her car, hoping that in five minutes she could drive toward them and ram their vehicle.

It was then that she heard the voice behind her. "Well, if it isn't Ms. Moneybags herself."

Elton had frequently bragged that he could move silently through the woods, just as he boasted he could dive from cliffs and ski jump like a pro. *I should have believed him.*

His red hair glowed like neon against the new fallen snow, despite the gloom. He was carrying a tire iron. "Give me your keys."

"What?"

"Don't stall, Callie. Your keys. And your phone."

Callie was once again thankful she was an accomplished liar. "I've already called everyone. They'll be here any minute." She backed toward her car.

Elton lunged at her, grabbing her wrist. "Keys. Phone." He held the tire iron high. "I will bash your head in, don't think I won't."

Is this how Harriet felt? Callie knew she was faster than Elton and probably stronger but if he hit her with that weapon, she would be disabled. "The phone's in the car."

Callie heard Meadow next. "Elton, the cops are looking for me." Meadow/Valerie appraised Callie as she approached. "Just kill her and let's go." She looked nothing like the faux-Mohawk child she had pretended to be. "We can hide the body and take her car. They'll find your Tesla but won't think to look for hers until they find her remains."

Callie raised a hand as if she wanted to be called upon. Valerie laughed. "I bet you don't agree, right? Tough luck."

Callie tried to act like she was negotiating a deal. "Why not take me hostage? You can last a lot longer in my car that way."

Valerie laughed again. "Let's not and say we did." Then to Elton. "Kill her."

"You do whatever she tells you? What kind of man are you?" Callie felt the slightest hesitation in the fingers locked on her wrist and knew taunting him was her only chance.

"Shut up, you." Now Valerie was ordering Callie around, too.

"That's it!" Callie had been a scrapper in her juvie days and had bested several guys Elton's size. Later, she'd taken self-defense classes designed to free her from attackers. Shifting her weight a smidge, she summoned every ounce of her well-toned body and threw all her weight into her foot against Elton's shin. She heard the crack of a bone. He crumpled a bit; she ran.

Behind her, he cried out in agony. Valerie followed her, having stopped only long enough to wrest the tire iron from her injured man. Callie probably couldn't have outrun Elton, but he now lay writhing and his girlfriend boss couldn't keep up.

Callie didn't stop at her car but headed into the woods, planning to stealthily traverse the few miles to Cooper School. The road might have been a wiser course but in the tiny partial second she had to plan, she decided the woods were more her friend than Valerie's.

It was dark now; the school was too far for her to see its lights. The moon hadn't risen, and starlight wasn't all the illumination it's cracked up to be. After an initial sprint, she had to creep to keep her sense of direction and to evade Valerie, who was fortunately broadcasting her presence by crashing through the brush and swearing.

Intent on her mission, Callie inched forward, feeling her way. Was it minutes or hours that she moved this way? *No idea.* Then she fell. It was a long way down. Her last thought was, *I'm not going to scream and tell Meadow where I am.* She pressed her lips together.

Then darkness. The real thing.

∞

CHAPTER 19

Whiteness.

Light.

Is this heaven? I didn't believe in it. Then Coop. *Is he dead, too? How did that happen?* "Callie, come back to me." His voice didn't sound all that dead.

She forced her eyes all the way open. Hospital walls. Coop was holding her hand, his hair greyer than she remembered. *Surreal but probably not the afterlife.* Callie squeezed his fingers. "What happened?"

"You're awake." Coop called something to someone and quite suddenly her quiet white room was like a Russian novel, full of people speaking incomprehensibly.

Dr. Chen said something that shut them all up.

Callie gingerly felt her arms and legs. Finding bruises and scratches but nothing broken and no bandages except the one on her head, she insisted again. "Really. What happened?"

Dr. Chen said to rest and avoid stress.

"No. I need to know." She had her full voice back now. Only her respect for the doctor prevented her from issuing all the ugly oaths she'd learned as a kid.

The shadowy figures around her materialized into Nora, Hazel, Craig, Lawrence, Phoebe, Alexis, and Shauni, each of whom had an opinion.

Coop never let go of her. "She does need to know."

The story that unfolded wasn't short. When the foreman

got home, he discovered he'd given Callie the wrong keys. When he couldn't reach her, he called Phoebe and left a voicemail explaining that Belanger had quit as patrol and Callie was at the site alone. Phoebe didn't listen to the message immediately, thinking it was likely to be some work detail she could deal with the next day.

In the meantime, Alexis learned that her department was looking for Meadow and issued an alert that appeared on every cell phone in a 50-mile radius and on the police scanners. She said later it was good she hadn't asked permission from the chief, who would have said to keep quiet until Valerie was caught. Alexis scoffed. "I have more confidence in ordinary citizens than in the Flambert police as he ran them."

Callie was distracted. "Are you fired?"

Alexis laughed. "No. The chief is fired. Belanger is fired. The mayor and the council president were arrested for conspiracy with the ski resort. I'm just fine."

"If everyone is gone, who's running the town?" Callie knew that wasn't the most important question but couldn't think clearly.

"An emergency meeting of the council voted Dorothy Kelly the council president. She begged the old police chief to come back from Florida just long enough for them to conduct a proper search for someone to fill the position. So prob a half a year to a year."

"I like that guy." By now Callie was sitting up. "Why didn't Meadow kill me?"

"She tried." Coop still hadn't let go of her.

Phoebe finally listened to the foreman's message and called Coop while Lawrence called the police chief and threatened legal action if he didn't send officers to the construction site. Coop and the cops converged on the center. They found Elton, who had hopped and hobbled to his car and was planning to leave. His luck ran out, though; Valerie had the keys and was still in the woods, cursing as she thrashed about. It took several hours to get a clear narrative from the two criminals and to realize that Callie was missing. A huge number of students and townspeople combed the area until they found her, passed out at the bottom of a ravine.

"Bad concussion. Blood loss. It was a miracle you survived."

Callie assumed Dr. Chen was exaggerating, though he rarely did. "How long was I out?"

Dr. Chen gave up trying to shoo people out of her room and instead made them all move back from her bed. "We put you in a medically induced coma for a few days so the swelling in your brain could subside."

Swelling in my brain?

The back story was even more complicated. Valerie met Elton long before she disguised herself as an indigenous teenager. Both had come to upstate New York to ski. They picked each other up at a bar and after discovering one another's ugly proclivities, they fell in love as much as psychopaths can. Valerie hired Elton on more than one occasion to seduce and murder various targets of her clients. Both of them found the details titillating and apparently videoed many of the murders to watch during sex.

The ski resort found Valerie's organization through unsavory connections (most on the dark web) and hired her to ensure their purchase of the land next to Cooper School. They told investigators they were unaware that murder was part of her arsenal of weapons. Their strategy was to ruin the school's reputation so that students would leave, the school would go under, and the ski resort could purchase that land as well. Valerie hit on the idea of the bullying website to start the ball rolling.

Then along came Callie and her women's center. "And the stupid city council," according to Valerie, "gave her the damned contract." The ski resort threatened to expose Valerie if she didn't return the money they paid her. According to ski resort personnel, Valerie countered that she would finish the job but if they opened their mouths, their children would be in danger. She accelerated her attack on Cooper School by directing Elton to seduce and kill Stella and then circulating rumors that the school was to blame for Stella's 'suicide.'

One of Valerie's earlier clients provided industrial poison that most small-town police labs would mistake for rat poison. Elton added the paralytic so he could sexually assault Stella without a struggle. He delighted in the uniqueness of his methods, designating himself "a killer artist." As an added measure, he stole Stella's diary and phone, poring over them to make sure nobody knew about him. The student had been gullible though, and apparently took seriously that he would know if she wrote about him, even privately, and would punish her.

The fly in the ointment was that Dr. Chen established that Stella had been murdered and then he identified the poison. Neither had happened in the earlier murders-for-hire. Valerie considered the doctor a threat and sent her boyfriend to eliminate him and steal his research. Elton's braggadocio saved the man's life. He reportedly planned to kill Dr. Chen with the same poison he used for Stella but didn't have time to administer it because he was nearly interrupted by the night cleaning crew.

Harriet's death was unplanned, though it served Valerie well, especially since Elton chose to kill her on school grounds. Unbeknownst to Elton, Harriet had seen him once when he was "dating" Stella. She recognized him again one night at the Main Street Bar & Grill and introduced herself, offering her condolences on the loss of Stella.

That meant Harriet had to die, and soon.

He told her he was never in love with Stella but that she, Harriet, was more his type. He flattered her and cajoled and promised her piles of drugs and gallons of alcohol until she eagerly promised to meet him in the woods near her dormitory so he could show her the ways of the world. He cautioned her not to tell anyone, lest they be found out and stopped. He brought a blanket and a roll of duct tape. Having no time for a proper seduction, he nonetheless managed to remove all her clothing before she became fearful and began to cry. To shut her up, he taped over her mouth. He could have killed her then, but he considered her nude body now belonged to him, like he created it. He, the artful killer. He raped her repeatedly, stimulated by her evident terror.

He was, as always, meticulous about the cleanup. He had to bash her face in to eliminate any DNA on the remnants of the duct tape he pulled off the bloody remains of her mouth. He was rueful about the DNA he missed but otherwise was rather proud to relate his depraved story to investigators.

Elton and Valerie weren't afraid of the Flambert police since the chief was too lazy to conduct a thorough investigation, but when Callie started "nosing around," they realized they needed to move quickly. Elton monitored Callie's progress when he could by eavesdropping, but when she hired Brant, he became hyper vigilant. The couple did everything they could to discredit the investigator, not realizing that Callie's contract with Brant had nothing to do with their crimes.

In the meantime, the ski resort told Valerie that they had not contracted for murder and said they'd get someone else who was more effective at attacking the women's center. The resort officials, now confessing like "freaking songbirds" told authorities that she again threatened them and their families, insisting that the deaths were minor hiccups in an otherwise successful venture.

Callie hoped Valerie and her clients would all rot in prison. "As if taking the lives of two young woman was just a tiny mistake, like a builder putting the wrong tiles on a roof."

Valerie's next step was to physically attack the building site. While Elton was tending to his aunt Jillian one evening, Valerie took a sledgehammer to the center site—unusual because she rarely did her own dirty work. Though she approved of Elton's methods and was sexually turned on by the videos of his "artistry," she needed to work out her frustrations at him having sex with other women. He'd done it before, of course, but never with women she knew.

Hazel growled, "Those videos ought to put him away for a couple of lifetimes."

"They will." Craig leaned against the wall next to his wife.

"Her entire organization is under arrest."

"They got caught because of you." Shauni spoke with conviction. "If you hadn't put together all the clues and confronted them, they'd be long gone."

"I'd like to take credit but like anything positive, it was a collaboration of good against evil." She had a new worry. "What about Jillian?" Callie knew that learning the truth about Elton must be a terrible blow.

Phoebe took up the storytelling. At first, Jillian had raged at police, lawyers, city officials, anyone she could reach. She said she would quit the project and work full-time on Elton's defense. She told Phoebe on more than one occasion to pack up and go back to the firm in New York City, which Phoebe ignored. However, Jillian was neither a criminal nor irrational, and as investigators privately revealed their evidence of Elton's misdeeds, her attitude changed.

"She told me that Elton's father, her brother, was what she called a no-goodnik. He was the reason she took such care of Elton." Phoebe sighed.

Callie sighed in tandem. "I feel bad for her." Then a heart-sinking realization. "Did she quit our women's center?"

Lawrence spoke with quiet assurance. "She'd find it expensive to renege on her contract with us, for starters. But this morning she told me she wanted to finish the project. She said she owed at least that much to you and the community for Elton's behavior."

Callie grinned. "Good. She does. What happens next?"

Dr. Chen was the first to speak. "This information about Valerie's syndicate might help solve some cold cases elsewhere now that police labs know what poison to look for. I've sent out a general notice offering to be a consultant." He raised a finger for another point. "I finally remembered what password I spoke with you about. It was to copies of all my findings in Stella's murder, which I'd saved on the cloud. All that evidence is available to investigators."

Nora was next. "Dad showed me Hale Brant's information about Arthur. What a two-faced jerk. I hate to admit that you and Dad saved me."

Alexis clucked. "They weren't the only ones who told you he was a mistake." As Nora sheepishly agreed, Alexis handed Callie a newspaper. "You can see a lot more coverage online, but this account is pretty accurate and puts you, the center, and the school, in an awesome light."

Shauni gave her partner a high five. "The vast majority of students are staying, and the national publicity means we're getting a lot more applications; both students and staff."

Callie felt a throbbing in her head. "I think whatever pain killer I got is wearing off."

Dr. Chen looked sternly at the group. "Time for everyone to let her rest."

Coop stayed at her side as the others gathered their things.

"Wait a second." Callie looked around at the people she loved, her chosen family. "Thank you all for—" She felt tears well up and choked. She saw her own tears mirrored in Coop's.

Coop gently blotted her tears and wiped away his own. "Honey, we thought you might not make it. None of us wanted to be anywhere else."

Murmured assents all around.

"Then just one more thing." Callie inhaled sharply, feeling love and pain in equal measure.

The room went quiet thinking she was in pain.

Callie found the eyes of the only person who mattered in that moment. "Yes, Harold Cooper, I'll marry you."

THE END

ABOUT THE AUTHOR

Jan Levine Thal attended a university high school that has some features in common with Cooper School. She lived in the Northeast for many years, and still loves the very specific turns of seasons in that region. She is more like Phoebe than Callie if you were wondering. Hazel was inspired by Jan's aunt, Selma Crevoshay, who taught English as a second language in public school. Harold Cooper is completely fictional, more's the pity. Jan was a full-time editor for three decades and has written several plays and essays in addition to the Cooper School books. Her website is: https://janlevinethal.com/

Cooper School has some very ambitious goals for the future: email the publisher to be put on a Book Launch list AND make sure you have read the first Cooper School Novel: *BONE DEEP* available where all major books are sold — and if you have some book club plans the publisher is delighted to offer group discounts.

ACKNOWLEDGMENTS

It takes a village and for once I don't mean Flambert.

My brother, Elliott Levine, provided great feedback about the law. His wife, Amber Perry Levine, has been a terrific sounding board for social work questions. My brother Sam Levine and his wife Lisa Levine (aka Captain Kirk) always believe I'll finish my projects, even when I don't. Callie's work ethic is modeled after my entire family, but particularly my brother Michael A. Levine and his wife Mirette Seireg. My fabulous son Jeremy Thal cheers me on with texts and photos from wherever he is in the world. My brilliant nieces and nephews have served from time to time as interpreters of youth lingo. Gail Sterkel's belief in me as a writer spurred me ever onward. Special thanks to Brendon Smith, who read the entire manuscript more than once. Steve Vig solved my technical issues so many times I gave him a t-shirt that read, "I'm here because you broke something."

I also thank my theater community – the playwrighting groups, the actors, the stage managers, the designers, the photographers, the crew. On and offstage collaboration has fed me through the loneliness of writing, especially during the pandemic. I cling to friends from high school, college, and my New York days. We're old fogies but we mastered Zoom and their company helps me feel loved and valued – these are writing tools for me.

My favorite compliment for the first book was from my friend
Molly Vanderlin who said that as she read it, she forgot that she
knew the author. So many others read the first book and urged
me to write this one.

Finally, this book would not be possible without Trish Lewis of
Van Velzer press, who caught many errors, such as when a
character was in two places at once. She also inspired significant
improvements.

Love Books?

SUPPORT AUTHORS - buy directly from

independent publishers. This puts more royalty

dollars into the pockets of your favorite author – and

gives them time to write their next book.

Visit us for links to our other books as well as many
other vibrant publishing companies to find the book
for you; join our Launch List to be the first to know
about new books:

director@vanvelzerpress.com

These ARE The Books You've Been Looking For.

Vanvelzerpress.com

A Cooper School Novel

Train Line

Cooper
School
Flambert
Lake Ontario
Poughkeepsie
New York City

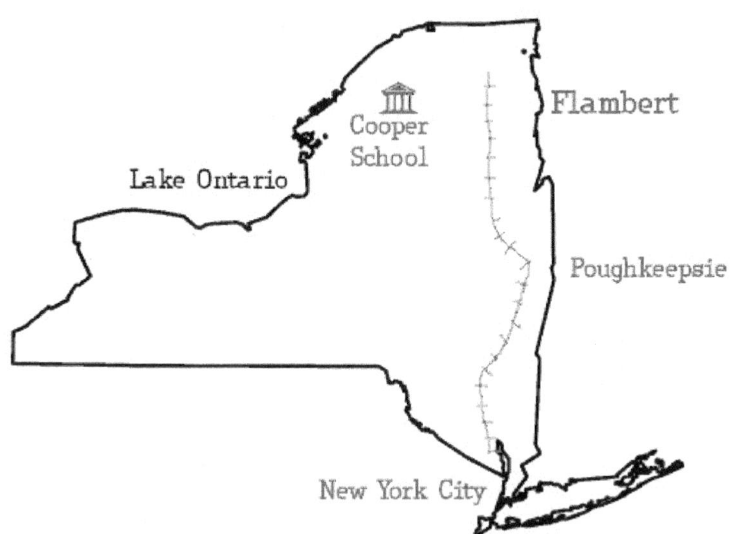